THE SYRIAN CONNECTION

Ross Meurant

SIBERIA WOLF PUBLICATIONS

Acknowledgements

Bev Robitai (www.bevrobitai.co.nz) for proof read; cover design; preparation of manuscript for ebook production and technical expertise.

Author's note:

This is a work of fiction. Most names, characters, businesses, places, events and incidents are either the products of the author's imagination or used in a fictitious manner. Where any reference is made to or about a *real person* and not a character in the novel, when the commentary is not obviously *artistic license,* it is either a matter of public record or personal knowledge of the author and other persons.

ISBN 978-0473-255510 - NZ National Library

ABOUT THE AUTHOR

Ross Meurant was a Member of Parliament for nine years. A stint as a Member of the Executive Council as Undersecretary for agriculture and forestry, ended prematurely when he refused to acquiesce the direction of the Prime Minister, to relinquish a position he took on the board of a Russian-owned (media-alleged Mafia) bank domiciled in Vanuatu.

Prior to entering parliament he was a commissioned officer in the NZ police. Subsequent to parliament, he owned equestrian facilities; was elected to local government as a councillor; consulted to several major fishing companies, was engaged by parliamentary services as adviser to Rt. Hon Winston Peters and emerged as a key figure in the *Scampi Affair*, which alleged political corruption.

From 2004 he lived and worked in Zimbabwe, Russia, Czech Republic and the Balkans. From 2007 he extended his business to Morocco, Syria and U.A.E. The author has a bachelor degree in politics and management, a master's degree in economics, statistics, law and policy and C.O.P's in law.

Other books by Ross Meurant

From the Beat to the Beehive - Harlen Press, 1988
The Red Squad Story - Harlen Press 1982
When Good Cops Go Bad (article) - ACP Media Ltd, 2011
Sex, Power and Politics – 2013, Siberia Wolf Publishing
The Syrian Connection – 2013, Siberia Wolf Publishing

Sex, Power & Politics and The Syrian Connection print editions distributed by www.**rossmeurant**.co.nz and www.letsbuybooks.weebly.com.

Also available in Kindle format on Amazon and in all other ebook formats through www.smashwords.com.

Dedication
A Russian Princess

Chapter One

2012. Palmyra, Syria

Palmyra, a metropolis of ancient Roman majesty and awe-inspiring dimensions, atrophied in the simmering heat. Alain and Egor maintained watch on a café along the street. At forty three degrees Celsius the sun was relentless.

Alain was a long way from his New Zealand home where disputes were settled by the rule of long-entrenched laws. Now he was waiting, well-armed, in a baking wilderness to negotiate a complex deal with Arab criminals. It was debilitating on his physical wellbeing and psychologically demoralising.

'Time?'

Alain responded in Russian to the demand of the younger man, *'Syeychas dva chasa'*.

Egor nodded imperceptibly but retained his vigilance, never taking his eyes from the café entrance some two hundred metres further along the street.

'You would do better to practice Arabic, my friend. The Russian these Syrians speak is as bad as your pronunciations.' He shrugged then extended a compliment. 'Most of the Syrian elite were educated in Moscow where accent could be absorbed in daily communications. They should have better ability. But you my friend learn only from the text book.'

'Assalaamu Aleikum', Alain responded to the challenge. *'Karshde dyen Yar gavoru kineega.'*

'Wa aleikum assalaam,' replied Egor. 'And peace be upon you every day you read the Cyrillic book.'

Suddenly Egor lurched forward, snatching off his precious Prada shades. 'English now my friend. Not make error at this time with speaking. Look', he said with urgency, 'The Devil's henchmen, they are arrived.'

. Instinctively Alain groped under his seat until he felt the reassuring coolness of the nine millimetre Makarov. For reasons of sentimentality he preferred its predecessor, the Tokarev, which had been standard issue to the Red Army during World Two. But either way, he had reflected when secreting the pistols, both versions had proven eminently successful as terminators of life.

From their vantage point in a dilapidated and inconspicuous blue grey Opel, the two men watched as a black Mercedes ML500 drifted to a halt in a cloud of dust, stopping directly opposite the Purple Camel café. Bodyguards poured like liquid into the street. One man, smartly dressed in Western clothing, took up position leaning across the bonnet of the ML and settling himself in a prime firing position with a Kalashnikov. The AK47 exuded a dullish gleam of sunlight on black metal. Two other men, also smartly attired, moved with alacrity across the street and disappeared into the café in a matter of seconds. Soon one of the men appeared on the roof of the single level café building. He remained there.

Without moving a muscle, Egor whispered in a calming voice. 'We have visitors. Don't move.'

Alain caught sight of movement in his rear-vision mirror too late. A large man in traditional Arab garb was already blocking any ability he had to exit the car. Damn, he thought, realising that he had been too preoccupied with the Mercedes and its occupants to check his rear.

'*Zdrastvooeetye*', said the man in a Western suit who had also appeared at the door on Egor's side of the car.

'*Zdrastvooeetye Tovarish*', Egor replied calmly.

'Please, for you to alight from the car, comrade,' came the reply in English, with an acknowledgment of the pronoun used by Egor. The use of English by the man with Arab features was competent and Alain thought he had heard the voice before.

At one hundred eighty three centimetres and one hundred and fifteen kilograms, much of it muscle, Egor's visual appearance left little doubt that he was an athlete in his prime. But the moment he stretched to his full height, the man with Arabic features, slightly built with shaven head and Savile row suit, hit Egor with such force in an unexpected palm-upwards blow under the chin that he was unconscious before he hit the ground.

The Arabic-looking man leaned into the car. 'Please to not reach for any weapon Mr Alain, and alight from this automobile,' he said in carefully enunciated upper-class English.

As he considered his predicament Alain noticed two more black Mercedes pull up outside the Purple Camel Café. Surreptitiously he watched Samer Kaakarli, his friend from a past escapade, being escorted toward the café. His mind was in turmoil as he watched him shuffle across the dusty pathway. Samer! He cannot have authorised this behaviour, Alain reasoned. This turn of events was totally unexpected.

Time seemed to slow as he considered his predicament, but in fact only seconds had elapsed. While regular swimming had maintained his cardiovascular and muscle tone, he was hardly equipped to engage his current adversary in combat. If this sharply-dressed man could put Egor out of action so easily, the chances of overpowering him were not in his favour. Thirty-nine years earlier, as a lieutenant in the New Zealand Special Air Services in Vietnam, a soldier trained to kill with bare hands, things might have been different. But the ravages of time had, as happens to all, taken their toll. Alain was aware that the adrenalin in his veins was dissipating as fast as it had arrived just moments before.

A commotion of dogs yelping and the security people accompanying Samer cursing was both the precipitator of a renewed burst of adrenalin and the distraction Alain had been seeking. With speed belying his age he scooped the Makarov from under his seat, at the same time catching the door latch with his right fingers. Forcefully he dropped his right shoulder to the door and, brutally slamming it open, crunched it into the shins of the man standing beside the car. Acting on instinct, he sprang from the Opel and slipped his right arm between the left arm of his guardian and the man's torso before twisting his arm up and over the other's left shoulder. Gripping the man close while thrusting the Makarov under his chin, Alain rendered the heavily-built Arab impotent.

The man with the Arab features and dapper dress on the other side of the vehicle never took his eyes from Alain. With care he took a Smith and Wesson .38 revolver from his belt and placed it on the roof of the car. Smoothly he then reached down and frisked Egor's limp body. Finding no weapon, he slid his hands under the driver's seat and recovered Egor's Tokarev. Alain uttered not a word, nor did the captive he had constrained.

With calculated precision, the man only a car's width away cocked the Tokarev. A Mexican stand-off seemed the outcome as he raised the gun toward Alain. A millisecond later, the heavily-built man in traditional Arab garb was dead, shot cleanly between the eyes. He crumpled, pulling Alain to the ground, locked as they were in a death embrace.

'That was foolish, Mr Alain,' said the gunman in a quiet but menacing tone. 'Your friend, his weapon has shot dead my associate. This not good for Russo-Syrian relations. You are now in much worse predicament. Please to place your weapon on car roof.'

At that moment, Alain remembered where he had heard that voice and recognised the man with Arab features.

Chapter Two

Thirty Six hours earlier: Central Intelligence Agency, Langley, USA.

'Quiet!'

The imperative from the Intelligence Analysis Head, devoid of florid imprecation but all the more commanding for that, drew instant silence at the table where five men and a woman had been convened at nine pm for a Code Red from Syria. 'Basil, you have the floor,' he said.

Shuffling his hastily gathered dossier on Syria the Head of Foreign Station Agents stood, adjusted his trousers, paused, took a deep breath and lurched into a fervent description of events in Syria which emanated from the arrival of a New Zealand businessman earlier in the week.

Six sets of eyes riveted on Basil. 'And?' questioned the Intelligence Analysis Head.

Cautiously Basil met the eyes of the other bureaucrats in the room, three of whom he knew to be *doves* and not *eagles*. 'Dwight is a good operator. I trust his judgment. I share his assessment that should this New Zealander be allowed to succeed, his actions will embolden the Russians, elevate Assad in the eyes of his people and most importantly, will serious undermine the credibility of the United States as leader of the Free World.'

'And?' the chief persisted.

Basil looked at his dossier on the table. He took another deep draught of air followed by noisy exhalation. 'I say take him out.'

The intensity of animosity exuded by Sally Jackson, Chief Financial Strategist and legend in her own time, could be felt in the room atmosphere without the need for her to articulate her opposition to Basil's solution. But she did.

'Chief,' she commenced with a withering stare at the Intelligence Analysis Head. 'Numbers,' she continued using the moniker given to her team of financial gurus as the only concession to camaraderie she would indulge in during a session she anticipated would boil over with passion, 'Cannot countenance such ill-considered response by the United States.'

The chief nodded; a gesture not of agreement but permission to continue. If time in the hot seat had taught the chief anything it was not to take sides too early or to obviously.

'The US has total control over transfer of US currency anywhere on the planet. All transactions involving the US dollar must pass through New York. This mechanism alone allows the United States to prevent transfer of money for purchase of goods or simply as a gift, between or among any and all countries. We have total control over payments which might be made by New Zealand to Syria for the purchase of fertiliser.' Sally Jackson was emphatic.

'Furthermore,' interrupted the legal officer, 'We have sanctions in place; internationally embraced by all but a few rogue states.'

The Intelligence Analyst Head produced a condescending grimace. 'Agreed the EU sanctions do endorse the thrust of Presidential sanctions but,' and here the chief paused for impact, 'we do not have UN sanctions in place on Syria, thanks to the Russians and Chinese and that opens the door to countries such as New Zealand which are not bound by EU sanctions or Presidential decree, to ignore the sanctions the US seeks to impose and I would hardly place New Zealand as a rogue state.'

Political Section officer Gustafson raised his hand to speak. The chief nodded in his direction.

'We are advised that the New Zealand government is aware of the initiative being taken by this chap in Syria and that they are opposed his actions but the government *per se* can do nothing because the man breaks no New Zealand laws! Nor does he break EU or US law as you rightly point out. Sir.'

Across the table Basil was shaking his head. 'This is not good enough Chief,' he implored. 'The fellow is a rogue. He has a shaft up our anus.' His tirade stopped short by a fierce glare from the financial strategist, Basil bumbled a sheepish "sorry" before continuing. 'There are other methods of payment than simply transferring US dollars. For example, the Russians could accept payment from New Zealand in euro currency and then transfer the price of the phosphate to Syria in roubles or buy Syrian oil as a barter trade for the cash from New Zealand.'

'But, my dear colleague,' interjected Sally with in a caustic tone, 'Syria wants US dollars.'

The legal section officer moved uncomfortably on his seat. 'I think we are missing a serious point here Chief. There is some evidence that this Kiwi fellow has set up bank accounts in various jurisdictions of dubious character around the globe. Belize for example, where half Mexico's drug barons launder their loot. This suggests to me that the issue is more a matter of shutting down options for the power elite within Syria from laundering the money through any number of ATM outlets in any country one cares to name. Surely this is our mission here; to stop this money laundering?'

The chief turned to the President's representative. 'Any comment Gerald?' he asked.

'No sir,' replied the young black man in dapper attire. 'I am here to listen only, Sir.'

Barry Sullivan swivelled his chair so that his back was to his attendees. There was no call for him to seek an opinion with the sixth pair of eyes in the room whose task was to record what transpired in the meeting. Often, when he looked out into the tranquil streets surrounding the CIA hideaway, Barry thought of American Airlines Flight 77 which crashed into the Pentagon on *Nine Eleven*. He remembered the Brothers-in-Arms just a way up the Potomac. How easily it might have been his cherished CIA headquarters and not the Pentagon. Animosity toward Arab states still languished deep in his soul. An ignoble sentiment, of that he was well aware, but he was also human and a warrior from deep in the forests of America's military complex with absolute belief that they were the chosen; the torch to lead a nation to lead the world to freedom and enlightenment. That the torch was Christian was axiomatic.

'Chief! Chief!' The decibels produced by his aide finally penetrated, rousing him from a virtual day dream of times past when America really was leading the devastated Allied Nations and defeated Axis from the ruins of World War Two. The

Marshall Plan which underpinned American economic aid to Europe and NATO which stood as the barrier against communist expansion across West Europe were the pillars of greatness. Those were the days when America really was at its peak. But Vietnam, *Nine Eleven*, the subsequent debacle of Iraq and Afghanistan and now Syria, not to mention the 2008 financial crisis! These events had seriously undermined the myth of American invincibility. And this stuck in the craw of retired Admiral Barry Stuttgart Sullivan, now Intelligence Analysis chief at CIA HQ.

'Where is your man in Syria now?' enquired the chief.

Basil squirmed. He didn't really know. Last communication was effectively that Dwight was already in hot pursuit. This put Basil's people out of the starting blocks before the gun. But political section officer Gustafson saved him temporarily by interjection. 'The last we had from the Ambassador in Damascus was that all troops were in bed waiting for the dawn's early light and direction from us, Sir.'

Barry let his gaze traverse the room. Unquestionably, Sally Jackson was not a happy camper on this one. If he authorised a hit on the Kiwi and it went wrong, she would be at his throat all the way to the President to whom Barry knew she had almost unfettered access. 'If it's all quiet on the Middle Eastern front, I propose to let things as they are until dawn,' he said quietly. 'We will re-convene at midnight. That should be breakfast in Damascus.'

Basil remained perturbed. Conflicting reports from Syria were not comforting. Basil knew well that the Ambassador in Damascus was quite a different character to C.I.A. field officer Dwight Arnold Jr.

Chapter Three

17 years earlier - 1995. Brac Island near Split, Croatia

His fair complexion absorbed the gentle heat as his eyes followed the constant procession of stunningly attractive women, some of who wore the smallest of bikinis. The gentle waves of the Adriatic, like a sea of diamonds, caressed his ever-browning skin under a benign but forty degree sunshine.

'Why for you look at other woman arse when I with you? Me not good?' his companion asked churlishly.

Alain lifted his hand from the white pebbled beach, a characteristic of Croatia. Carefully he removed his designer sunglasses and looked across to Valentina Goloshapova who sat upright and petulant on her beach recliner. She was a stunning woman - not beautiful but attractive. Slim and tall with height in her legs, she had blonde hair and eyes as blue as the cloudless Arctic skies which hovered above her Russian homeland. Her lips oozed sensual viscosity.

'Valya', he said with deeper resonance than usual. 'You are Russian princess. These peasants are washer-women compared with you. *Teebyar oochen kraseevarya.* You are very beautiful.'

The thirty-five year old tourist consultant from St Petersburg glared with mock hostility, which slowly gave way to an arrogantly sensuous meander from his chest to his groin. '*Yar galordnee,*' she said.

'It is not time for dinner,' he replied, knowing full well that when she said she was hungry, it was not her appetite for food to which she was referring.

Propping himself on his elbow, Alain reached out to touch her impeccable skin – like satin or velvet he was uncertain. But what he was sure of was that its texture was unlike anything he had savoured. Touching her thigh and feasting his eyes on well-proportioned breasts immediately created a throb, then swelling, in his swimming trunks. 'Pass my towel please. I must cover up before I stand and then I will mount you the moment we return to the room.'

Dinner once again consisted of fish. Though the country was at war, the fisher fleet still managed to supply restaurants with a constant supply of fresh catch. Salads however, were something on which he had needed to instruct the chef. Diced onion alone did not suffice and nor was such a diet conducive to the velocity of lovemaking he was required to sustain.

Alain leafed through the well-worn menu in a perfunctory gesture. The waiter knew the wine they preferred. No order was solicited nor placed. A bottle of Macedonian red would soon appear.

Only now, at nine in the evening, was the heat beginning to abate. Eating earlier was uncomfortable. Besides, they had both fallen asleep after yet another torrid session beneath the sheets. Alain shook the vision from his mind. The constant lapping of the sea nearby reminded him of the gentle slapping of their bodies and the excessive juices they produced as he had thrust incessantly into her. Never had he experienced such a compatible and synchronised partner in bed, nor one with such an appetite. Her lust was not due to him failing to satisfy her; on the contrary her orgasms were powerful and persistent. He concluded she simply liked sex. But then, so did he.

Few others were dining that evening. After all, there was a war going on and a brutal encounter it was. A general, Ante Gotovina, commander of Croatia's premier Black Battalion, sat in a corner with several noisy aides. The Black Battalions were named not for the colour of their skin, but for the deeds they perpetrated. Both Serb and Croat had these units of death. Gotovina was reputed to be the Croatian equal of Ratko Mladic, but it was the Serb not the Croat who was the reason Alain had been sent to the Balkans.

'These are tragic lands,' the New Zealander said in a reflective mood as they waited for dinner in the State owned hotel, a building as worn out and as flat as the service staff.

The look of utter contempt on Valentina's face caused Alain to pause. Her blue almond shaped eyes had captivated him from the moment they had met, but their lure disguised a razor sharp intellect which dissected debate with lethal logic.

'What? Have I offended you?' he asked.

With a characteristic throw of her head and flick of her hair Valentina leaned back from the table, paused and delivered an acerbic glare. 'Western people are same. Shock at violence when people fight for their land. What is tragic? Serbia she fight and Croatia she fight for land what they make dispute over four hundred years. Is normal to fight for home,' she said with a hint of contempt. 'Like Russia fight Bonaparte and Hitler when these vermin invade my Motherland,' she continued, the venom in her voice betraying latent animosity towards Germany and possibly towards France.

'Russia fight and Russia win. Russia maybe twenty million dead in Second War. What is number killed in Bosnia? Maybe one hundred thousand? Huh,' she said contemptuously. 'Even Polish they make nine million dead and France seven million and Yugoslavia have one million people dead during World War Two. How much British dead? Maybe half million and includes bombs blitz casualties. Small number. Very big different when country is fighting an invader on own sand.'

'Soil,' said Alain to assist her translation.

Valentina nodded. '*Nyemitz*. Eleven million dead to defend their Fatherland when Russians come.'

'*Nyemitz*?' queried Alain, answering himself. 'Germany. Yes. They lost eleven million in World War Two.'

Alan knew Valentina was accurate with her total number of German dead. Knowing the sensitivities of Russians over which nations had suffered the greatest casualties and who made the greatest contribution to winning the Second War, he said: 'America. They claim they won that war but arrived late and lost only three hundred and forty thousand.'

She ignored his reference to America. 'So? What is problem Serb and Croatia kill each other fighting for homeland? Is normal!'

The waiter arrived with their wine. Both were silent as he placed the bottle on the table and walked away. It's typical of the service here, thought Alain, non-existent. Workers consider all to be equal so guests must pour their own wine.

'Jews lost a few people too, come to think of it,' Alain added belatedly, 'and they weren't even fighting for land!'

Valentina was not finished. 'Jew fight for their own land. Jew not problem for Balkans. Balkan is fight for land and revenge. Muslim Turk invade this lands four hundred years behind.'

'Before,' interjected Alain. 'Four hundred years before.'

She glared at him with simmering hostility.

'Catholic on west of Balkans now Croatia. Christian Orthodox Russian on east where now is Serbia. Austria invade from north and captures and makes own empire. Croat and Serb fight but Austria have big friend with Magyar; how you call, Hungary? Together these Europa countries dominate Balkans until Islam come from Turkey in south. Then more fighting and Austria go home and Ottoman rule Balkans four hundred years and make many people Islam.'

Valentina fell silent. His interjection seemed to have disrupted her thought process.

'You were saying, the Turks came to the Balkans. That was four hundred years ago I think,' he prompted.

Valentina nodded and took a sip of wine. If Russian men had the reputation of being among the world's heaviest drinkers, Valentina did not extend that idiosyncrasy to the fairer sex.

'Turks come and – how you say,' she asked searching for a word in English, 'inseminate. Today United Nations say this is rape. Turk make rape of women to put little Islam in belly of Croat and Serb woman.'

Valentina fell silent again and took another sip of the red wine which had become their repast.

Quietly now she continued. 'Time now for, how say you, paying back. All invaders go home. Only Balkans people here and now they fight for territory. On Bosnia where Turk made most babies are now many Islam peoples. Kosovo. Place on history where Turk make big battle with Serb. Now is paying back time. Rape by Serb now to destroy family of Muslim. Rape is weapon of war. History of Balkans repeats. Father to son, mother to daughter. Remember many generations. Balkans like Irish and English. Peace for small time but much hatred always make for killing some time. America not fix Balkans.'

That night they did not make love. Valentina was restless in the hot night air and Alain could not sleep either; their discussion unsettling him for reasons he had yet to fully comprehend.

War, he thought as he lay, sleep evading him. How different was the perspective of his father, a Kiwi who had gone to North Africa with the Second New Zealand Division to fight the German, Field Marshal Erwin Rommel, in 1941. Alain remembered well sitting on the steps at his home one Christmas while his father and uncle told stories about their adventures in far-off places like Egypt's Alexandria and Cairo, getting drunk and dancing with ladies with veils. His recollection was that his father and his uncle had a great adventure at the war and were unhappy to be back in New Zealand milking cows and drinking warm beer. To each of them, Rommel had been a soldier to be admired, the Desert Fox as much a hero as a villain to most New Zealand soldiers who had fought against him. Alain realised that his father's understanding of war had been very different to that of peoples whose country had been invaded. Valentina had made that clear earlier in the evening.

This had also been the case in his war, Vietnam. He accepted that the reasons the French and then the Americans had been defeated by a relentless enemy in that Asian conflict, were the same reasons as those spoken of so passionately by Valentina a few hours before; to expel an invader who had not won the hearts and minds of those being subjugated.

The early hours did bring some sleep, but before the wind got up to ripple the mill-pond stillness of early morning Adriatic waters, Alain and Valentina had swum two thousand metres. One reassuring aspect of these Brac Island waters was that there were no sharks, unlike his native New Zealand. At breakfast, when Alain raised the spectre of sharks, Valentina could not understand how he could be more concerned about being attacked by these massive killers of the depths than by being shot by a sniper or driving over a land mine.

'You go today?' she asked timidly.

Alain nodded. Although theirs had been a chance encounter, he was now infatuated with this Russian princess.

'You will go to Split and make travel arrangements for "approved" Soviet tourists to visit Croatia?' he asked, emphasising the word approved in something of a barbed jest.

She shook her head as she poked a fork in her fruit bowl. 'Is not true,' she said finally.

Pausing over his coffee, Alain felt the first twinges of anxiety. Was this feeling remorse for betrayal of his wife? But it could not be, for he'd been widowed two years after his return from Vietnam when she and their unborn child died during the delivery – an event which had propelled him into near suicidal depression. Perhaps it was anxiety at their imminent parting for their chances of meeting again were remote. But Alain instinctively knew the anxiety he felt had to do with danger, not emotion. Involuntarily he glanced around.

'None of my people are with us,' she reassured when she observed his furtive glance.

Confused but now alert, Alain tilted his head, his body language demanding explanation.

'You silly man Alain Foveaux. Believe chance we meet in Split? You general in Oman army!' the Russian proclaimed.

'Lieutenant Colonel,' he corrected.

'What matter,' she shrugged. 'Bosnia Muslim people many killed. Rape. Sarajevo where Serbs make war crimes. Now is Croatia also jumped into wagon, how you say. Croatia also make war crime in Herzegovina across border not far. General Gotovina you see last night at dinner. He now make war crimes on Muslim near Mostar. Today you go to Mostar. I know. You go to find Muslim general and offer weapons from Arab peoples. You mercenary for Arabs. You white man, Christian. Make good spy. Croat not thinks you emissary for Islam.'

Her emphasis on the middle syllable of the word emissary momentarily evoked in Alain a fleeting carnal desire. Something in her speech pattern he found most seductive, but that dissipated almost as quickly as it had manifest.

Suddenly the breakfast seemed no longer palatable. Many thoughts now raced through his mind. Of course, a chance meeting with a beautiful woman in a war-torn city could have been coincidental. Had she been Croatian she may have been "on the game", as the British had termed it, or perhaps a war widow, but she was not; she was Russian. He knew, of course, that the Russians were not flavour of the month in the Croatian sector of former Yugoslavia, given the Russian help being provided to the Serbs. At that moment, Alain realised his companion was not in Split to re-establish travel links for Russian tourists who had in past years flocked to the beaches of the southern-most ally of the Soviet Union.

The "Mission of Friendship", as she had described it, was a fallacy and a calculated one at that. Now, as he prepared to move across the frontier into Bosnia-Herzegovina and the mist of passion and play time abated, he could see all too clearly.

Feverishly he concentrated, desperately seeking to remember what he had told her in the hours of self-promotion he had spent indulging himself between her thighs. Equally turbulent in his mind was how he might have compromised his mission. What secrets had he imparted that she did not already know? Slowly, but surely, it was dawning on him. Valentina was an agent, and the Russians at least, knew exactly why he was in the Balkans.

'I am not a Christian,' was all he could manage in response.

Valentina seemed shocked. 'Why you not like all Americans and British? You are Muslim?'

Alain shrugged dismissively. 'I was brought up a Christian but I no longer believe. But nor do I believe in Islam and I am not a Jew.'

Waiting and watching him like a cat waits for a mouse, finally she said, 'This things I know,' confirming Alain's instinct that she was an employee of the FSB, the agency that had taken over from the former Soviet Union's KGB secret police. 'You must go now. Your driver is waiting on fish market in Split. Ferry make one hour. No time for more sex,' the Russian declared in not-negotiable terms.

Alain felt his world fall away. How could the Russians know so much of his plans and about him personally? A feeling of claustrophobia engulfed him, causing his blood pressure to drop, or so it seemed.

Across the breakfast table sat a woman of absolute confidence, in control of her surroundings and her emotions in every way. He could see she was not afraid, but he was.

She reached out, placing her hand on his.

'You in no danger from Mother Russia. Russia has big friend in Syria. Syria is Arab. Arab not liking what happens in Sarajevo. Serb kill many Muslim but Serb is also Russian friend. Serb are Slavic people, like Russians. Strong bond. This makes problem for Russia. How to help Muslim friends of Syria and keep Serbia friend?' Valentina allowed the question to linger. 'But now Gotovina, Croatian general, make war crimes on Bosnia Muslim. So now Russia can help Syria who is Arab and Muslim to fight Gotovina because he is Catholic.'

Alain felt his blood pressure settling back to normal. Valentina's English was difficult to follow sometimes, but she got the message through. Because Mladic was Orthodox Serb, Russia could not help its Islamic friends against Serbia and the genocide. But when Mediterranean Catholic Croatia, in the form of General Gotovina, perpetrated war crimes against Muslims in Bosnia later in the conflict, Russia found a way to help its Middle East ally.

'So,' ventured Alain cautiously, 'the Omani speaks with other Arab states about Bosnia. That includes Syria. But the Arabs have a problem sending an Islamic escort with me. Islam is not popular at this time in the Balkans. Instead, Russia offers you to be my guardian in Croatia?'

Valentina did not answer. Standing up, she prepared to leave the table. 'You are much good lover Mr Foveaux. *Oochen xharosho*,' she said. 'I must make walk on promenade. *Plaisir d'amour*. When I return on room you are gone. *Da sveendanya tovarish*.'

Then she was gone. Like gentle wind on water. Sudden perturbation followed by stillness.

Alain gained entry to Herzegovina at the Croatian border control at Metkovic, a region known as Dalmatia. He was conscious of a strong kinship between the northern part of New Zealand and Dalmatia. In his homeland many immigrants from this region had settled in the north in the early twentieth century, working as a peasant class digging for kauri tree gum. Inured to hardships, the Dalmatians had persevered, growing their own vines and over the decades emerging as a wealthy land-owning class of commercially-astute wine makers. As he sat huddled under sacks of potato on the rear of a vintage truck, seeking to pass interminable hours, he tried to recollect the names of they who had arrived in his country from Dalmatia.

Marinkovich, Simunovich, Franich, Matich, Radich, Simich; there were many. Most had changed the spelling of their names to include an 'h' attached to the ending of a name, to capture in English the phonetic sound of 'ich', which often characterised the last syllable of Croatian language.

A sudden bang on the door of the truck in which he was secreted snapped his mind from esoteric entertainment. Adrenalin surged through his body. After five hours of inertia it took only the slightest variation from what had become routine, to cause alarm. In spite of demonstrable family links between the people who manned the border post and his homeland, he had no illusion that he would not be protected from brutal treatment if he was discovered now. He was, after all, about to unlawfully enter a country where his mission was to offer weapons to those being vanquished.

'*Bog, bog, bog*', was all he understood the guard saying. His pulse slowed. '*Bog*' meant good or okay as he had understood people on greeting each other in the cafés he had enjoyed with Valentina. Soon the truck rumbled forward again and two hours later he was offloaded, ostensibly as a sack of potatoes, into the cellar of yet another café.

Once darkness had descended he was hustled onto the deserted street. The air was still warm and the city seemed at peace.

'Stari Most', explained the man who extracted him from the potato pile. 'The Turks built it in the sixteenth century. An iconic crossing place of the Nerevta River. An old bridge, as its name describes, that has carried many invaders. Turk. Austrian. Bulgarian. Then Germans and the Soviets. Now United Nation troops.' Spitting on the ground Samer cursed in Arabic. 'They are all the same, whether in this place or my country of Syria, where French and English and German once looted.'

Bullet holes peppered the stone and plaster walls of almost every building in sight. Fifty-millimetre machineguns, he estimated, and mortar damage also. The contrast between the tranquillity of the evening and mortars in Mostar was profound.

'Beneath Stari Most the river glideth at its own sweet will,' said Alain.

'Excuse me?' his companion uttered.

'Today it is so peaceful here. Such antique beauty. Astonishing architecture and, as an English poet once wrote, a river doing its own thing,' Alain replied.

Nodding in agreement, Samar collected his cigarettes from the table.

'I could stay here forever,' the New Zealander observed.

'Ha,' replied Samer. 'Do not mock death, my friend. The black camel will kneel at your tent soon enough. This is a dangerous place at this time. If your dinner companion from Brac Island found you here now, you would be a dead man. And it would be a slow and painful death.'

'General Gotovina, you mean?' Alain enquired, although he already knew the answer.

Samar nodded again. 'Ratko Mladic committed unspeakable atrocities in Sarajevo over two years. He is now infamous for these things and one day Allah will punish him. Hundreds of Muslim brothers shot by his snipers; women and children. But they were the fortunate who were shot. Many were raped. It was a ploy to destroy the fabric of Muslim families. It is a most vile weapon of war.'

'And Gotovina?' prompted Alain.

'Mladic is a Serb. Historical enemies of Islam. Gotovina is a Croat. For many years Croatia were brothers in blood with Bosnia Muslim against Serb dominance of Yugoslavia. Even at the outset of this war, which started on the death of President Tito and gained unstoppable momentum on the collapse of communism across the Iron Curtain countries, Croatia left alone its Muslim allies in Bosnia-Herzegovina,' explained Samer after pausing to light a cigarette.

'It was one year ago now, 1994. Croatia supported our forces fighting Serbs at Bihac. Not far from where you make love to Russian spy,' he added, with a smile of approval.

Again, Alain wondered at the extent of information the people he was meeting knew about him.

'Croatia took full advantage of our victories and launched attacks to recover Krajina from the Serbs.' Samer leaned across the small table and spoke quietly. 'But Gotovina lost control of his troops. They massacred many and not all were Serb. Only last month in Knin, which is very near to Split. Terrible things, my friend. Terrible things,' he repeated as he swayed back on his chair. 'Only two weeks ago my friend, in this very town, Gotovina celebrated his victories.'

That statement surprised Alain. 'But was that not a victory for Croatia over Serbs who had secured a military presence on the Croat Bosnia border?' he countered.

Samar lit another cigarette and inhaled deeply. He was of swarthy dark hair and complexion with the hooked nose so common among Arabic peoples of Syria, which he claimed as his nationality.

'It was a victory for the Croatian state but the general they hired reverted to his criminal past as a youth and a French Foreign Legion mercenary in Zaire, on the Ivory Coast, and later Argentina and Guatemala where he fought for Far Right Governments.'

Pausing to inhale again and more reflectively now, he continued. 'General Gotovina brought his Ustashe from the battlefields of Dalmatia to Mostar where he made war on our women.'

'Come,' he said after a time of silence, when only the turbulence of water passing beneath the Old Bridge could be heard. 'It is time to go. Abdul will drive you. Go east, then south through Montenegro and Macedonia where our Muslim brothers are now in control. He will leave you at the frontier with Greece where we have peasant herdsmen on our payroll. They are loyal because the money is big. It is only a short crossing of the mountains to Salonika and a fishing vessel will find you and take you to Cyprus. From there it is a simple task to fly to Damascus.'

Alain tightened his grip on his satchel. Toiletries and a change of underwear and socks was all that could be carried. 'So, I came here understanding Mladic's atrocities were the justification for the Arab world to support its Muslim brothers and sisters. Now you explain there is more than one villain loose.'

A knowing smile creased the ruggedly handsome face of the clandestine emissary.

'You will not ride with us? Your home is Syria?' Alain asked as he stood up.

Samer shook his head. 'Look at me,' he smiled jokingly. 'I am overweight, forty, with legs too short to climb mountains. Besides, I have business to attend with the Brotherhood.'

Alain watched his host, searching for any hint of betrayal yet to come. But he found none in what seemed a genuinely friendly face. 'Tell me Samer,' he finally asked. 'Will this be the route to send back the weapons?'

A darkness seemed to pervade Samer's person momentarily, replaced by an expression of understanding. 'Yes, as we have discussed. Send us only one cache successfully. That is all we require. We have sufficient Kalashnikovs from our Russian friends. These are fine weapons for the ground fight. But urgently we must have anti-air. Your Redeye Forty Three C with infrared homing is good. Much better than anything Russia can give us if she would. But she does not provide this technology because the Serb is also a Slav.' Samer shrugged. 'Russia will not provide this level of sophistication for use against another Slav. So we must get anti-air missiles from you, my friend.'

'Well, as I explained, Samer,' said Alain, 'Oman is replacing this weapon with the upgraded Stinger Ninety Two. So I have access to surplus Redeyes. They are still very effective. It is the gift I have been tasked to provide you with.'

As they talked, a small battered Citroen trundled across Stari Most and stopped. Alain entered the car cautiously. A youth of perhaps sixteen years smiled without teeth. A scar from his mouth to his ear made it appear he was always smiling.

'*Assalaamu aleikum*,' said Samer. 'You are always welcome my friend. May our paths soon meet.'

'*Wa aleikum assalaam*,' replied Alain.

'*Laa bas*,' waved Samer and they parted.

Chapter Four

2011. Auckland, New Zealand

Bryce paced relentlessly across the Persian carpeted floor of Doug's office. A stiff breeze rattled the rigging wires on yachts of all sizes that cluttered the harbour basin quay. Spring was in the air. Temperature hovered around twenty three degrees Celsius. Not hot in comparison with European summer temperatures but the humidity was energy-sapping.

'For Christ sake, sit down,' Doug rebuked. 'My man will be here as traffic conditions permit. It's still not three o'clock.'

'Sorry,' Bryce retorted, perching himself on the arm-rest of a sofa in the corner of the office.

'Nice carpet,' he observed, pointing to the floor tapestry. 'You get this from Syria?'

Doug shook his head. 'Iran mate. Land of the Ayatollah. A gift for services provided to a mutton-buying expedition some years back.'

Bryce nodded. 'I seem to recall we were doing live sheep exports to Iran when I was still at school, back in the nineteen nineties.'

Doug acceded. 'We were doing a big trade with Iran well before that when the Shah was in power. Large volumes of second grade mutton left over from the stockpiles we and the Aussies created with ill-considered subsidies to greedy farmers who kept producing lambs neither country could sell on the world market. A simple case of over-supply – the consequence of politicians deciding they know better than the market what should be produced and how much should be made or grown.'

Bryce shrugged. 'Yeah. What happened to that trade? We must have sold the surplus by now?'

Doug continued the history lesson. 'The Ayatollah took over from the Shah and the focus moved strictly to halal-killed meat. Until then we hadn't given a damn about their religious edict, but the new regime changed all that. Overnight we started building halal plants and brought in Islamic slaughter men by the score. We also jumped on the Aussie boat, literally, and started selling live sheep as well.'

'I remember there were issues with animal cruelty for a while,' Bryce offered, wishing to make a contribution to the discussion.

'Yep,' Doug said, anxiously looking at his watch. 'Bloody animal rights lobbies reckoned too many sheep were dying when the ships got into the hot weather. They claimed that hundreds of carcasses were being dumped into the Red Sea. Finally we pulled out.'

'And the Australians?' Bryce enquired.

Doug shook his head. 'Those Aussies are made of sterner stuff mate. Where there is a dollar involved they are hard to stop.'

A gentle door knock disrupted the conversation. A pretty young receptionist poked her head through the gap. 'Your three pm is here Doug. Shall I send ...'

Doug interrupted, wishing to get on with what he viewed as a serious meeting. 'Send him in, and Lisa; coffee for all of us please.'

The man who entered Doug's office was known to Bryce, but only as a result of the news items on which he had featured over a period of years. The intruder looked older than Bryce recalled, but time takes its toll, he thought. That aside, Alain Foveaux remained a strongly-built man. His steel blue eyes were slightly hooded, gravity taking over the eyelids as the years passed. His dress was casual but neat and he walked with a slight limp.

'A pleasure to meet you Mr Foveaux,' said Bryce, welcoming the new arrival.

Alain nodded politely, grasping first Doug's hand then Bryce's in a firm grip.

'We have been detailing some of our nation's recent trading patterns and partners, for the benefit of young Bryce here,' Doug said. 'For a young fellow who has recently taken over from his father, the more back-grounding he gets about the wider aspects of fertilizer application, the better he will be able to put his doctorate to proper use and make serious money.'

Alain raised his eyebrows in recognition of the younger man's academic achievements. 'A Doctor; medical or PhD?'

Bryce shuffled uneasily. Proud as he was of his academic achievements, a clumsy humility often overcame him when he became the focus of attention. 'Economics,' he replied, then for no reason added: 'Former Prime Minister Muldoon once said, "There are two kinds of doctors – those who make you well and those who make you sick." Muldoon obviously didn't like economists, you see.'

Alain grinned and Doug tapped the young man on the shoulder. 'Your old man would be enormously proud of you Bryce. He always understood he had been lucky, not smart. He wanted you to be the clever one.'

Again the young man's lack of confidence became apparent. Of slight build, with sharp facial features, and already balding, Bryce projected anything but the macho image revered in a country where sporting achievements were more highly valued than academic or artistic talent.

'I am impressed,' Alain said by way of congratulation. 'A lot of hard work. The best I could manage was two B passes for management 101 and C minus in a maths paper the army thought might be helpful for me to calculate the trajectory of artillery shells.'

Feeling more at ease, Bryce laughed. 'They should have enrolled you in physics if that was their aim.'

Alain smiled. 'I also managed three B passes in Russian language. At the time we were in Vietnam fighting another of America's world crusades. The choice was either Chinese or Russian. Both have baffling alphabets but fortunately for my future life as it unravelled, I took the latter. But that was the end of my university. You must have been at the books for, what, eight years at least?'

Bryce nodded. 'Nine and every one of them paid for by my Dad.'

There was another knock at the door and Lisa presented coffee and a choice of cookies.

'Come gentlemen,' instructed Doug. 'Enough of this academic banter. My education stopped after I learned to read a rugby programme. Coffee and to business.'

'Though I have to say,' Doug said as a way of concluding the banter, 'I have difficulty these days reading a rugby programme. There's too many names with four A's: Liavaa'a, Vaa'agna and Maa'a Anau. Not like our days of amateur rugby. Too many Samoans and Tongans lured here by the professional money and now we can't pronounce half the names. They're much more baffling than your Russian or Chinese.'

Bryce cleared his throat with an embarrassed pseudo cough. 'My wife is from the Cook Islands,' he confessed.

'Well,' Doug replied with a smile. 'At least she has a good Irish surname now, doesn't she Mr Brady?'

Alain broke the silence, directing his gaze at Bryce. 'The problem, as I understand from Doug, is that you are being forced out of raw phosphate supply countries by major players in the industry.'

Doug chipped in on behalf of his young compatriot. 'That's right my friend. Bryce's father saw the opportunity some years ago, when evidence began to emerge that soil was being damaged by application of fertiliser mixtures containing cadmium, being sold by the majors in the industry.'

'Majors?' queried Alain.

'Big companies. The conglomerates,' Doug explained. 'Some have become very aggressive in defending their turf. This monopolistic commercial behaviour is symptomatic of small countries. In our country dairy, meat and timber industries are classic examples. Major players, who in many cases acquired their monopoly as a result of past government protection, don't take kindly to the loss of that protection under new millennium free trade policies and will sabotage emerging entrepreneurs when they can.'

Taking up the narrative with enthusiasm now that the conversation had turned to his advantage, Bryce said: 'Five years ago the scientific community was the only group who accepted the research which showed fertiliser application on New Zealand soils was destroying the bio vegetation; the humus, fungi and microbes. All of these are growth enhancers which are proven to control plant pathogens and the worm base and therefore the ability of the soil to repair itself and regenerate. So my father started sourcing phosphate which can be applied to our soils in its natural state and without damaging the ecosystem.'

'But is that not precisely what the big companies do?' Alain asked.

Bryce shook his head vigorously, speaking with passion. 'No. You see, some of the big boys bring in phosphate which lacks the RPR component we seek. These phosphates must be put through a steam and crush process which bleaches the impurities with sulphuric acid. But that produces an even more damaging substance which leaches into the soil when this manufactured fertiliser mixture is applied to our farms.'

Alain held up his palms in mock surrender. Shaking his head he implored: 'Too fast. Too much information. Please start again. Take me through the chemistry.'

'Good idea,' Doug asserted. 'This is a very important issue for our country and global environmental concerns. It's best that you understand the science properly.'

Bryce moved to a whiteboard. He was feeling more at ease now and on environment issues he was most passionate. 'Carbon emissions are an internationally-recognised problem,' he stressed. 'Hence we now have Kyoto, followed by trading emission schemes where carbon emitters may buy credits in countries where enterprises retain carbon. Re-planting forests is one manifestation of carbon retention and this creates carbon credits. Big emitters, or polluters, like many American companies, seek to offset the damage they cause to the environment by simply buying into a forestry block in New Zealand, as an example.'

'So moving right along,' Doug interjected, 'Let's focus on one aspect of the wider problem - fertiliser in our back yard.'

Bryce smiled perfunctorily. 'The company Dad set up, Kiwifert, is able to make a positive contribution to the release of harmful carbon into the atmosphere which happens when fertiliser degrades. It does this by selling fertiliser which increases carbon containment in the soil. RPR phosphate is the key to achieving this outcome.'

Alain turned to Doug, his look of confusion prompting an explanation in layman's terms. 'RPR means Reactive Phosphate Rock. In its natural state it can be applied to our soils. The leaching rate under rain for example is thirty per cent less than the leaching rate of fertiliser mixes produced by many other companies.'

Alain nodded. 'Raw phosphate applied in its natural state must contain RPR if it is to reduce leaching and thereby minimise damage to the soil,' he reiterated.

'Crudely put, yes,' confirmed Doug. 'Before buying raw phosphate product, Kiwifert tests for RPR to ascertain how good this soluble small rock is. Phosphate deposits are either Reactive Phosphate Rock or not. Then it is a matter of how good the RPR consistency is. Vietnam and Algeria have good levels of RPR. Egypt does too but they produce a very dusty output. Morocco on the other hand is not high in RPR, nor is that product from Saudi Arabia.'

'Phosphate lacking the RPR constitution is less expensive to buy. Australia and New Zealand drenched themselves in this toxic nightmare during the century they exploited the deposits of bird shit on Nauru Island, but after we neo-colonialists destroyed that Pacific island paradise, we moved into the Middle East. It makes good economics today to buy the phosphates lacking the RPR because it is cheaper and also because infrastructure or plant to process the stuff already exists.'

The sound of wire rigging ropes slapping against masts persisted unabated. 'Doesn't that start to annoy you after a while?' Alain asked of his host.

Doug looked at him perplexed 'What are you talking about my friend?'

'That noise. What is it? Slap, slap, slap.'

'Oh I see,' Doug proffered. 'It's the rigging wires on the rich boy's toys anchored in the Basin. It never stops – a bit like tinnitus. You learn to live with it or you go mad.'

The three men lapsed into a silence, ostensibly listening to the yachting rigging but also cogitating on the matters being discussed. Bryce continued, circumspectly. 'The most compelling reason for continued application of RPR deficient phosphate is not that it is cheaper, nor because plant facilities exist to mix their cauldron of bio-damaging fertiliser.'

Looking directly at Alain to command his attention he continued. 'The most compelling reason is that their PRP deficient fertiliser damages the soil so much it cannot repair itself. That means the only way that soil can reproduce crops is by continued annual application of the same fertiliser which destroys the underground bio-life. It's an endless and self-fulfilling regime.'

Alain nodded sagely. 'It also seems to be as good as any formula to print money. Do all our major fertiliser companies behave like this?'

Bryce shook his head. 'Not all, but some, and they are a very powerful force.'

After another contemplative silence, Alain went on. 'So how do I fit into this affair? I don't even know the chemical formula for water.'

Doug nodded his assent. 'Like to try the formula for whisky?' he joked. 'But seriously my friend, I have asked you here to help out the son of an old mate. As impressive as Bryce's academic qualifications are and as passionate as he clearly is to salvage his father's legacy, he is looking at oblivion at the hands of some who, in my opinion, behave as if they were some sort of phosphate mafia."

Turning to his two seniors, Bryce said humbly. 'I am asking you to help us source RPR phosphate from Syria.'

A smile crossed Alain's ruggedly-featured face as the irony of the situation become obvious to him. He and Doug had been formidable adversaries as uncompromising rugby centres. It would be interesting, mused Alain, to go into battle again, but this time with his old foe on his flank, not opposing him.

Bryce began to wonder if the man Doug had brought to Auckland to discuss his problems had lapsed into a day-dream. But Alain, this man of many rumours, suspicion of black deeds and dubious business deals, finally roused.

'Thanks for the compliment, but this is a serious undertaking,' he said emphatically. 'What in hell's name makes you think I can operate in Syria? They are on the verge of civil war. How would I get a shipload of phosphate out of the country?' He paused. 'I suppose we are talking here about many shiploads – a continuous supply of the RPR. How would I arrange the transport of cargo through a bloody war zone?'

Leaning forward in earnest, Bryce took up the challenge. 'Doug tells me you were recruited to the Sultan of Oman's army after your tour of Vietnam. Many would say you were a mercenary in a region most New Zealanders regard as unstable, uncivilized and outright dangerous. Doug says the New Zealand government's subservience to American foreign policy renders them worthless as envoys on our behalf in Syria, so the best option is to use the experience and contacts you must have accumulated in the Middle East.'

The cacophony of rigging slapping against masts continued unabated, dominating the sudden silence in the office.

Rolling out of his recliner chair as graciously as his damaged knees and arthritic hip would allow, Doug got to his feet. 'That's a bit over the top Bryce,' he suggested, somewhat embarrassed by the bluntness of the younger man's approach.

But Alain raised a hand to stay him. Perhaps there is more to this boy than first meets the eye, he mused. Pausing for a few moments, he responded. 'No, the boy is right.'

Smiling now, Alain rose from his seat with more grace than Doug. 'And yes young man, I did take a job in the Oman desert cavalry. I began as a logistics major and completed my second tour as lieutenant colonel in military intelligence.' Turning to take in the vista of yachts and the sparkling waters of the Waitemata harbour, Alain continued. 'As a point of order, there is actually no such thing as military intelligence any more than there are criminal lawyers or military music. There is information reviewed by the military, lawyers who practice criminal law and military bands.' Again he paused for one of his periods of reflection. 'But in that job I did come to understand the dynamics of other cultures.' Turning to face Bryce he confessed. 'As it transpired, this opened doors I never knew existed.'

He had not seen her since Croatia in 1995. But since the season of Arab Springs, she had begun texting. Alain figured that she had been assigned to Syria shortly after NATO invaded Libya. He also concluded that the Russians were not about to make the same mistake in Syria they had made when they abstained from voting to block international intervention in the land ruled by Colonel Muammar Gaddafi. More than occasionally he had thought about her. Messaging between them was perfunctory and never more than half a dozen words of cryptic text language, but that was enough to evoke old memories and a dull ache in his loins.

'Yes,' said Alain with anticipation. 'I will go to Syria and negotiate to get you access to this RPR phosphate.'

Chapter Five

Damascus, Syria.

Nothing much had changed since he was last in Damascus. The passport control seemed to have been neither painted nor improved in any way in the seventeen years since he'd flown into this city from Famagusta. That had been the culmination of a journey of a lifetime as emissary for an Arab arms supplier. From Masqat in Oman, to Frankfurt, then on to Split in a charter flight, and a glorious stopover on the island of Brac. Days later, secreted under potato sacks on a lorry, he'd crossed the Croatian border into Herzegovina. By dilapidated Citroen they had surreptitiously made their way through war-torn Bosnia, Serbia and Montenegro before the relative tranquillity of Macedonia, seemingly spared the excesses of that brutal Balkan conflict, and finally into Greece.

Joining a very slow-moving queue of passengers fanning themselves with any apparatus they could grasp in a bid to combat the stifling heat and absence of air conditioning, Alain deliberately slowed his mind to calm his tense physical state. It was going to be a long wait. He knew from experience there was no point in getting agitated and confrontational with officials who had never lost a dispute. During the wait his mind rolled back the years to events which had preceded the day when he had last stood before this same passport control.

The passage over the Greek mountains seventeen years ago had been refreshing contrast to the turbulence of the Balkans through which he had just passed. An agreeable friendship had developed with the old man who guided him during the week it took them to make the crossing. As a much younger man, his Greek escort had guided over these same mountains New Zealand soldiers escaping the Nazi forces invading Greece, but in reverse, to a Yugoslavia unaffected by war at that time.

The New Zealanders, abandoned and trapped in Greece when the main British and Australian force fled to Crete, had been consigned to becoming prisoners of war for the duration of the conflict, by British Prime Minister Winston Churchill. The same man who as Naval Secretary had planned the disastrous assault by Australian and New Zealand troops in the Dardanelles against Germany's ally, Turkey, at the outset of the 'Great War' two decades before. That World War One military disaster of monumental proportions, had endured in the psyche of Australian and New Zealand as 'Gallipoli', to become the foundation stone of the ANZAC military spirit.

Alain had made the crossing in late summer. A winter crossing, as his countrymen had endured fifty-five years earlier, would have been bitterly cold and miserable with a myriad of dangers facing the ill-prepared. He and his guide had come upon the graves of many of the New Zealanders who had died trying to escape their Nazi pursuers.

Once across the mountains Alain had boarded a small fishing vessel in Salonika. This rendezvoused at sea with another vessel near Cyprus carrying him to the port of Famagusta in the Turkish enclave. From there he had been flown, as a tourist on a small charter aircraft, to Damascus.

No. Nothing much has changed in this place, he thought to himself as he shuffled forward at a snail's pace.

'Passport and visa.' The demand jolted Alain from the state of automatism in which he had ambled forward. It was finally his turn to make his declaration. He presented his New Zealand passport containing the visa certified for Syria which had been issued in Canberra as he had passed through Australia.

Without taking his eyes from him, the Customs and Immigration officer held Alain's passport to his shoulder. Moments later a tall slim dark man in a lightweight fabric suit and adorned with a pencil moustache came forward, took the passport without looking at it and signalled Alain to follow him. None of the other people in the queues seemed to take any notice whatsoever.

The official walked rapidly and Alain had trouble keeping up. At one point he completely lost sight of his escort, only for the man to reappear suddenly around a concrete pillar near the baggage section. He assumed he was getting this preferential treatment because he was someone who was willing to ignore the pleas of America not to trade with Syria and was here to do business. The alternative of finding his way from the airport to the Damascus city centre, while not daunting, would nevertheless have been time-consuming and irritating. After flying from Singapore to Abu Dhabi, then being forced to wait three hours for his connecting flight to Damascus, Alain was drained. He was tired and in need of a shower and sleep.

'How big luggage?' asked his escort in English, but with a distinctly French accent. Alain signalled with his index finger and they waited. The conveyer belt was not operating, but soon a reliable old Massey Ferguson tractor appeared, just like the machine his father had used on the family dairy farm many years before. Fortuitously, he noted, his bag was still perched on the trailer and had not toppled off, as was the fate of many in a trail of baggage spread across the tarmac.

Moments later they were again walking at brisk pace, into the harsh sun of the Middle East. When he stepped out from the protection of the terminal the brilliance of the sunlight temporarily blinded him. A wave of heat stifled his breathing. Pausing to get his bearings and recover his senses, Alain was suddenly confronted by his escort blocking any further movement. With hand turned open but close to his belt, secreted from all but someone passing very close by, the escort need not have spoken to make his intention clear.

'One hundred dollar for airport tax. Please you make pay to me,' the escort announced without any hint of diplomacy.

The demand neither surprised nor upset Alain. 'No American dollars, I deal only in Euros.'

'You have one hundred Euro?' the thin man solicited.

Alain produced one hundred Euro. The change of currency and exchange rate appeared to have no relevance to the quantum demanded. 'You will drive me to Omayed hotel, correct?' Alain asked as he tendered the note.

The escort nodded. Alain extracted another hundred Euro note from his pocket. 'And you take me to sexy girl, correct?' The driver demurred, glancing furtively about. As if, thought Alain, taking him to a brothel would be a greater sin than demanding money from a businessman sufficiently well connected to have a chauffeur provided by Syria's Foreign

Affairs Ministry. The escort nodded, took the money and placed Alain's luggage in the back seat. Taking the hint, the New Zealander sat beside the driver. It was a Mercedes 280SL, vintage indeterminable.

'Women are good at this place?' enquired Alain with more than a touch of lascivious anticipation. The driver nodded.

'Syrian girls?' Alain asked.

The driver shook his head and frowned. 'Korea and Russia - no Syria.'

Alain let the kilometres pass in silence. It was a good to be back in the land where Jesus and the Prophet Muhammad had once walked. Although he was not a religious man, the fact that these figures in history trod paving which was still intact astonished him. Later, he decided, he would renew his acquaintance with the Mosque of Saladin and the Old City. Sensing a relaxation from the driver, Alain kicked off the dialogue again. 'Do you work with Government?'

The driver laughed. 'All peoples here work with Government. Private business very small.' After a hesitation he added 'Bar girls, private business,' accompanied with raucous laughter at his own joke.

'I am called Alain. It is French but I am from New Zealand.'

The driver nodded. 'I am Ahmed. I know you name is France. I speak France. You speak France?'

'I speak English and Russian,' Alain replied.

'Ahh!' said the driver as he turned his face toward Alain. '*Ya torsha*', he said in Russian. 'You have been on Moskva?' Without waiting for a reply he continued. 'I have been on Moscow. Many Syria peoples are on Moscow Institute for Technology. I am graduate agriculture science.' The driver's pride in his qualification was not lost on Alain, who confirmed that he too had been to Moscow.

On arrival at the Omayed hotel he gathered his suitcase and shook hands with Ahmed. 'You want I wait for you go to ladies house?' the driver asked.

'No. I have changed my mind Ahmed,' Alain lied. 'I will have sleep. It was good to speak with you. Please be my friend while I am in Damascus.' Ahmed nodded vigorously. Being a guide to a foreigner was inevitably a lucrative pastime.

'What is your mobile number?' enquired Alain. Ahmed again cast furtive glances, then smiling he wrote his mobile number on a card. He did not return the second hundred euro note.

Alain knew that the pay packets of these people were far from overflowing. This seemed to be the case in most countries he had visited where corruption was rife. Low pay to public servants was inevitably a contributing factor to corruption. Taking Ahmed's card he said in a conspiratorial manner, 'If I need help one night, I will call you.'

Ahmed's smile provided Alain with a level of comfort. He knew from experience that the best way to get out of a bad situation in a strange city was to have a friend in need. If he called Ahmed at midnight, the driver would suspect no more than that he wanted to visit a brothel. So far, things were moving ahead as planned.

What was not planned or expected was finding a tall slim long-legged blonde with almond shaped blue eyes standing in the hotel foyer as he entered the Omayed.

Valentina!

After all these years, his Russian princess was standing not ten metres away from him. She looked immaculate, from her designer label attire to her astonishingly well preserved physique. Alain was aware that, unlike virtually all his age group in New Zealand, his torso was well-preserved with neither paunch nor much muscle wastage, although his face was beginning to show his age. But Valentina – she had to be fifty years old at least, yet could pass for forty in even the brightest sunlight.

Alain pondered, how did she know he would be here, at this time in the Omayed? Why was she here?

He dropped his suitcase on the marble tiles, anticipating moving toward her, but the slightest movement of her body and a head inflection caused him to freeze. She showed no sign of recognition and then she looked directly at him with a blandness that shouted warning. Instinct told Alain that now was not the time for a reunion.

He confirmed his reservation while Valentina sat in the ante room where departing guests assembled. She appeared to read a magazine and Alain appeared not to notice her. But Valentina was not to be his only surprise of the day.

'Mr Foveaux', said an unmistakable American accent. Alain paused, glancing in the direction of the voice. An athletic male in his mid-thirties had pulled himself to a halt after rushing into the lobby. Proffering a hand and a charming smile the American volunteered, 'Hi, I'm Dwight Arnold junior. You are Alain Foveaux?'

Alain nodded and accepted the extended hand. 'Welcome to Damascus,' said the American, as if it was his own private fiefdom. 'Sorry I couldn't meet you at the airport. Damn road blocks – you never know where they are going to spring up.'

'Something these people learned from the Americans when they were in Iraq, no doubt,' Alain replied with a disarming smile.

'Huh? Well. Maybe,' replied the younger man, a little confused. 'Anyway,' he continued preferring to ignore any slight or misunderstanding. 'Great to have you here. I'm with the US Embassy - third secretary agriculture. I've been assigned to provide you whatever you need while in this fascinating corner of the world.'

Alain made a quick assessment. Definitely CIA. 'Thanks for the offer,' he finally replied. 'Tell me Dwight, what have I done to deserve the services of Uncle Sam?'

'We keep tabs on the nationalities entering and leaving,' Dwight Arnold junior revealed. 'You Kiwis don't have a diplomatic mission here so we are happy to do pick-ups from the airstrip for our allies in Afghanistan.'

Alain noted the American did not mention Iraq, a conflict New Zealand had refused to get involved in by sending combat troops to a war the UN had said was illegal.

'I am authorised to offer you transport anywhere you want to go while you're here,' the amiable well-dressed young man offered, confirming Alain's belief that there was more to this matter than a simple friendly gesture from an ostensible allied brother in arms. 'Thanks, I'll keep that in mind,' Alain replied as he made his way to the elevator, observing from the corner of his eye that Valentina was nowhere to be seen.

Hours later – many hours later – an Imam calling to the faithful pierced the warm air and ended his fitful sleep. It had been a choice between a noisy but effective air conditioning system or silence and fresh warm air wafting into his room through the opened balcony. The warm air had prevailed but the five am call to prayer also found the open doorway. The chant was soothing and peaceful, imparting to travellers that this was a timeless land where some things remained as they had been for many centuries.

Alain's mobile phone buzzed and rattled on the dresser. Still in a state of semi-consciousness, he mumbled while fumbling for his connection to the outside world before reading the text that had just arrived.

"Zavtrak vorsem saladeen carfye," he read in phonetic Russian. "Breakfast eight – Saladin Café." Alain threw back the sheets and despite the ungodly time of day, headed for the shower in anticipation of a meeting of much promise. Perhaps, even a liberal dose of pleasure.

When he entered the café, she was already seated at a table near the waiter's access to the kitchen. Always with an escape route, he concluded. She hasn't changed at all.

'It's good to see you *Tovarish*,' she said in the dulcet tones that had always turned his legs to jelly. 'How you make good conditions on body?' she said, her eyes roving over his torso before resting on his crotch.

'Swimming,' he replied by way of explanation. 'How make you so slim after so many years are gone?' he asked involuntarily, emulating her jilted English.

'Not make babies. Not find Russian man make good husband. Men easy for sex but not good for husband,' came her blunt reply, which for some reason injured him. She did not stand to embrace him nor did she offer her hand. Awkwardly Alain took a chair and sat.

'No children – me either,' he replied meekly.

Valentina tilted her head in surprise. 'You not have wife? You not have children?' She seemed disbelieving.

Alain told her in subdued and unemotional terms what had happened to his wife and child.

Valentina remained silent for some time, never taking her eyes from his face. Her scrutiny made him feel naked and vulnerable. 'Valya has many children,' she eventually said, with no suggestion of jest.

'How?' he began, relieved to have the focus off him but a little alarmed at her revelation.

'Valya has ten children at orphan home. She sends money for children who have no mama and papa. Orphan children in Russia very sad.' Her confession of compassion touched him. Astonishment? Respect? He could not quantify and let the moment pass.

She was still a stunningly attractive woman, perhaps more so than she had been on Brac Island when she had been in her mid-thirties. Maturity had enhanced her appeal. Alain was completely overwhelmed by her presence and embarrassed that his infatuation was so obvious.

Valentina waved to the waiter, always a man, never a woman in this part of the world. She ordered coffee and croissants in fluent Arabic with no opportunity for Alain to approve her selection.

'Why America CIA on Omayed? You work now for America?' It was an accusation, not a question.

'Hey,' Alain protested, with gestures of denial. 'I did not know that American. I not know he come to meet me,' he said, again lapsing into a form of broken English. 'I was as surprised to see him as I was surprised to see you.'

Coolly she appraised him.

'Come on Valya. I am not anti-American but nor did I arrange to meet that fellow, or any other American while I am here,' he protested.

'You not tell me you come on Syria,' she said accusingly, and with some petulance.

Alain opened his hands in a gesture of incomprehension. 'Valya. We have not spoken since that day in 1995 on Brac Island. I had no way of finding you. I could hardly go to the Soviet or Russian Embassy like a love-sick child to plead for your address! That may have even been fatal for you. How could I know?'

He lowered his hands and his voice tone. 'The first time I have contact with you is a text, maybe two years ago. "Hello comrade on Brac" and nothing more. Brac was the key and I assumed it was you, but it may have been the fellow I meet in Mostar. I did not know and replied, saying only hello. I recall that response and waited for weeks for your rejoinder, but nothing. Then one day months later more text – "Is good on Damascus comrade". Again I replied, with just one word – "Fine".'

Shaking his head in exasperation he continued. 'So, tell me! Was I supposed to send details of my trip to Syria at this dangerous time to a stranger who texted me occasionally? Valya,' he said now with emotion. 'I hoped it was your text and I hoped to find you here, but I could only hope. I am very much happy that you have found me.'

The tension subsided but a frown creased Alain's brow as questions occurred which he felt he should ask. 'How did you know I was coming to Syria? You were at my hotel – you knew about my trip,' he said, virtually in accusation.

Valya did not respond immediately, opting to wait until the coffee and croissants had been served. She leant back as the waiter spread a napkin on her lap. The waiter ignored Alain's napkin. 'Russia vets all visitors on Syria. Russia is friend for Syria. Co-operate is good. Your name is known to FSB,' his breakfast companion proffered.

'And you are FSB,' he said knowingly, and with satisfaction, as if he had solved a complex riddle.

Ignoring his accusation she pressed on. 'America not have co-operation with Syria. Not read visitor manifest. How America know *you* are on Omayed?'

Alain shrugged, again. 'I suppose they read the airline manifest in Abu Dhabi. The United Arab Emirates is pro-American. You know this. It is logical U.A.E. will share passenger lists for Syria with America.'

But still Valya pressed on. 'Omayed hotel is not on airline manifest.'

Alain had not thought of that and he immediately sensed her gloating at his discomfort.

The coffee was thick Arabic and in short measure. Alain consumed the entire cup before realising it was empty. With some disdain at his lack of finesse Valentina signalled for more. The waiter returned, leaving the pot on the table this time, accustomed as he was to the Western penchant to drinking coffee like beer.

After some moments of visual assessment of each other, Alain could contain himself no longer.

'Valya, it is so good to see you. I missed you very deeply after Brac. I thought about you constantly, for weeks, months and even years later I lamented our lost chances. If only I had stayed in Yugoslavia.'

'Hvartska,' she corrected him.

'Whatever. I could have secured employment in one of the armies marauding through that broken region.'

'*Nyet*,' she answered. 'All Balkan armies are patriotic. New countries have no money for pay mercenaries. Not wealthy like Oman.'

She was not making things easy, that much Alain understood. 'I had no idea where to look for you Valya,' he said, with a touch of pleading in his voice.

'I return Soviet Union where is big changes. Very dangerous times. Yeltsin not keep good controls. Bandits steal, how you say, State assets – oil, gas, control of railways, minerals. Many state assets of new Russia are stolen. I make small shadow, not make noise and get killed,' she paused, searching for a simile, 'on cross-fire.'

Alain recalled reading about the death toll of entrepreneurial figures who had emerged from the smoke and dust caused by the re-birth of Russia. It had, he recalled, mounted swiftly during the halcyon months of changing the guard from Gorbachev to Yeltsin, and then Putin, who had emerged, seemingly from nowhere. 'You survived,' he said, stating the obvious.

'President Putin is good for Russia. Make Russia strong. Is good for me. My colonel was *droog* for President Putin," she explained, using the Russian word for friend. 'My colonel make work for me find bandit thieves of Russian assets.'

'And now?' he asked, 'What is your job in Syria?'

'Now I am colonel,' she tossed back.

'That does not surprise me,' he said with genuine feeling. 'But what is your job?'

'Assassinate enemies of Russia who are spies for America,' she said with a serious glare, before bursting into laughter. An insipid grin lingered on his face as he endured her humour, knowing that it was at his expense.

'I am FSB colonel. That is all you must know. Is why I ask questions, why is America CIA met you at hotel?'

'I have been thinking about that too,' Alain replied. 'This can only have come from New Zealand Foreign Affairs speaking with the Americans. Since the changing of the government in my country, relations with America have improved.'

'Is this good – you approve?' she interrupted.

Reflecting on this loaded question, Alain replied. 'I think the country was comfortable with having a foreign policy independent of America. Our Labour Government was not defeated because of its refusal to send troops to Iraq. Their foreign policy reflected the will of the people. But now we have a Prime Minister who is Jewish, so I am not surprised he has been overtly courting America.'

'What you think, America is good for New Zealand?' his interrogator continued.

Alain rubbed his chin, before answering, carefully. 'Short answer – no. I think New Zealand travels best outside America's umbrella.' The stunningly-attractive, but determined woman opposite him smiled.

'But,' Alain continued. 'Personally I have no gripe – ah, no hostility toward America.' Her smile dropped away. Finally she declared. 'You stupid man Mr Foveaux. You come on Syria buy phosphate. This I know. Today you meet Minister Mines and Minister Agriculture and maybe also Wakid Mashreq. He top man foreign investment and military intelligence.'

Alain raised his eyebrow, both in astonishment at her knowledge of his affairs, but also at the mention of Wakid Mashreq.

'Perhaps you will have reunion on military intelligence,' she quipped, referring to his former role with the Omani military.

'No such thing,' he said waving his finger in an admonishing gesture. 'But tell me Valya, why I am stupid?'

'You not tell New Zealand Foreign Affairs you at Syria for phosphate?'

'No, it is none of their business and they don't ask,' Alain replied. 'I considered it prudent to advise them that I was travelling to this increasingly dangerous zone, but not why.'

'Then your government tell America you are in Syria! This correct?' the Russian countered.

'Probably,' said Alain, considering whether New Zealand's officials would convey that information to the Americans. 'Not as a department policy, but an individual might have.'

'Why you not tell America? Why you not make friend on America, ask permission you can buy phosphate?'

Exasperation and irritation began to show in his manner. 'It is nothing to do with America where we buy phosphate. What is more, America has no control over who I trade with, nor does America have a right to poke its nose here.'

'Ha,' she said contemptuously. 'America soon make financial transaction blockade. Stop all payment to Syria for exports.'

'You are joking,' Alain replied, with genuine astonishment. 'How can they do that?'

Valentina shook her head. 'I tell you again, you stupid man Mr Foveaux. America constantly interfere all countries. CIA make problems on all countries where America not like regime. When America make world financial blockade, big problem for you to make payment for phosphate.'

Alain did not like the way the conversation was going and shifted uncomfortably in his chair. There was no denying America had the world by the throat when it came to transferring the currency that underpinned world trade. This was, he agreed, an unpalatable situation for many nations and was leading to initiatives by Brazil, Russia, India and China – BRIC by acronym – to set up their own international monetary fund.

'*Tak*,' she continued, reverting to Russian idiom for an expression similar to the English word, so. 'Someone on your country not want you make buy with Syria. These people tell America. It is true, I know this thing.'

Alain was unsure whether she meant she actually knew, as the result of information or intelligence the Russians had received, or whether she was speaking intuitively. Either way, her deduction unsettled him. The fertiliser industry in New Zealand was worth a billion dollars a year in revenue. Industrial espionage and sabotage for such a prize could certainly not be discounted.

Seeing she had hit a nerve, the Russian pressed home her advantage. 'Now your competitor has an ally in Syria who is also interested to stop you.' Alain said nothing, his second cup now containing cold coffee.

'Mr Foveaux,' she said leaning forward earnestly. 'This is very deadly place you come to at this time. Many people have died in this country recently. America uses this killing as step stone get on Syria. America tells world this for democracy. Same America what kidnap freedom fighters in Iraq and Afghan – fighters who say, "America go home". These fighters America name terrorists. Not make these fighters prisoner of war where are some Geneva Convention rules. America takes these people on black flights – aircraft with no identity. America take these men to prison farm in Romania where no democracy and also Poland and Lithuania, which wants war with Russia. At prison farm America torture these man. Make water-board torture. This not water ski but wet cloth on face make not breathing. Later these men they are dumped at Guantanamo Bay. You know what is Guantanamo Bay, Mr Foveaux?'

Alain nodded.

'Guantanamo Bay prison is outside jurisdiction of America law. Very convenient place for people America take terrorist because American constitution not applies.' Alain nodded once more, visions of protests in his own country against his war in Vietnam, flashing through his head.

'You here on Syria and buy phosphate. When blockade come you break blockade and make very big insult on America. Loss face, how you say. Best for America stop you before you make embarrassment on them.' Leaning back, she appraised Alain with mock contempt. When she continued her voice contained a measure of menace. 'Be very careful Mr Foveaux,' she said softly.

Collecting her jacket from the back of her chair as she stood to leave, Valentina reached out to touch his shoulder. Her first sign of consideration for him, he mused. But he lamented that it seemed not to rekindle lost feelings.

'You must be careful Alain. America will assassinate you. Not Russia, not me and not Syria. You are small cog in big wheel. You also now old man. Not like Vietnam. Not like Oman. Not like Balkans. This is dangerous place Alain. Russia is your only friend. *Dos vydahnya*.'

And just as many years before, in an instant she was gone.

Suddenly Alain felt very alone, deflated and uncertain. Dare he concede, he also felt very old.

Shahbander and Ali Abed and Joul Jammal and Baghdad. At least I can remember the name of the fourth street, Alain thought as he set out to find the intersection of four streets or avenues some seven hundred metres from the Omayed. As he walked past the Fardose Tower Hotel, a mere hundred metres on, security guards toting sub-machineguns languished in the shade. Alain did wonder why the Omayed was free of the same level of security as the Fardose, but such was the inexplicable case at several buildings he passed on his way to the roundabout of the four intersecting roads, only one of which he could remember by name without reference to his written directions.

Turning right into Baghdad Road he felt more at ease. The street was wider, carried more traffic but seemed less angry, and he could remember that name without his notes. Outside the entrance to Ministry Agriculture he stopped. It was eleven forty five am. He was early but he decided to enquire at the reception desk of a building with a confusing entrance foyer, where the office of the Minister Agriculture was actually located. It was a fortuitous precaution for the address he had been given was incorrect. The Ministry was situated in another nearby building in an alley with an unpronounceable name. Agitated, Alain drew a map in his diary as best he could follow the instructions of a woman who had little ability, either in the English or Russian languages.

Twelve minutes later Alain entered a nondescript but well-air conditioned building. This time his first stop was at a security desk with x-ray facilities, although they were inoperative. The guards however searched his person methodically and perhaps more thoroughly than the machine would have done. He wondered what process was adopted when a female came to visit the Minister. On the third floor he was again subject to security checks, but this time, only his passport and letter of introduction provided by the Syrian Ambassador in Canberra were scrutinised. Moments later he found himself in a large, well-worn but very outdated office, where three men sat waiting.

'Hello, I am Alain Foveaux. I am from New Zealand and I have an appointment to see the Minister Agriculture,' he said politely, but firmly.

The three men all smiled, greeting him in Arabic. Alain waited for the English version but it did not come. *'Kator Meenistre'*, Alain fumbled, in Russian. 'Who is the Minister?'

'Patorm', replied one of the men indicating that the Government official would be there soon.

An awkward few minutes passed with Alain making perfunctory attempts in Russian to discuss the weather. Then a man of ample girth, but of impressive stature, swept into the room. Dressed immaculately in suit and tie, he was followed by another, equally deserving of immediate respect. Alain caught sight of two strapping younger men waiting outside the room as the door closed.

The Minister's English was passable but his Russian was better, so Alain found himself slipping between the languages as the meeting progressed. The second man never introduced himself and took a seat behind the trio who had been in the room when he arrived. Alain did not need two guesses as to who was the chief of spies.

An attractive woman in Western clothing entered, bringing mint tea. She was a stunningly attractive woman, possibly aged forty, with olive complexion and deep brown eyes matching her dark brown hair. Alain was momentarily transfixed by the grace and elegance of this apparition – a younger version of Sophia Loren, he thought.

The meeting with the Minister lasted thirty minutes. Most of the discussion was on world affairs and how New Zealand viewed Syria in its present situation. There was particular interest in why New Zealand and Australia held such divergent positions on America and Iraq, and ten minutes was devoted to what Alain thought about Europe's financial crisis. Reference to the sale of phosphate was fleeting, which was an irritant to someone who had travelled half-way around the world for exactly this purpose. During the meeting, the three men who had been in the room prior to his arrival scribbled notes incessantly, the initial language difficulty apparently no longer affecting them.

As quickly as the meeting had commenced, it ended. Alain found that he was the only person remaining in the office. The whole affair seemed surreal. Was it real? He wondered.

When the stunningly attractive woman re-appeared in the doorway, he knew it had not been a dream, but any thoughts he may have had about time alone with her at a nearby café were quickly dispelled. The woman was polite but beneath the veneer of feminine allure, Alain perceived a professional who believed in her religion, and any familiarity beyond handing him a card with an address and a time for the next meeting, would have been his imagination.

'This meeting will be with managers from the phosphate company,' she said by way of alerting Alain to the possibility that Ministerial oversight of export business did not include the distasteful business of setting prices and payment regimes. 'These managers are not proficient in English. We can provide a translator but you might wish to engage an interpreter from one of the agencies in the city. They are accustomed to this work and speak more fluently than our Government interpreters,' she said with a haunting smile and impeccable English.

Alain meandered back to the Omayed hotel. This was a fascinating city in a fascinating part of the word. He remembered his promise to himself to revisit the Old City and to tramp its kilometres of crowded ancient passageways. Meanwhile, all about him were the sounds and smells of a civilization confident of its place in the world in spite of its internal problems. The people of Damascus seemed pretty happy to him.

The woman from the Agriculture Ministry had unsettled Alain more than he realised at the time. Sex, he considered, was like oxygen. Not important until it was not available. As a young man in his twenties, sex had come and gone, according to one's luck at the rugby club or chance meetings through friends at work. When he and Kay married after his return from Vietnam he had been twenty-five. From that moment on he had been monogamous, the sex they shared being frequent and beautiful. When she'd died in childbirth two years later, he'd been devastated and for some time completely lost that carnal urge.

In Oman sex was intermittent. Sleeping with the locals was a definite no-go zone. For reasons of religious divide and family honour, making advances to local women would have been distinctly injurious to his health and wellbeing. In lands where promiscuity was an option only of the privileged in illegal but classy bordellos, for foreigners such adventures were also off limits. There had been a few passing affairs of course, mostly with German nurses on contract to the Arab Emirates. But his work had been absorbing, demanding and often isolated him from opportunities to indulge with the fairer sex. And so he had been a virtual monk – most of the time.

But then there had been Valentina. Like a Goddess she had invaded his being, dominating his thoughts for months after their liaison in Croatia and setting a benchmark no other casual affair could match. Disinclined to lure a juvenile 'bride' from the Ukraine or Thailand to fill a void, Alain had, as he reflected, had over recent years been near suffocation, to revert to the oxygen analogy.

Looking forward to a cold shower and an afternoon nap, Alain waited patiently as the antique elevator answered his summons to join him in the lobby. He was surprised however to find not only Dwight Arnold junior but also another younger man with spectacles and greasy hair watching him from across the foyer. Both wore the unmistakable garb of United States Embassy staff. Alain had already correctly placed Dwight as being an employee of the CIA. He placed the second American as technical, possibly language and possibly an economist.

'Hi Alain,' Dwight greeted him like a long-lost friend. 'Thought we had an agreement?'

'Oh!' said Alain, now genuinely surprised.

'We're here to help you find your way around the city. You gonna need a driver to get to Homs?'

'Sorry?' said Alain, now even more genuinely confused. 'Homs?'

'Site of the big phosphate mines,' his self-appointed American guardian retorted. 'Plenty of trouble up there too. You are gonna need our escort my friend.'

Alain looked at his shoes, twiddling the signature ring on his finger. 'Who is your friend?' he decided to ask, before challenging the brazen American.

'Hey, sure buddy. Very rude of me. This is Wilbur. He is our resident linguist. Totally fluent in English, Arabic, Russian, German, Italian and Spanish. That's where he gets his complexion. Back home we'd call him a Spic.' Dwight laughed too loudly.

Wilbur and Alain acknowledged each other with a nod but there was no attempt to shake hands. 'Dwight, this is going a bit fast for me,' Alain professed. 'Your friend, is he Puerto Rican?'

'My parents were, Mr Foveaux,' Wilbur replied, with a degree of dignity.

'You work for the CIA too?' Alain flicked back.

Dwight and Wilbur exchanged glances. 'We are both with the Embassy, Mr Foveaux,' Dwight interjected. 'We're here to help you negotiate with these wogs. This is a hard land. They will sell you fifty tons but send you forty tons.'

Alain waited for the moment of extreme irritation to pass, and said, 'Listen Dwight. Why don't you chaps wait for me? I want to shower. I'll come down shortly and we can sort this out.'

'Sure thing Alain,' Dwight replied. 'Sure thing. We'll be in the bar.'

Arriving at his room, Alain turned the key, pushed open the door and waited a moment for his eyes to accustom to the darkened surrounds. Instinctively he knew someone was already there. He had no weapon so he balanced on his toes prepared to deflect a blow.

'*Prevyet*,' said a voice he knew. Then he smelt her perfume.

'Valya,' he replied, hoping the relief didn't show in his voice. 'Today is turning into one big surprise.'

'Your meeting is good?' she enquired, with no explanation of how she had come to be in his room.

'Which meeting are you referring too; with the Minister or with the Americans?' he asked.

'You have meeting with Americans?' she probed with alacrity, and some alarm in her voice.

Alain tossed his notebook onto the dresser and began to undress, heading for the bathroom.

'Yes, they were waiting in the lobby. They probably couldn't get the spare key to this room because you already had it,' he responded with sarcasm.

'You are telling me true Alain Foveaux? CIA is in lobby?' the Russian probed.

'Look Valya,' he said with undisguised annoyance. 'I am in this country to buy phosphate. What is so sexy about manure? Why am I all of a sudden a big celebrity being shadowed by the CIA and the FSB? You people think I am going to make bombs with this stuff? I am not a bloody terrorist you know.'

Moving across the room, Valentina picked up his trousers from the floor and folded them over a chair. Alain stepped out of his designer underwear and headed for the shower.

Fumbling with the antiquated controls, his thoughts returned to the wander down memory lane he had indulged in on the walk back to his hotel from the Minister's office. Almost starving for oxygen for months, now in less than an hour his loins had ached at the sight of a Syrian beauty and now this Russian, so close to him. Quickly twisting the tap to cold, he entered the shower without hesitation.

It was an older style shower with confined space but Valentina reached in to adjust the water flow to warm and then made room for them both. Water cascaded over their bodies, noses touching, eyes closed. Without warning, Valentina took his erection into her womanly sanctuary, producing what both of them had known would be an inevitable outcome.

It took time for the emotion and excitement to dissipate, but when it did, he remembered his promise to the Americans.

Leaving his Russian love-mate in his room he went down to the lobby. Dwight and Wilber had gone, but the receptionist handed him a folded piece of hotel paper. The message, scrambled in hand, was simple. "Thought we'd let you sleep. Will call at 8 pm. Please, be our guest for dinner. Our treat. Dwight."

Alain returned to his room and showed the note to Valentina. 'Okay', he said, taking a seat at the writing desk as she faced the mirror applying facial cream. 'You have made me an offer.'

'Russia make offer, not Valya. Russia have big interest in your project. Is why Valya has license to make deal. Valya only Colonel. This deal from '*glarvnee obizyarn*'.

'Chief Monkey,' Alain translated aloud. Perhaps she means Putin. Perhaps she means her general. But either way she is correct. What Valya had offered had to have come from very high up the tree. 'Did Russia make me the offer of Valentina too,' he asked, but immediately regretted his banality.

Leaning back from the mirror the Russian gazed into his eyes, pouting her lips. He had anticipated a caress but his head reeled from the effect of a slap across his face which knocked him out of his chair.

'Tomorrow you go to Homs with CIA.' Her manner was composed as if his faux pas had not happened. 'Not important for you visit Homs. Contract signed here in Damascus. But Russia want you tell Valya what is America show you in Homs. Is propaganda I think. America not have access to phosphate mines and managers not speak with CIA. Visit in Homs very interesting for Russia. Russia make translator for you. From New Zealand. Understands rugby,' she said, uncharitably Alain thought.

He cocked his head in genuine surprise. 'When do I meet this translator? What is his name?'

'Egor. Tomorrow you are in Homs. Return late. Long drive. If no trouble you in bed two am. Next day you have meeting with phosphate managers, office in Baghdad Avenue. Noon. Always Syria meetings noon. Egor he will meet you on Minister's address eleven forty five am. He know All Blacks' names. Code words,' she said cheekily, with still no sign she had been offended by his earlier unfair barb. Collecting her cosmetics, finally she confronted him. 'You are *durak*, Alain Foveaux.'

Alain nodded. 'Yes, I am a stupid man Valya.' He followed her to the door.

'You make good plan for phosphate, you Russia friend. When all finish maybe you make home Rostov na Dona.'

'Why would I live in Rostov on Don, Valya?'

Pausing in the corridor she smiled. 'Valya now live Rostov na Dona.' And she was gone.

Chapter Six

Auckland, New Zealand.

Life in Egor's new country was far easier than the letters from his sister Marina had suggested. For a start the roads were in much better repair than the roads in Russia. At another extreme the level of crime was amateur in comparison to the intensity of crime back home. Often Egor had scoffed at the low mentality pub and club violence he had witnessed in his new land. Predominantly Polynesian gang members would fight each other over a table to drink at in a bar rather than battling over which bars and clubs would pay protection money.

Most astonishing had been the laid back attitude of New Zealanders to education. A belief that a student must never be failed because of the psychological damage it might do was a characteristic of the education system which seemed to pervade other aspects of life. The attitude that competing was important but winning was not was a shock to the Russian. It seemed to Egor this ethos emanated from a misguided belief that irreparable damage could result if a young person was pressured to do better.

Egor realised early that his Russian university degree was worthless in many Western countries which measured academic qualifications on the reputation of an institution being "acceptable" rather than the levels of academic achievement the university attained. In Auckland he enrolled to repeat the courses he had passed in Irkutsk. On a weekly basis he cruised through the mathematics and physics examination in the top deciles, demonstrating to himself, if not to his lecturers, that the level of academic delivery in New Zealand universities was well below that of Russia. This was particularly evident in the technical disciplines, and especially physics and mathematics.

Egor realised quickly that the influx of Asian students - particularly from Korea, Taiwan, China - who flooded the universities, were also far ahead of New Zealand students academically. Most Asian students, he concluded, attended New Zealand universities, not for the academic excellence they promised (but did not deliver), but either to satisfy residence criteria for immigration qualification or because they had failed to achieve the very high pass marks to gain entry to universities in their home countries.

Egor could have taken advantage of a student loan scheme to fund his studies but it was easy to secure employment as a café kitchen hand instead because many New Zealand students seemed not inclined to work. Also, for indigenous New Zealanders it was a relatively easy option to get onto unemployment or sickness benefits. He soon realised that Welfare payments were more than a motor mechanic was paid in Irkutsk. The result was plenty of low paid jobs which Egor was very willing to accept.

Egor resisted invitations from other young men for him to join a rugby team. Obsession with the game seemed to border on religious fervour. Mothers and grandmothers seemed to know more about rugby than they did obstetrics. Well-muscled, tall and solidly-built, Egor was told he would make an excellent lock forward or flanker, but the promise of adulation from the calibre of young women he had seen hanging from the arms of intoxicated rugby heroes in the clubs he sometimes frequented, lacked appeal. The solitude of karate lessons with an ageing Japanese master to improve the karate training he had obtained at officer school in Russia, had more appeal and within a year he was ranked black belt *chidokan*.

The first crisis Egor faced in his new land was a health scare. His mother failed a breast screening which had been offered free of charge, part of a campaign against this ravaging type of cancer. Early tests indicated his mother would need surgery, but in spite of the Government's enthusiastic endorsement of breast cancer awareness, getting her into a public hospital proved problematic. Very soon he learned that being Caucasian or white, and in particular being from Russia which most New Zealanders still viewed as a Cold War adversary, was not good pedigree for gaining admission to public hospitals. Queues of Polynesians from nearby Pacific Island states consistently cluttered the entrance ways to public hospitals and emergency facilities. Irrespective of the growing seriousness of his mother's condition, somehow the authorities simply did not help.

One day as he sat in a café opposite a bank, he could not believe the lack of security he witnessed when a uniformed crew stopped to replenish an automatic teller machine. A seed was sown in his mind at that moment. He knew then that he would not stand by and wait until his mother's condition was beyond repair. He would get the money for the private hospital care which was out of reach of his immigrant family.

That evening he told his mother of his plans. His mother's anguished cry brought his sister rushing into the lounge. Fearing the worst, grief showed on the young woman's face. 'Mama,' she screamed.

Egor stood like a colossus over the two women in his life. 'It is not Mama,' he said softly seeking to reassure his sister.

Wide-eyed, Marina looked at him. 'What? What is it then? What have you done?'

Egor tried to explain but Marina cut him short. '*Durak!*' she shouted. 'Fool.'

Turning to her mother she implored. 'Mama, you must tell him. He is right to get money for you. But not this way. You must tell him.'

Resignedly their mother signalled Egor to lift from the dresser a matrushka doll. Inside the largest doll were not smaller dolls as was customary, but a folded document, which she handed to her son. It was embossed with the Russian State coat of arms and beneath Egor recognised the address of FSB, Moscow; successor to the KGB.

Egor pushed the buzzer on the entrance gate to the Russian embassy in Messines Road, Wellington. A voice asked him in English to state his name and business. Egor answered in English. The reply came back in Russian and the gate opened automatically.

Inside the gate Egor stopped to savour the feeling of being on Russian soil once again. The neat buildings and gardens nestled on a hill, providing a stunning view over the capital city. A large ferry made smoke against the still harbour vista, as it glided silently across the water. Egor breathed deeply and walked with purpose to the Ambassador's section of the compound.

The Ambassador, urbane and mid-fifties, seemed a pleasant man and Egor waited for the diplomat to explain what Mother Russia wanted of him.

After perfunctory and polite chat the Ambassador said, 'Alexi is Third Secretary and responsible for matters which will involve you. Alexi has full authority from the Kremlin to process your case.' He paused then said, 'Look after your education and the work you should carry out. It has been a pleasure meeting you young man. I am impressed with your commitment to Russia and to making a success of your life in New Zealand.'

The Ambassador stood and walked to the large window. Alexi moved behind the desk vacated by the senior diplomat and opened a folder. He looked at the Ambassador and appeared to be waiting for him to leave the room. When the Ambassador remained looking out of the window, Alexi shrugged imperceptibly then addressed Egor. His manner was brisk but not unpleasant, yet Egor sensed he lacked the graces displayed by the Ambassador.

'I am Alexander Chernusskiy. I am FSB Major. Moscow directs me to offer you a commission as lieutenant, FSB. What is your response?'

Egor demurred. His plan prior to arriving at the Embassy was simple. Offer his services on condition money be advanced for medical costs for his mother. But now, in the lion's lair, he felt uncertain. He had expected to be told that the Motherland wanted his services, but it was one thing to think about demanding money before he obliged and another thing entirely too actually do this.

'What will I be required to do?' he asked.

The major smiled sardonically. 'You do not expect me to discuss FSB duties with someone who is not FSB? Surely?'

Egor's head dropped slightly, his body language signalling clearly to the major that he had capitulated.

'I have papers for you to sign. Here,' he indicated with a pen.

Egor demurred again.

'Come,' encouraged the major in a tone which resembled an order but was not.

Egor stood and lifted his head. 'I am willing to serve Mother Russia, comrade major, but I must first know what is expected of me, and before I make any final decision I wish to negotiate allocation of funding to meet urgent medical costs for my mother.'

The Third Secretary seemed incapable of response. Lower jaw dropped and mouth ajar, slowly he stood. Pressing his knuckles onto the desk top he leaned forward in an unmistakeable gesture of conflict.

'Your mother is unwell?' asked the Ambassador interjecting from the corner of the room.

Standing to attention Egor turned his head and replied. 'Yes comrade Ambassador. Her medical condition requires surgery, immediately. Her medical costs will exceed forty thousand dollars. Our family does not have that money.'

'But what of this fine public health service? Will that not accommodate your mother?'

Egor shook his head. 'No com...'

'Enough of that comrade nonsense,' the Ambassador barked harshly. 'That went out the door when they set fire to the White House,' he said referring to the Parliament in Moscow fired during the halcyon days of transition from the Union of Soviet Socialist Republics to Russia. 'Sit down please. Explain. What is your motive for responding to the Kremlin invitation,' he said with only the slightest trace of sarcasm.

Egor explained his mother's plight.

'So, you will also wish to nurse her as she recovers?' enquired the Ambassador. Before Egor could reply he asked, 'How long will it take to complete your second degree?' This time there was no mistaking the irony that a student whose standard of mathematics and physics won a pass in a Russian institution must endure the ignominy of re-sitting a degree to obtain a certificate accepted in the West.

'Two more years sir and yes, I do wish to be with my mother as she recovers. My sister is at school. I must also work in the café. We have no money.'

'Wait outside please,' instructed the Ambassador.

Later that day Egor bought eleven roses from a florist at the Auckland airport before taking the bus into the city. An equal number - a dozen such as seemed the custom of New Zealanders - would be a bad omen. Odd numbers for health and happiness was an entrenched Russian custom and it would be unwise to ignore this on such an occasion.

At Newmarket he got off the bus and walked five kilometres to their apartment in Meadowbank. Egor smiled to himself. His mother had sacrificed much to ensure the family had accommodation in the Eastern suburbs of Auckland. Even if their home was not luxurious and only on the verge of the dress circle of fine houses, private schools, well-paid executives, tennis-playing wives, zero crime and the greatest number of Ferraris per head of population in one suburb in the world, the Rostov family avoided the fate of most immigrant families - residence in a poor suburb, with the inevitable consequences.

Over dinner Egor explained the detail of the contract he had made with the Government of Russia. All conversation within the family was in Russian so expression of feelings and explanations flowed in a highly-educated vernacular.

'I am to complete my degree at Auckland University. This time frame should also permit me to obtain New Zealand citizenship and a New Zealand passport. The major insisted a New Zealand passport would help me travel internationally without the need for visas, as is the requirement with our Russian passports.'

In silence his mother ate the borsch entrée but Marina fidgeted nervously.

'What else?' she demanded. 'What more must you do? Is your pay sufficient to cover mother's medical procedure?'

Savouring the moment, Egor pushed a piece of beetroot around his plate with his spoon. 'I am officially a second lieutenant FSB but I have no pay.'

Marina was aghast. Dropping her spoon into her soup, she stifled the urge to shout at her brother.

'I have received a loan from my employer. The loan will be sufficient to pay all invoices for mother's treatment.'

At this Marina did scream. Leaping around the table she hugged first her brother then her mama. But her euphoric display was cut short by her mother.

'And what else, my son. What must you do? To save my body what price has been paid for your soul?' she asked and her eyes demanded no obfuscation.

Egor pushed his plate away. 'I am at peace Mama,' he said. 'I must serve Mother Russia as directed but this is not to me a burden. It is what Deyduschka wanted. And it is what I want.'

In explanation he spoke. 'New Zealand is pleasant land but its people are foolish in many ways. For one, they insist they are not racist, but they are against immigrants. Coloured skin Pacific Islander people are tolerated if they play rugby but are avoided by whites with influence and affluence and abused by the white manual workers who compete for the same jobs. Asians are reviled, ridiculed for their facial distinction, condemned for their self-imposed isolation and despised because they operate a black market economy and avoid taxation. But also white Caucasians, like us, our accents are a beacon for New Zealanders to treat us as inferior. Have you noticed how they resort to their monosyllable manner of speaking to us, as if we were children?'

Marina giggled at this last comment, causing Egor to glare at her long and hard.

'This makes it very difficult for you to succeed, Mama, and me also. Marina is younger and has no accent,' offering a barb to his sister. 'But for me at least, I welcome the chance to serve the Motherland, to gain employment where my education and potential can find its level and not be limited by prejudice of people who really are not highly educated in spite of their self-perception.'

'Of what else do you not approve in this land of plenty?' asked his mother.

'Most perspicacious of you, Mama, your phrase, "Land of plenty". If Marx were to visit he would consider he had found the utopia he proclaimed,' scoffed Egor. 'But,' he continued with less enthusiasm. 'Like all forms of communism or state socialism where the State provides, sooner or later, over spending and under productivity combine in a toxic economic mixture.'

'What do you speak of?' enquired his sister, somewhat confused.

'Kiwis already they lose the drive to succeed. "She'll be right!" You have heard this expression? But it is more. It has become an idiosyncrasy which characterises the nation. They won't or don't want to work hard. For people who do wish to get ahead it becomes too hard to work two jobs. Soon they too lapse into a routine; as long as they earn sufficient for the man to have a beer at the rugby club each Friday night where he is content to watch another game on TV! For young people, it is too difficult to study long hours. Last week parents and students complained the examination of French language was too difficult for school finals! So! New Zealand students will be set easy examinations in French next year! But this of course will be of no use when they must seek employment where language fluency is required,' he concluded with a shrug.

'And for these calibre of reasons you will leave our new home?' asked his mother in a tone of which Egor knew to be wary. 'This category of malingering people also exist in Russia where most find solace in vodka.'

'Mama,' he said. 'It is best for us to be in New Zealand. This I do not dispute. Although this may be a fool's paradise, it will survive for some years to come and you have brought us from a land we know the faults of too well; uncertainty of pensions and banking integrity; crime which invades the best homes in more brutal ways than these people can imagine; corruption from the lowest council employee to the most powerful politician; from police in the street to industry inspectors or customs and excise agents. To say nothing of the extremes of weather all must endure. Russia is a harsh land, I can see this clearly. You have done well to bring your children to this sheltered land and I do hope Babushka will join us soon.'

At the mention of grandmother all fell silent. It was proving a mammoth battle to bring the old lady to be with the family.

Egor recalled his poignant departure from Russia and his grandmother. He had struggled with the enormous feeling of guilt at leaving Mother Russia. Though he was leaving to join his mother and younger sister in New Zealand, it was difficult for him to suppress a feeling of shame. He could not help feeling that he was deserting his country in time of need.

Unlike some families who emigrated as a means of keeping a son from conscription into a military service not known not for its sensibilities in training, this was not the case with Egor. He had refused to join his mother in New Zealand until he had completed his officer training. At least he retained that level of dignity but he had also fulfilled a pledge to his grandfather who had been a general for both the armies of the Tsar before the revolution and the Red Army after the revolution: "Serve the Motherland, my son." The time frame of his military service also gave him time to complete an engineering degree at Irkutsk University. For all its faults and hardships, Russia had equipped him well for life and for this he was grateful. His heart was in Russia and forever would he be Russian.

Embracing his babushka, her frail frame had collapsed against his strong torso. He struggled to hide the emotion of the moment.

'Babushka,' he said plaintively. 'You must please reconsider. Please come to join mama and Marina and me. Mama writes she can have you join us under family reunion; it is a special category of immigration for families who are apart.'

Babushka heaved a deep sigh. 'I must stay and tend to dyedushka and your papa,' she said resignedly. 'They would be lost if I were to leave them.'

Closing his eyes tightly shut had been no barrier to tears which trickled down his cheeks. Both his grandfather and father had been dead for several years but still the old woman spoke of them as if they were waiting for her in the car.

A hand on his shoulder separated him from his grandmother. Larisa, his mother's sister, guided babushka from the passenger embarkation gate. She had smiled but did not speak. Forlorn Egor had waved to two friends since childhood who had come to farewell him. Then he'd walked through passport control.

Helping herself to salad, the mother poised with fork in hand. 'But?' she asked.

Egor smiled. There would be no rebuke that he sensed from her changed tone of speech.

'Russia wants me. This country does not. Russia has offered me employment commensurate with my education and my aspirations. I want to help build a nation and be permitted to make the contribution my personality and my skills affords. Russia offers this. New Zealand does not.'

'Well,' said Marina. 'Mr Superman. What will you do for your foreign employer? Spy on your new countrymen?'

'Ha!' scoffed Egor. 'The last Kiwi to be arrested for spying on behalf of the Soviet Union was an economist. Dr Sutch! He was accused of passing secrets to the Soviets about prices New Zealand would accept for meat. For me to get into such a position I would need to be employed by Foreign Affairs. The chances of me! A Russian immigrant! No little sister. I am of no use as a spy in New Zealand.

'So? What must you do?' Little sister would not be dissuaded.

Egor sighed. 'First I must be with mother as she recovers. This is the instruction of the Ambassador. Then I must visit the Embassy once a month for a weekend. At that time I will be indoctrinated,' he said with a trace of cynicism. 'By major Chennusskiy. What he will impart I can only guess.'

Egor's mama watched her son in silence.

'Perhaps I will travel to Moscow during a university vacation; they do not wish to prolong my study period by taking me away from university during semester.'

'They will teach you how to shoot,' suggested Marina.

'That I learned in officer training before I departed Russia,' responded Egor somewhat annoyed at his sister's childish remarks. 'Oh!' he exclaimed as he recalled one other requirement. 'I must enrol in Arabic language.'

Chapter Seven

Damascus

Announcement of imminent landing brought Egor back to the present. Having boarded the noon Singapore Air flight out of Auckland, he had arrived in Singapore in time for dinner.

After a surprisingly inexpensive taxi ride from Changi Airport to his hotel on Orchard Road, Egor was out on the streets of the city which still offered glimpses of British colonialism in the architecture of many preserved building facades.

'This is how the world should be' said Egor to himself as he meandered down a boulevard, made a right turn and found himself at Raffles. Famous as a setting for the romanticism of British colonialism by the pen of Somerset Maugham and infamous as a brothel for the Imperial Japanese conquerors who in 1941 emphatically exposed the fragility of British, Dutch and Portuguese imperialistic designs, the venue now served as a tourist rendezvous.

By the time Egor returned to his hotel he had fucked two Chinese and one Russian whore.

Before breakfast Egor worked out in the hotel gym then swam one hundred laps of an annoyingly short twenty five metres pool. By check out, he had fucked two more Chinese whores both at the same time. At two pm he took a taxi back to Changi airport and hung about to catch the second leg of his Auckland to Abu Dhabi economy class flight.

During the eight hour flight to United Arab Emirates, in a state of hedonistic euphoria, Egor masturbated in the toilet convincing himself he qualified for the Mile High Club. In Abu Dhabi he crashed out for almost twenty four hours in the Sheraton Khalidya before boarding his Etihad connection to Damascus.

When he looked upon Colonel Valentina Goloshapova with lascivious intent he made his first mistake.

The Russian embassy in Damascus was quite a different beast to that which he had become accustomed to in Wellington. The prefix "comrade" was, as in the case of Wellington, extinct, but the ethos was most certainly alive in Syria. In his first unarmed combat refresher Egor came to understand quickly that application of the cavalier New Zealand standard of "She'll be right mate', had no place with the Russian mission in Syria. Only the timely interruption of Colonel Goloshapova at the gymnasium to deliver manuals for his study, saved him from severe contusions and possible joint dislocation at the hands of a brutal Alpha Force instructor, Sergei. When it came to the shooting range, Egor was barely able to focus on the target, so physically exhausted was he.

Two weeks after his arrival in Damascus Egor had his first formal briefing from Colonel Valentina Goloshapova. Though wearing casual civilian clothing, Egor stood rigidly at attention, eyes focused on the wall portrait of President Putin.

Ignoring his presence, Valentina took her chair at her desk and proceeded to flick through leaflets in a ring bind folder. After some minutes she lifted her gaze to appraise the young man. He was a strapping physical specimen and handsome too. His academic record was impeccable; straight A student at Irkutsk University and straight A student at University of Auckland. Mathematics, physics, engineering. Objective subject matter; none of the subjective easy subjects like law and social science which seemed too often for her liking to adorn the curriculum vitae of new recruits to the Federal Security Service.

His conduct in Singapore, as reported in his dossier, was that of an immature *derevnarar mooschek* or hayseed, but his application to training and his grasp of instruction in trade and financial transactions, was "commendable" according to his instructors. Language acquisition in English; excellent. Language acquisition in Arabic; pass. There were no reports of indiscreet behaviour during his leisure time roving the bazaars and enticingly exotic alleys of the Old City but the report from Singapore told a different tale.

'Be seated,' she ordered. Egor sat.

'You have been living in New Zealand now for five years. You have New Zealand citizenship. Tell me Lieutenant, you know well your new countrymen?'

Egor was cautious. From the moment he'd made the mistake of looking upon the colonel as something to bed, he'd felt, metaphorically, a knife at his throat. Every comment he had subsequently gleaned from casual conversation or overheard among colleagues, warned him to tread with great care. By physical appearance she seemed to be no more than five years his senior but his research placed her at least being mid-forties so his first indiscretion had been excusable. At least that is how he had reasoned to himself.

He had learned that she trained as a medical doctor before being recruited to the KGB. Her commitment to Mother Russia was unyielding. His Alpha Instructor had warned him never to touch the colonel, even in banter, for she resented unwelcome male attention and had the "martial arts skills to match her mental determination"; a phrase the instructor had left linger. Egor realised he was afraid of this woman.

'I have lived with them colonel, and observed their idiosyncrasies. It is safe place for my mother and sister to live.'

'Would you, how shall I say, spy on your new country for Russia?'

Egor had anticipated a question of this nature and had resolved not to prevaricate if asked. 'I have New Zealand citizenship but I am Russian and will always be. I joined FSB to serve Russia and I will do what is asked. But in New Zealand there is little I can do to help Russia in a covert way. I would need to be an employee of the government with access to information on trade or government intentions to sell state assets as is their way to repay international debt. But I am none of these things,' he replied. Then he added as an after-thought; 'Their military capacity is fisheries protection of their economic zone; that is all.'

A few moments later he said, 'I would prefer not to be asked to spy, as you say, on my new country.'

Valentina appraised her subordinate in silence for some time. Finally she said, 'Actually Egor,' using his first name for the first time, 'We intend you to help your new country. In doing this you will also assist Russia to help Syria who has long been our ally. This is why you have been brought to Syria.'

'I am ready, Colonel,' replied Egor.

Valentina handed a dossier to Egor. 'This is a dossier on Alain Foveaux. He has been engaged by a small fertiliser company in New Zealand to secure a consistent supply of RPR phosphate. Your task Lieutenant is to make yourself indispensable to the man.'

'How?' asked Egor after hesitating.

The colonel eyed her subordinate. 'I worked with him briefly on an operation in Bosnia during the Balkan conflict. I have made contact with him again. He is a little out of his depth. I will arrange for you to be assigned as his translator when he begins negotiations to buy phosphate. You should use that relationship to foster camaraderie. Stay with him in his leisure time. Make him like you. Make him rely on you. Make him trust you. We need him on our side. He could be the catalyst to several opportunities being considered at a higher level than mine.'

Chapter Eight

Homs, Syria.

'This region is combustible,' Dwight explained with apparent enthusiasm. 'A powder keg.'

It had been an early start. The Americans collected Alain from the Omayed at two in the morning. He had not returned to his hotel bed from dinner the previous evening until ten pm so he was grateful to snatch sleep intermittently as the large Dodge four wheel drive travelled north on the Aleppo highway. Dwight and Wilbur also seemed comfortable snoozing while the driver piloted his big Dodge machine with commendable skill.

After several hours Dwight entered into a desultory narrative as they approached the environs of the third largest city in Syria.

'The place dates back two thousand years,' he volunteered. 'The Romans were here, as they were everywhere.'

Profound, thought Alain.

'The Muslims took over when Islam began to pollute the globe, back in the seventh century or thereabouts. The Crusaders arrived in the eleventh century and for a couple of hundred years brought Christianity back to the stomping grounds of Jesus, Our Lord.'

Reference to the Christian religion and the Crusader cause was a constant theme. Alain recalled descriptions of former President, George W Bush, comparing the mission of America in Iraq with the Crusades of a thousand years before.

Dwight went on. 'Krak des Chevaliers, a Crusader fortress, is in this region. It's worth a visit. The Templar Knight Crusaders were impregnable in that garrison, from which they sallied forth to save the peasants from the brutality and barbarity of Muhammad and his followers.'

Alain resisted the urge to challenge this interpretation of historic facts. The castle had been the base for some two thousand Knights Hospitallers, not the Templar Knights, and they had raped the land far and wide, extracting tribute from the peoples whom the Crusades were ostensibly saving from perdition, until 1271. The fortress was then captured by the Mamluk after a siege lasting thirty six days.

When Dwight expanded his commentary, declaring that the 'Crusaders finally vacated Jerusalem after a Muslim general, name of Saladin, starved the city – a victory of logistics rather than superior fighters,' Alain could endure no more in silence.

'Yes, I am aware of the role good logistics plays in warfare,' he said casually. 'I was in fact logistics commandant in the Omani army, and as with most if not all problems we face today, history was my guide book to success in that role.'

'Please explain, Mr Foveaux,' asked Wilbur, the more studious of his two travelling companions. 'I too have studied many civilizations, it is part of linguistics. I am interested to hear why you place such importance on logistics in the subject of preservation of civilizations.'

'I do not have a PhD Wilbur, but I was smart enough to understand that of the three elements which defeated Napoleon in Russia, the one over which he had total control was logistics. He had no control over the Russian winter or over the Russian army, but provision of appropriate supplies at the appropriate time was an element he did control. He got it wrong and lost the war.'

'The same thing happened to Rommel against the Eighth Army in North Africa. Hitler denied him fuel supplies. Logistics! The telling factor of that theatre of war was supplies to Rommel and not the late arrival of American forces in North Africa,' he said, adding a snarky barb. 'Logistics or supply of such elementary items like winter clothing and anti-freeze oil was also a critical factor in Germany's implosion on the Eastern front although I'm sure the roused and angry Russian Bear was certainly the dominating factor in that theatre.'

They drove on in silence, the Americans uncertain how to respond to Alain's less than subtle rebuff.

'So, my friend Dwight,' the New Zealander said in a conciliatory tone, 'to suggest that Montferrat the Crusader commander at Jerusalem was defeated by logistics and not superior fighters is tantamount to suggesting that planning to have sufficient ammunition is not part of battle strategy.

Superior planning is always the difference between victory and defeat.'

A minute or so later Alain delivered the coup de grace. 'Saladin was smarter than the Crusaders. He is also remembered for his humane treatment of the vanquished when he retook Jerusalem. Something the Crusaders did not afford the occupants of that city when they captured it a century earlier, raping and pillaging with typical Christian zeal. Hence his epithet - Saladin the Merciful.'

Rather than subdue Dwight, Alain's rebuff seemed to have goaded him into adopting a more provocative manner. As the day wore on, this deteriorated into bullying and intimidating behaviour. The less Alain was inclined to heed the advice of his American friends, the less they were inclined to maintain a facade of congeniality.

As the day passed, Alain viewed oil installations, cement works, heavy industry factories and ultimately regions demarcated as phosphate mining operations. Only once were they confronted by protestors or terrorists, depending on which side of the conflict one viewed events from. Some twenty or thirty young men, all wearing variations of turban - some chequered red and white, some black and white and some plain dull colours but dirty. None of the militants he saw carried firearms, but in their faces they carried defiance.

Later that afternoon the trio took refuge in a shaded café. The heat manifest in a simmering haze and the yellow and gold desert environs of the countryside blended into the city as if part of one large landscape. Alain drank mint tea while the Americans drank Coke.

'So now we are here, you are sure there is no phosphate official you need to meet?' Dwight enquired.

Alain sighed audibly. 'Gentlemen, as I said last night at dinner, my next meeting with the phosphate people is tomorrow at noon, so the sooner we head for Damascus, the better. I do appreciate the tour and the time you have given me. I have noticed many of the sectors of this city are off limits. Perhaps that's what you wished me to witness first hand? But I am not in this country to try and solve their internal problems. I simply want to buy manure.'

The way Dwight was shunting his drink around the table top with the knuckles of his fist graphically captured the frustration Alain sensed building was building on the American side of the debate.

'Listen my friend,' the American began, but paused as a woman in full burqa hurried by, sheltering her child from the infidels with arm over shoulder and body between the foreigners and her offspring. 'We have tried to help'.

'Help what?' interrupted Alain.

Dwight took the bottle in his hand and squeezed, deflating the container with a crackle. 'Last night over dinner we pointed out that the American people want to help the Syrians bring democracy to this land of denied freedoms, religious extremism, and brutal repression of opposition.'

Alain sought to interject again, intending to make a comparison with American policy of kidnapping people in states beyond their jurisdiction for rendition to the black prisons Valentina had spoken of, or to Guantanamo Bay, but Dwight had the floor and would not brook dissent. 'To help the people of Syria topple the tyrant who rules by the barrel of a gun, the American people have enlisted the support of their loyal allies and that includes your country, Mr Foveaux - New Zealand.'

The American was now in full swing. 'Our people will also gain support through the European Union mandates, which freeze financial transactions affecting Syria. What this means in simple terms, Mr Foveaux, is that the free world has imposed sanctions on Syria. These sanctions include a trade embargo which you come here to break.'

Glaring now across the table Dwight let the New Zealander know exactly how vulnerable was his position.

'If - and I stress the word if - you were to make a deal with these Worthy Oriental Gentlemen or WOGs as they are better known, you don't seem to comprehend the practical obstacles which confront you to physically transport the phosphate to New Zealand. And ...'

Alain interrupted. 'What would the American people do, Dwight, blockade the ship on the high seas? That's piracy.'

Smiling now, Dwight leaned back in a less aggressive posture. 'So, you get the picture my friend. But it wouldn't get that far, quite simply because you will not be able to guarantee payment to these WOGs and if there is one thing a WOG wants, it is payment. These WOGs more than ever want foreign currency, but the American people have decided that they will not allow financial transactions to flow to Syria. Do you understand now? You cannot defeat the American people.'

Momentarily Alain rested his chin on clasped hands, elbows resting on the table. If ever there had been any residue of affinity between the two men, it was now totally dissolved.

'Now it is your turn to listen, if that is possible. Forgive me that I take refuge once again in history. It was not the barrel of a gun or American military jingoism that brought down the Soviet Union. It was in fact their own flawed socialist or communist economic philosophies, very similar I might add, to the socialistic interpretation of Keynesian economic utopia which brought my own country, New Zealand, to its knees in 1984.'

Alain riveted Dwight with a withering stare and continued. 'In Korea and Vietnam, America's superior firepower ultimately proved irrelevant to who won the war. Nor was it American military might which brought a tsunami of democratic euphoria across the Middle East in 2011, extending to the present time. What precipitated that "Arab Spring",' he hurried on, 'was a young Tunisian by the name of Bouazizi whose self-immolation stirred up a hurricane which blew through the Arab world.'

Alain had finally stunned his tormentors into silence. Angry now, he continued. 'I recall well an Australian Formula One driver, Mark Webber, questioning the integrity of holding the 2011 Grand Prix in Bahrain where human rights were being so badly abused. He was right to ask this question, for in short time medical doctors who attended combatants on both sides of the divide in that state were sentenced to death; an injudicious initiative soon overturned by someone who recognised that such a level of banal conduct by the absolute monarch of a minority Islamic sect where the US navy has its base, was not good PR.'

'We intervened on that one,' Wilbur inserted into the discussion with alacrity, seeking to claim some credit for Uncle Sam.

Alain continued uninvited. 'Later I was in contact with an old friend, a German nurse who had been detained as virtual captive at her medical post within Bahrain for several months. She told me about the intrusion onto that State by battalions from United Arab Emirates and Saudi Arabia, whom she said were impeccable as keepers of the peace. But,' he said raising his voice with emotion, 'A black battalion from Pakistan, so named not for the colour of their skin but the calibre of their deeds, murdered, raped and tortured Shia Muslim who happened to live in Bahrain.'

Leaning forward to emphasise his caustic invective Alain hissed, 'If ever there was a message for the people of the Middle East, whether Sunni or Shiite, it is to develop a nuclear capability as soon as possible and never give it up.'

Shock registered in Dwight's face, soon replaced with a contemptuous sneer, then after what seemed a month of silence, the CIA man said, 'I can see we have not convinced you Mr Foveaux.'

'Profound,' said Alain, for the second time that day in response to his escort's perspicacity. Beyond the point of cosmetic diplomacy he snapped. 'Now, are you sons of bitches going to return me to the Omayed, or rendition me out of here as a bloody terrorist?'

Fifteen minutes later Alain was riding in what seemed to him to be some form of unlicensed taxi on the road back to Damascus, thanks to hurried arrangements by Ahmed, his driver from the airport the day he arrived in the country.

Chapter Nine
US Embassy, Damascus.

Porter Julian was a career diplomat. Period. Unlike many of his peers who lobbied for ambassadorship to benefit their private sector commercial empires, he had put his name up for diplomatic service because he believed in his country.

Porter was a Democrat through and through, a founding member of the Democrats Club at his High School in Berkley and chairman of the Democrats for Change during the time he was at Princeton University. He had remained an avid committee person at Yale Law School where he completed his doctorate. While a lecturer on legal ethics at Southern California Law School, he enrolled in the Military Police reserves, avoiding all training postings to active service during the summer vacations but allowing him enough time to indulge in a hobby which absorbed him completely – learning the Arabic language.

In the Arab quarter after sunset Porter would explore carpet shops, antique bazaars, cafés with coffee strong enough to make one's hair stand on end and simply divine pastries. For hours he would peruse leather-bound Arabic text, practice his vocabulary on sweet young girls at the serving counters and absorb the mannerisms of handsome young dark and mysterious men. Deeper into the night and the labyrinth, he reclined with a shisha water bowl hookah pipe and feasted on beefy women who shed veils and gyrated to strange but relaxing music. And as the months passed and his hosts discerned his preference, he began finding refuge in the arms of the forbidden pastime of boys barely past puberty.

At a fundraiser for his local Congressman one summer, Porter was invited to deliver a speech on 'Conflicts of Interest - US Foreign Policy in the Middle East.' Not long after earning a standing ovation for that dissertation, he was asked to present a paper for the Leader of the House, a Democrat. His subject matter was whether politics were ethical. At thirty nine years of age it was suggested to him by an aide to the Leader of the House that he should put his name forward for political office. He did, and became Ambassador-elect to Egypt. Twelve months later, with a change in the Presidency to the Democrats, Porter Julian's mother attended his swearing in as United States' Ambassador to Syria. His father would have been so proud, she kept telling him.

What bothered Porter Julian most, was dealing with the unnecessary hostility bequeathed to his Government by its predecessor. Porter had admiration for the peoples of the Middle East whose civilizations dated back eight thousand years. 'Who was George W to come over here and seek to impose his version of civilization and his preference of religion on peoples who designed reticulated sewerage even before the Romans, but who found a different pathway to the same God we worship?' he would rhetorically demand, pacing his bedroom suite as he did so often in the early hours of morning, robbed of sleep by the legacy of a bigoted foolish Texan. At least presidential candidate Ron Paul promoted a message he and other younger Americans understood – "Who are the US to go into other countries and tell people how to run their affairs?"

As the son of a small time lawyer on the outskirts of San Francisco, Porter was a Christian and for a long time he believed the Catholic version that Jesus was the son of God, even if some of the explanations stretched scientific credibility to breaking point. But then, he had never considered an alternative pathway to God than Christianity – whether one preferred the Catholic or Protestant version. It wasn't until he dabbled in the Arabic language and studied their culture that he began to realise there was an alternative.

Like the majority of Americans, Porter was myopic when it came to geography and knowledge of distant civilizations, all of which had crumbled at some stage. By logic of many Americans, these were civilisations that must have been inferior to the United States, which they viewed as leader of the free world today. But discovery of Arabia and the Asia sub-continent awakened Porter's mind to an astonishingly world. This old world, new to him, was rich in life's experiences and cultures, which when measured in timeframes of durability, dented somewhat the myth of America's assumption of supremacy.

More significantly, Porter's study of the Middle East religion Islam, created a pathway to God by a more credible route. Rather than a man, allegedly conceived and born in defiance of the indestructible elementary rules of human propagation and later named Jesus, Islam held to the more scientifically palatable belief in a man born by conventional biological wonder, who was later anointed as God's messenger on earth. The prophet Muhammad.

As Porter listened to his senior CIA officer on station in Damascus, he could not help compare the traits of a former President with the embittered, prejudiced and ignorant oaf, seated across his desk and on whom he must rely for the intelligence on which to base decisions which could reverberate around the globe in a flash. And it could be a nuclear flash, he concluded, if those Israelis were let any closer to the levers of power.

'This New Zealander is a terrorist in the making,' the CIA operative declared. 'The man simply won't listen to reason. He has three goals – he is seeking to embarrass the United States by subverting our trade and financial blockade on Syria, and wants to accumulate a stockpile of a deleterious substance which can be used by terrorists to make bombs.'

'Like McVeigh did in Oklahoma?' said the Ambassador, referring to the American who had obliterated a downtown city building by detonated a truck loaded with explosive, including fertiliser, destroying one hundred and sixty eight lives in the process.

Dwight nodded, in absolute agreement.

Porter pressed his hands together making the shape of a church steeple. 'That's two reasons, chief.'

Bewildered, Dwight looked askance at his Ambassador. Long ago he had figured the man as a pansy, although he had never been able to collect sufficient evidence against him. He also reckoned the Ambassador as a WOG sympathiser and had reported as much in confidential cables to his bosses.

'Well, he spluttered, 'to make money selling the stuff of course.'

'Selling the stuff to whom?' Porter persisted.

'Well, God damn, to the farmers back in New Zealand.'

Porter stood, stretched, and then walked to the bomb-proof window which permitted a distorted view of a palm-studded lawn basking in the yellow reflection of millions of surrounding acres of sun-reflecting desert.

'A couple of points, chief,' said the Ambassador as he turned to face his CIA intelligence guru. 'We don't have the financial transaction blockade in place, yet. Oh we will have, but a physical blockade is not likely in my view. The Russian already have naval vessels in the port of Tartus and they are very keen to return to the days when they had an entire battle group stationed there. Another point. This is not US soil. We can't arrest him. None of our anti-terrorism laws have any effect here.'

Dwight felt his throat constrict with frustrated anxiety. This Ambassador was one son of bitch. 'That's not entirely true, sir. If this man is deemed to be a threat to the United States of America we can take him home to stand trial.'

Porter shook his head in dismay. The senior CIA officer on station in Syria had an uncanny knack of emulating his hero, George W, grasping at the most remote and unlikely opportunities to build a case against someone who would not salute the American flag.

'So you're suggesting I authorise you to rendition him out of here. Do you want a few hours with him in the basement before he is flown out?' Porter added sarcastically. 'Perhaps a session on the water board might make him see reason?'

'Well,' vacillated for station chief. 'No, I don't think that is the best option, I disagree with you there.'

Spinning on his heels the Ambassador composed himself to avoid delivering an outburst he might later regret. Contempt seethed through his body but he was able to maintain a professional veneer.

'Listen chief. Put what you say in writing; your recommendations on how you believe this problem should be handled. A maximum of, say, five hundred words. Have it on my desk when I return from my next appointment. I'm meeting with the Minister of Education for lunch.'

Dwight sniggered, just loud enough to compel the Ambassador to react.

'You have a problem with me meeting the Minister?' Porter enquired.

'He's a queer, sir,' the CIA man retorted.

'Pardon? What do you mean, chief? Is he of unsound mind?' the Ambassador enquired, knowing full-well the insinuation was referenced to the Syrian's homosexuality as well as his own. It was dangerous ground for them both.

'Not sure about that sir, but he is a homo,' gloated Dwight, letting the diplomat know that he knew the ambassador's own dark secret.

Pausing at the door, Porter replied. 'There are no homosexuals in Syria, or Iran for that matter. Have you not read the edicts emanating from the religious leaders?'

'That's rubbish,' Dwight retorted, 'and well you know it.'

Pulling the door to near to closed the Ambassador had the last word. 'There must be better ways for you and your men to hone your surveillance skills than spying on the sexual preferences of our host nation, chief. After all is said and done, with Obama's gay rights approach to the military - it might become a capital crime for homophobes like you to speak your mind!'

Chapter Ten

Damascus, Syria.

Placing a conference call to New Zealand via the Omayed switchboard should have been a relatively straightforward exercise, but as Alain was learning, nothing in Syria was straightforward. Resorting finally to his cell phone, Alain set a time for Doug to set up a conference call with Bryce, fifty minutes later.

To kill time Alain smashed a punch-bag in the tiny hotel gymnasium. He left the gym reeking of body odour and drenched in perspiration, but infinitely less stressed having completed such a strenuous workout. A quick cold shower and he lay on his bed, trying to decipher a missive delivered to his room during his absence.

"Plan change. Egor Rostov will meet you on lobby at eleven forty-five am and accompany you in meeting with Minister Mines. Egor is translator. My protégé. He make delay at Minister. More time we need for make plan. Russia your friend."

The note was signed, Supetar. Only two people in Syria knew about Supetar, the love nest on Brac Island seventeen years ago, so Alain accepted the note as genuine from Valentina. But what the hell was she talking about?

Five minutes later Alain was woken from a deep slumber by the incessant buzzing of his phone. He quickly briefed Bryce and Doug in developments, traversing events since he'd arrived in Syria five days earlier.

'So in fifteen minutes I go back the Minister's office, or more precisely an office used by him for discussions with people like me. There I will meet, I presume, with the officials who were present at our first meeting and possibly some hot shot from Homs or the head office of the phosphate mines division.'

'Great,' Bryce said enthusiastically. 'You have done well. Just remember we need the stuff landed here in New Zealand at US two hundred dollars a ton CIF.'

'And that is payment, where? On arrival in New Zealand or at port of departure?' Alain knew the answer but experience had taught him pedantic analysis of each contract was advisable to confirm that nothing had changed and to remind all parties what had previously been discussed.

'I need to make this payment at port of destination, New Zealand,' insisted Bryce with some trace of annoyance that he was being grilled to confirm what had previously been decided.

Alain hesitated before replying. 'I'm not so sure it will be as simple as that. These people are international pariahs at present. Trading partners are in short supply and they do need hard currency payment for their exports, which suggests any outfit willing to upset the Americans and trade here should be able to get a good deal. But I don't get the feeling these people will be taken for suckers.'

'It's not that we want to take them for suckers,' Bryce retorted. 'It is simply that US two hundred dollars a ton CIF is my highest price payment landed in Auckland. Otherwise I will have to put up with the dusty crap I get from Egypt. That costs more to prepare back here but at least I can land Egypt product at US one hundred and ninety five dollars CIF a ton.'

'And payment?' asked Alain.

Bryce confirmed what he had told him prior to his leaving New Zealand - payment by an irrevocable letter of credit deposited with an agreed bank to be released when the product landed in New Zealand. Alain felt uneasy – he knew the product from Egypt was strictly cash up front, before loading commenced at Alexandria, and he had no reason to believe any Arabic state would deviate from these entrenched trading protocols, namely money at point of loading.

Alain did not need a young buck flexing his muscles miles from the action, but Doug entered the discussion just at the right time.

'Yeah Bryce, but for the sake of US five dollars a ton, settling for the crap Egypt exports instead of this top rated RPR stuff out of Syria, I have to say, that doesn't make a whole lot of sense. You have to pay Egypt up front and if Alain can negotiate a price of US two hundred dollars a ton for prime phosphate

CIF, is it not smarter to go for the prime product and pay Syria at port of loading?'

Bryce fumbled for an immediate retort but finally resorted to the rationale Alain had intuitively divined when he raised the issue of Syrians not being taken as suckers. 'For Christ's sake, these people are in no position to impose draconian trade conditions. Who do they think they are?'

Alain watched the numbers on the digital clock move inexorably toward eleven forty five. 'Tell you what Bryce,' he said finally. 'You have the option to go back to Vietnam for your supply. The Vietnamese accept payment thirty days after delivery in Auckland. But of course the problem you encountered there was that your supplier ultimately chose your opposition back home because the opposition buy more product and threatened to blacklist the Vietnamese if they supplied you. You are a small fish and the Vietnamese fellow wants to keep his hook in the big fish.'

Alain allowed time for his message to sink in. 'You can cut off your nose to spite your face and pay US five dollars a ton less but on payment at point of loading port in Egypt. But remember there is a strong probability some farmer's neighbour will invoke some obscure Greenie bylaw and have your Egyptian solution banned because of the dust removal process you must go through once the product is in New Zealand. Or you can let me find a solution here in Syria and not tie me to this issue of payment only when the product hits the port in New Zealand.'

Two minutes later, when the red digits told Alain it was eleven forty five am, he broke the silence. 'I have a car waiting to take me to these negotiations.'

'If I pay up front in Syria and they don't send the product, I am stuffed,' an exasperated Bryce declared. 'I couldn't recover my losses. A Syrian court – no chance,' he said derisively. 'Tell them I will pay by irrevocable letter of credit via any bank in Germany, conditional on the money not being reversed out of that bank if the product is delivered to Auckland within sixty days of leaving the Syrian port. Payment in full will be made by the German bank to the Syrian phosphate company the moment the product hits the wharf in Auckland.'

Alain shrugged, concluding that he would adopt the same stance it is was his money at stake. Perhaps I was a better soldier than I am an international trader? And perhaps I was better trading in political intrigue, he mused as he reflected on his mission in Bosnia, than I am trading in hard currency. Perhaps I can still learn from that young fellow?

'Why specifically a German bank?' Doug asked after the call to Alain terminated.

'They are the only banks trusted by countries either side of the East-West divide,' Bryce explained.

As Alain alighted from the elevator, an athletic young man greeted him. 'Mr Foveaux,' he said with only the slightest trace of an East European accent. 'We must hurry please. A driver is waiting. This way.'

The dash from the hotel lobby to the grey Mercedes was a mere ten metres but it created sufficient exposure to an asphyxiating heat, devoid of the humidity which plagued Singapore, but nevertheless sufficient to leave him feeling like he was in a blast furnace. He was thankful for the air conditioning which was standard in the German car.

'Hello Mr Foveaux. I am Egor. I live in Auckland. I am brought to Syria by Russian government to help you make phosphate purchase.'

'*Prevyet*,' replied Alain in Russian. Then in English he asked 'What the hell is going on? They fly you from New Zealand to help me negotiate a modest commercial transaction of phosphate! I am not buying uranium!'

Egor smiled his easy smile, and Alain quickly calculated that the boy could have any woman he wanted. 'While you were sleeping Mr Foveaux, the Americans imposed a financial transactions blockage for all US dollars routed into Syria or known Syrian bank accounts. We anticipated, sorry, the Russian Government anticipated this some time ago. The world will be told of this within forty eight hours.'

Adopting more of the third-person stance he continued. 'The Russian Government is still smarting from being duped over the NATO no-fly missions over Libya, which turned into overt hostile combat against anything with Gaddafi's name attached. We have no intention of making the same mistake twice. If you do buy phosphate it will be in direct violation of American plans. Our task is to help you achieve your mission. One small step for Kiwifert Mr Foveaux, one big step for mankind. The rest of the world does not like to be bullied and intimidated by America.'

'You mean if I buy phosphate in Syria, the Yanks won't let us send the money? When did this happen? I was just talking to New Zealand and they never mentioned it,' Alain asked, ignoring for the moment Egor's speculation about Russian motives, but appreciating the boy's clever plagiarism of the words of some American who had claimed he walked on the moon.

'As I just said, the world will be receiving the news about now,' Egor replied. 'Please, I must ask you to listen. Colonel Goloshapova instructs me what is Russia's proposal.'

Things were going a little too fast to protest. Alain didn't like the Americans telling him what the rest of the world could do, but by the same measure he did not like the way Valentina and her bosses in the Kremlin were assuming the role of mentor where he was concerned. But there didn't seem to be many alternatives as things were clearly being played out between the two superpowers. He sat back and tried to concentrate on the voluminous but rapidly delivered equivalent to an Orders Group he was accustomed to from his military days.

On arriving at the Syrian Minister's office, it became obvious that the people Alain was to meet were nervous. Anxiety was in the air, almost palpable. The same three officials who had been present at his first meeting were there again but sat sombrely at the rear of a well-appointed office different to that which he had been ushered into three days earlier. Another man – Alain placed him as being in his mid-fifties and wearing the standard dark blue suit and white collarless shirt with no tie, buttoned at the neck – sat to the left of the ornate desk which took centre stage. No sooner were Egor and Alain seated than they stood again as the Minister entered.

The Minister took his place behind the desk, which also served as a conference table. He was accompanied again by Wakid Mashreq but his body language left no doubt that it was he who was the man who would make the decisions this day. Curt acknowledgments with head nod and perfunctory salutation concluded and those in attendance took their seats. Egor was not introduced and Alain concluded from the way his translator was ignored that formalities surrounding his presence had already been reconciled by the Russians.

'Mr Foveaux,' the Minister of Mineral Resources stated formally. 'We have concluded enquiries into the company you represent. Due diligence you might say,' he said with the trace of a pleasant smile. 'It is important that we only do business with companies which are in a position to make good any undertakings given and agreed to in a contract.'

Alain returned the pleasant smile.

'Allow me to introduce Bassam Sulaiman,' he continued, gesturing with an open hand toward the man with the white collarless shirt. 'He is chief executive of Barsik Enterprises, one of the most efficient phosphate mining companies in Syria.'

In an unexpected gesture the man in the dark blue suit reached across the table and shook Alain's hand. *'Zdrastvooeetye. Minya zavoot Bassam. Ochen preeyatna. Kak Dela?'*

'Hello, pleased to meet you too Bassam,' Alain said, returning the welcome in Russian. 'I am Alain. It is a pleasure to be here.'

Alain turned to his interpreter saying, 'Perhaps it is better to speak in Russian but my interpreter will translate to English for I may easily miss important words if I rely on my own ability in Russian.'

Bassam nodded understanding as the Minister took the lead in negotiations. 'We have the RPR phosphate you seek Mr Alain. It is the best on the world market.'

'Our research confirms this,' Alain responded.

'What quantity do you require over the period of each year, please?' Bassam asked.

'We want to take one hundred thousand tons per annum to begin with, Alain replied. 'We hope that a reliable supply of well-priced phosphate with high RPR and some sulphur content will result in our company being able to supply a demand in New Zealand for a more environmentally-friendly fertiliser end product. We anticipate taking five hundred thousand ton per annum after five years.'

Alain watched translation of the dialogue. The expressions of those in the room ranged from utter delight from the officials, to a more measured reaction of approval by the Minister. Wakid Mashreq produced a barely perceptible flicker of recognition.

Fifteen minutes later Alain and the phosphate merchant had specified, by chemical analysis, the precise content of minerals Bryce required and had carefully quantified the volumes to be transported. But the price and conditions of payment still hung over the negotiations like a guillotine.

'For the sake of clarity and so that we are all on the same page, by my definition FOB means Freight on Board at port of loading,' Alain proclaimed. 'The seller is responsible for placing the goods on a ship at the port of shipment and retains ownership of and responsibility for the goods until they are so loaded.'

Egor translated and all were agreed.

'Where a deal is done FOB, once the goods are on the ship, the vendor has no further responsibility and where a sale price is negotiated FOB, once the goods are on board the ship and the Master notifies the bank holding the letter of credit, the bank releases payment to the vendor,' the New Zealander went on.

There was no dissent and Alain continued his dissertation. 'CIF means cost, insurance and freight. Where a price is negotiated CIF, the seller is responsible for arranging the freight and insurance for the goods to destination port. CIF means the vendor is responsible and liable for the goods until they are loaded on the ship, at which time responsibility for loss or damage of the goods transfers to the insurance company as part of the CIF deal.'

Everyone is the room understood these established conventions of trade by shipping. The contentious part invariably centred on when payment was made.

'We seek to negotiate a CIF price to the port of Auckland, per ton, but payable at port of destination,' he ventured, testing the waters gently.

Alain's request for variation of payment convention seemed not to perturb Bassam, the Barsik Enterprises boss. 'What is your CIF price per ton at port of destination and, at what point will payment be made?'

The sting was in the tail, thought Alain, like a scorpion. 'We must have a CIF price in Auckland at US one hundred and eighty per ton.' His reply generated audible air, streaming inward over clenched teeth.

'Mr Foveaux,' commenced Bassam gratuitously. 'US one hundred and eighty per ton FOB with you to pick up your own freight and insurance costs, maybe. But US one hundred and eighty per ton with us picking up the freight and insurance costs? Come now.'

Alain did not enjoy haggling over terms and conditions. He was a facilitator. He arranged meetings in strange places among even stranger people, but he let those strange people reach their own strange agreements. In days past he had seen tribesmen turn very nasty quickly as Kalashnikovs were un-shouldered amidst torrents of indecipherable yelling. No-one in the room was carrying a Kalashnikov but Alain was pleased no one seemed to be in reach of such a weapon.

'What is your starting offer?' retorted Alain, anxious to get out from under.

'Let us move swiftly here,' interrupted Wakid Mashreq. The man stood now, rather than leaning against a pillar as he had been, silent and contemplative. 'This is not time for gamesmanship. America plays this with our country on the international stage. One eighty is not good enough Mr Foveaux. We did not expect you to start bidding at your final offer but, please, we agree now or my time is best spent elsewhere.'

When it came to rank, Alain thought the Minister had it. But the Minister never blinked, let alone cast a glance at Wakid Mashreq for impertinence. Was it not unusual for those with real power to lurk in the shadows, beyond the glare of publicity?

Alain was of a similar mind to Wakid Mashreq. Haggling over prices was beneath intelligent people and Wakid Mashreq gave every sign that he was an astute man.

'Two hundred US CIF New Zealand,' he exclaimed, wanting to bring the matter to a swift conclusion.

To his surprise it was Bassam who answered. 'You have a deal.'

'The more important questions,' Wakid Mashreq retorted, 'are when and how?'

Alain was impressed with Egor - the young man had not missed a beat. Translation was virtually all Russian to English and vice versa but frequently he switched to Arabic. He was very capable, almost invisible, but was the essential means of communication between the parties.

'Is it accepted that we will make payment to Barsik Enterprises by way of irrevocable non-transferrable letter of credit deposited with a German bank approved by both parties?' Alain looked at Wakid Mashreq for confirmation.

Wakid Mashreq nodded assent.

Not wishing to delay the proceedings further, Alain went straight to the bottom line.

'Our final position,' he said making eye contact with Wakid Mashreq in a gesture of approval of his style of negotiation. 'The letter of credit will pay out when the ship docks in New Zealand.'

'Not good enough,' responded Bassam without any encouragement from Wakid Mashreq. 'Pay when the vessel enters New Zealand territorial waters. That way we get paid irrespective of any industrial disputes your country might be exposed to from those militants in the wharf workers' union we have been hearing about. And we won't be caught up in delays caused by your competitors paying off people so a shipload of our product sits for days waiting to dock.'

The militancy of the wharfies' union had occurred to Alain, but the thought of commercial sabotage by competitors, as elucidated by Bassam, hadn't entered his head. It was pretty obvious that Syria's commercial intelligence was better than his own. The Syrians had calculated the pricing for phosphate to exactly the dollar as calculated by Bryce but had also taken into account exceptional events, such as demurrage costs of delays on New Zealand wharves.

'Agreed,' Alain said.

Unexpectedly the Minister interrupted the flow of negotiations at a critical stage. 'No doubt you will lodge the letter of credit the day you place your order.' It was a statement rather than a question.

Alain nodded acquiescence. Having scored a point, the Minister informed the group that refreshments would be served in an adjacent reception room, during which there would be no further discussion on the matter of phosphate.

Wakid Mashreq looked at his watch, appearing to Alain to be about to object, but changed his mind and, placing his arm on Bassam's shoulder, walked with him to the banquet table chatting amiably. Alain accompanied the Minister with Egor at his elbow.

Luncheon was a seated affair. The spread of food was impressive - salads, cold roast lamb on the spit, fruit in abundance, fish, and a refreshing cold drink of mint, lemon and as best his tastebuds could discern, sweetened with sugar - lots of it.

'This is not your first visit to Syria,' said the Minister as a matter of fact, with a smile.

'I passed though in 1995' replied Alain, aware the Minister would already know of this. 'Not much has changed.'

'Not much on the surface, Mr Foveaux. Syria is a timeless land in that respect. You must visit Palmyra to appreciate what I am saying,' the Minister advised.

'I would like to do that,' Alain said. 'But what is beneath the surface, Minister?'

The Minister was contemplative but eventually he did answer, with Egor doing his best to maintain the flow of translated dialogue.

'Syria is not much different to America or Russia or France, when it comes to where the power lies,' the Minister said with a knowing smile. 'America, for example, has their fabled military industrial elite; a matrix through which people move upon retirement from the military to executive status with a munitions or aircraft manufacturer. It is important of course for a manufacturer of military hardware to have a network linking back from its board room to the military officers' messes so that when time comes for decisions to be made by the senior officers which tank or which helicopter is preferred, that information is available to the manufacturer.' The Minister shrugged dismissively. 'The deciding factor, as always Mr Foveaux, is money, paid to those with influence.'

Prostitution is reputed to be the oldest profession in the world, thought Alain, but a close second would be corruption.

'The manufacturer makes money by securing a contract to supply military equipment. If the cost of securing a billion dollar Government contract to make coastal gunboat is the additional cost of paying a bribe to several well-placed military officers, then that expense can always be recovered when overrun costs are levied. This matrix of network of power elite invariably embraces Congressmen who want industry to remain in or relocate to their constituencies. This dimension opens another Pandora's box.'

Attacking a rack of lamb, the Minister continued. 'This, how you say, racket, is rampant among Americans who proclaim their true raison d'être is propagating democracy as they define the concept and not gaining riches. It is the subject of many textbooks, my friend.'

As something of an afterthought, the Minister added 'The French - well! They were our most recent colonial, shall I say, advisers. And I can tell you Mr Foveaux, when it comes to corruption, the French have no peer - Russians or Chinese included. Do you know, the French make and sell armaments to countries that are at war with them? Trust me. We know.'

Alain bounced back. 'Smarter than the Americans, I am sure. They *gave* armaments to Saddam and the Taliban to fight Iran and the Russians respectively, but were soon facing their own weapons when the fortunes of war changed. At least the French were smart enough to sell military hardware to their future enemies.'

Appraising an apple in hand, the Minister then gestured with it toward Alain. 'Corruption. Deception. Ahh, these are the true fruits of life!'

Alain digested this information at about the same speed as his orange. Wiping juice from his chin he asked. 'May I conclude from your dissertation Minister, that beneath the surface of Syria, it is too business as usual?

'How perceptive of you, Mr Foveaux. French is it not?'

'If you are referring to my surname, yes. Unlike most New Zealanders, my forebears did not hail from England, Ireland, Scotland, Holland or Dalmatia, which is Croatia today. My antecedents are French, and it was a distant relation whose name now graces the seaway between the South Island of New Zealand and the former sealers base of Stewart Island at the bottom of our country. It is known as Foveaux Strait.'

Casting a glance to his left to make eye contact, the Minister asserted. 'Then as a Frenchman you will have no difficulty with our session after lunch.'

The first difficulty Alain had with that session after lunch was the problem of trying to stay awake on a full stomach of exquisite tasting food. The appearance of Colonel Valentina Goloshapova joining the group was the second.

Wakid Mashreq took centre stage, the Minister to his right and a man Alain had never seen before to his left. The three officials and the phosphate seller, Bassam, did not return to the post-luncheon session. But it was the face, or more accurately a personality, which dominated his attention. The man was unmistakably astute and ruthless, his appearance never to be forgotten. The coldness of his gaze sent a shiver down Alain's spine. Introduced only as Yasin, Alain realised immediately that the first name appellation should not for a moment be taken as a sign of affinity. A man of distinct Arabic features, medium height and slim but tensed physique, brown thinning hair and eyes of a zealot, this new arrival left no room for mistake that his purpose was business and that killing was his business.

Valentina seemed not to be perturbed by the man. Ostensibly busying herself with paperwork in a dossier, she ignored his presence.

Watching Egor furtively, Alain could see his guardian also calculating the changed dynamics of the meeting. Only once did he catch Valentina and Egor making eye contact. Resplendent in her colonel's attire, Valentina remained slightly aloof but even the Minister was clearly smitten.

Wakid Mashreq took the floor. 'Much progress was made before the adjournment. With the co-operation of Mr Foveaux we have settled on the specifications and price for export of phosphate from Barsik Enterprises to New Zealand. Shipping detail is yet to be finalised, but this is not an insurmountable task. What is more difficult,' he said rushing his delivery a little, 'is the transfer of payment from New Zealand to Syria.'

Wakid Mashreq took the time to make eye contact with the five people remaining in the room. Looking now directly at Alain, he said, 'Mr Foveaux, you come well recommended by our friends from Moscow.'

Alain began to feel the hairs on his neck shift and, possibly, a drip of cold perspiration between his shoulder blades. For reasons not yet clear to him, he felt his life was about to change, irrevocably.

'This morning I appreciated your rejection of pedantic posturing to reach a price and conditions which we agreed, swiftly. This is the sign of intelligence over emotion.'

Alain accepted the compliment with stoicism but he remained anxious.

'I wish to continue discussion in the same spirit. I seek to find a solution to the problem of transferring payment of the phosphate to Syria without posturing. The Americans have imposed a currency transaction blockade on Syria,' continued Wakid Mashreq. 'I seek your indulgence, in confidence. You are free to walk from this room whenever you chose.'

Making eye contact with Yasin, who now bore down on him with a malevolent brooding stare, confirmed Alain's gut instinct. The tenor of the meeting had changed.

Alain fiddled with his pen on the desk in front of him. He took a dim view of the Americans sabotaging the best chance young Bryce had of breaking, what some referred to as the fertiliser mafia, in his homeland and waited for the solution.

'Shoot,' said Alain, a response which seemed to take much of the confidence away from Wakid Mashreq.

'What?' he asked.

Egor explained that it was a colloquialism, an invitation to proceed, not to embark on something more sinister.

Wakid Mashreq visibly relaxed, offering a rare smile. 'If your company tried to send payment to Syria or any bank accounts known to the Americans they would block the transfer of that money.' The Syrian paused and frowned. 'At this point I could remonstrate Mr Foveaux but it would serve no purpose. We are not politicians here.'

A Freudian slip, Alain thought.

'There are forces working behind the veil, if I may speak metaphorically. Over recent months American sanctions against our businesspeople and politicians, preventing them from transferring money and freezing assets they have beyond Syria, have been creeping over us like a mist. At this very moment we know allies of America are bowing to their master and are introducing similar restrictions against Syria. This is disappointing, but what is most concerning is that our Arab brothers, under pressure from America, may also impose sanctions on Syria and its leaders.'

As Egor translated, Alain was left in a state of disbelief. The Arab Union, taking a unified front against Syria? He interrupted the speaker.

'I find this difficult to believe. Why would they do this?' he asked.

At first his interruption was poorly received. Alain could see this from the bland expression which came over Yasin's face, but after translation, the tension in the man with the distinctly Arab features relaxed.

'I am relieved to hear your genuine concern Mr Alain,' Yasin offered, speaking for the first time. 'This strategy of united Arab opposition was not possible against Iran, my home country, where we are not Arabs but Persians. You know this of course.'

Alain was aware Iranians deeply resented any suggestion that they were Arabs. Iran's peoples were indeed of Persian descent, speaking the Farsi language and not Arabic and being predominantly Shiite Muslim, whereas most Arabs occupying the states to the west were Sunni. Alain likened this religious divide to the Protestant-Catholic division in Christianity.

'The Arab Union does this because it is under pressure from the Americans,' explained Yasin, whose calm manner Alain realised was maintained only by intense self-control.

'King Hammad of Bahrain is leader of a minority of privileged Sunni, and with the aid of Saudi and United Arab Emirates troops recently brutally crushed protest against his regime. It was important for America to retain King Hammad in power because it has its Gulf navy fleet stationed in Bahrain. It was also important for America to crush the Shiite majority whom it fears will side with Iran.'

Aware of this, Alain nodded acquiescence.

'But very little is said of the brutal treatment of Shiite in Bahrain. This is because America makes every endeavour to, how you say, shut down bad publicity for such a loyal ally.' Yasin shrugged indifference, yet his eyes conveyed anything but.

When Yasin spoke of Sheikh Hammad bin Khalifa al Thani's call for intervention of the Arab military in Syria, his venom was undisguisable. 'Qatar is also a puppet of America. America has its air force command in Qatar. The relationship is intimate, like lovers, perhaps reminiscent of illicit love between a black slave and a white master in America's Deep South before its own civil war? This liaison will surely end in tragedy as is the case with any mixed marriage. Do you not agree Mr Foveaux?'

Before Alain could compose a response, Yasin continued.

'Turkey, foolishly part of a NATO which neither trusts nor wants them as a partner other than to have some control, is supplicant to America because of these latent pressures. But Turkey has its own demons. For centuries it has fought a war of genocide against a very large Kurdish minority on its North Eastern provinces. It now has a Kurdish enclave refugees establishing on its south eastern border. This will be a problem for Turkey.'

Opening the palms of his hands Yasin said, 'Fortunately for my country, not all trade partners are susceptible to American bullying. China for example has refused to heed the oil embargo America has imposed on Iran.'

Alain sensed Yasin's reference to how the Arab states were turning on each other, in contrast to Iran, which was not an Arab state, was more to score points over his Syrian business partners than to contribute to the theme, however relevant.

The immediate reaction to Yasin's barb was palpable so Alain sought to dilute the effect. 'Perhaps the recent French legislation making it a crime to deny Turkish genocide of Armenian peoples last century will undermine the relationship Turkey has with the West?'

Unexpectedly it was Valentina who spoke next, mitigating further the intensity which had pervaded the room. She spoke in Arabic so Egor translated for Alain.

'Mr Foveaux. The business plan you provided to support your application to the Minister of Mines projects expansion of the volume shipped to your New Zealand company of five hundred per cent. This is in five years. This volume makes significant sales for Syria and large transfer of foreign exchange to Syria.'

'One hundred thousand tons to five hundred thousand tons. On today's agreed price, from US twenty million dollars to US one hundred million dollars per year,' Alain chipped in to help her out.

Valentina smiled to show her appreciation.

'So, Mr Foveaux, this is big money and in many years may constitute very big earnings for Syria,' the Russian continued.

'As we are now meeting in confidence and are being frank,' interrupted Alain, making a statement rather than positing a question, 'the political triumph of a Western country, being my country New Zealand, to act in defiance of the United States and collaborate to break the stranglehold on world money transfers, would probably be worth more than the monetary value of the transactions.'

'Ahh!' The sound of a part exclamation and part laugh emitted from the Minister. 'Your sagacity again Mr Foveaux,' he said waving an admonishing finger. 'Yes, there is a political advantage. A scoring of points, is that how you say?

Alain nodded, looking directly at Yasin before returning his attention to Valentina, who moving across the room to a whiteboard which had been installed during their absence at lunch, took a black felt pen and began to draw.

Five minutes later she stepped back and read through the five options she had listed in English. The fact that her handiwork was not transcribed into Arabic did occur to Alain and alerted him to the possibility that, as the Government officials and Bassam had not returned to the meeting following lunch break, those who remained were all multilingual.

Momentarily Alain wondered just how many on the board of big companies or financial institutions or even parliamentary committees in his own country would be other than monolingual. He lamented that this was major a disadvantage for his countrymen and women. Most Caucasian New Zealanders would have a pejorative regard for Arabs or peoples of Asian ethnicity – born out of ill-conceived xenophobia. Yet here he was sitting at a top corporate table and all had more than one language. Distance between the South Pacific and the centres of humanity, regarded by many antipodeans as a Divine gift, was in Alain's view also a curse: a curse in terms of economic costs for transportation of exports and a cost in terms of isolation from the reality of needing more than one language.

Chapter Eleven
Auckland, New Zealand

A slowly-cruising yellow, blue and white squad car drifted past Bryce as he aimed the key fob at his Audi and depressed the button. The heads of two figures huddled in greatcoats traversed to the right, then tilted to the rear vision mirrors as the police car stopped twenty five metres further along the street. City lighting glimmered in the puddles of recent rain and it was cold - too cold for any sensible person to be loitering in a lower city street at four o'clock in the morning. Unsure whether to ignore them or wave, Bryce chose the latter but the squad car remained stationary, emitting steam from its exhausts. At the point in time where Bryce calculated the police would reverse, Doug splashed his way through a puddle as he nosed his Toyota into in a space marked "reserved".

'Jesus it's cold,' Doug exclaimed as he clambered from his car. 'This better be worth the bloody effort mate. Why couldn't he wait another four hours?'

The two men hurried to the entrance of Doug's office. 'He said it was urgent. He said he was making the call from the Russian Embassy,' Bryce said, raising his eyebrows in a gesture of exaggerated surprise. 'He reckons it's the only place he can call with a secure line. He said he needs us both on a speaker phone. He had some serious propositions put to him. Your office is midway for us both.'

Pulling the door shut behind them, Doug gestured at the police car as the heating within the building afforded instant relief from the cold. 'Lucky I came along,' he said as he threw a glance over his shoulder at the police.

Doug switched on the lights then examined his desk phone. 'Three minutes to call time. Hope this bloody thing works properly or I will be really pissed off.'

Three minutes later the phone hummed and blinked. Doug pushed buttons, shouting all the while, 'You there mate? Are you there?'

Alain responded, Doug stopped shouting and the conversation began to flow.

Alain outlined the progress he had made at the meeting with the Minister and the price they had agreed with the chief executive of Barsik Enterprises.

'That's great,' a relieved Bryce shouted, also believing that if he shouted it would make him more audible in Syria. 'Well done. We have at least ten dollars leeway in that price. Bloody marvellous. And they went with the letter of credit payout at port of destination?'

'Yeah,' shouted Doug from the corner of the office, 'but couldn't that have waited until daylight out here?'

'Payout in territorial waters of New Zealand,' Alain said, correcting Bryce's assumption the deal had been done port of destination, before going on to explain why.

Over the following fifty minutes Alain talked while Bryce and Doug listened, with only the occasional query.

'So that's it,' Alain said finally. 'I suggest you both go have breakfast at the Hungry Horse, make a decision and I will call back ten am New Zealand time.' The line went dead.

'This is dangerous stuff my friend,' cautioned Doug. 'I think the first question to answer is what trouble could this cause? It is a good price and none of your competitors will get a look in if you go with their option. You will be right inside the tent, but is it worth the serious shit which will follow?'

As was his habit when under pressure, Bryce paced the floor, conceding that of course Doug was right. A good price for excellent quality RPR and no show of being pushed out by a competitor. But breaking a financial transaction blockade? Was this blockade legal? Who do those Americans think they are? Was this just an American thing or was it supported by the United Nations or anyone else?

'I suggest we get a legal adviser down here,' Doug said. 'Someone good on sanction busting.'

Bryce paced the room again, engrossed in thought. 'I know! I've got it. We'll slip up to the university café for breakfast. I'll call my wife Susan. She's doing politics there and has a good relationship with one of the senior lecturers. We can discuss this over breakfast with an armchair expert.

'Right,' said Doug. 'This may take longer than the six hours Alain has given us. I will make sure my secretary takes Alain's call and he will simply have to wait. You need to get accurate advice here. Are you sure a university lecturer is the right person to bring in on this? I mean, a lawyer is subject to confidentiality, but a lecturer has no legal obligation to stay silent.'

'I've been thinking about that,' replied Bryce. 'This stuff is not off-the-shelf for lawyers. They would take a week and charge like a wounded bull. Susan's lecturer does this stuff every day. US foreign policy stage three. They love the subject, so her advice will be as good as any. But will she stay quiet?'

A disarming smile lit Bryce's boyish features as he answered his own question. 'If I don't go with this I don't give a damn whether this lecturer runs to the media or not. If I do go with the Syrians, what the local media contribute from any interview with the lecturer will be pushed off the front page by the CNN story and the noise the Yanks will be making. I have got to call Susan then we can take a stroll up the hill.'

The university coffee shop was not quite as Doug had imagined. Sure, none of its denizens wore business suits, but with the exception of half a dozen or so, all the male students had short hair and most of the young women were eminently suited to bedroom duties. He didn't notice anyone smoking cannabis and no-one stood on a table and preached Mao. Bryce's wife may have been registered as a Cook Islander but her petite frame and olive complexion suggested some ancient mariner of European blood had spent his time well in that tropical paradise. Sarah Middleton, on the other hand, was anything but petite and came very close to his perception of what a professor might look like - untidy, disorganised and some time since she had bothered to hide the grey hair with an agreeable hair colouring.

Within thirty minutes Doug had decided Professor Middleton knew her stuff. He also concluded that she was balanced in the manner in which she presented the pros and cons of American foreign policy post-World War Two. On the one hand she argued that America did indeed have a role to play in world reconstruction as the only country after 1945 that was capable of confronting the Soviet Union occupation of countries it had liberated from the heel of Hitler's Third Reich. But she barely suppressed her contempt of the superpower's foreign policy relative to its behaviour in recent conflicts, such as Vietnam, Nicaragua, Somalia or Bush senior's arming of Iraq's Saddam as a foil against the Iran's Islamic republic after the fall of the Shah and of the subsequent US invasion of Iraq. All of this, insisted the professor, called into question the integrity of American motives.

When it came to putting before her a number of hypothetical scenarios involving transfer of goods and subsequent payment for the goods, blatantly in breach of a self-styled American blockade, professor Middleton unravelled history as adeptly a nurse might unravel a bandage. 'The US adopted sanctions against Syria as far back as 2009. Iran, Myanmar, Cuba, Columbia, Somalia and North Korea are also subject to similar measures,' she advised. 'The justification for the sanctions appears to rest on whether a country fails to comply with advice given by the US and whether it is perceived as a danger to America, rather than because of any alleged abuse of human rights. Take for example Zimbabwe, where Mugabe rules in a time-warp of paranoid brutality against his own people. This madman does not attract as serious US sanctions which apply to the Taliban against whom the Americans crusade in the name of saving women yet kills them with impunity as "collateral damage" to drone attacks.'

Peering across the bridge of her glasses, she added, knowingly. 'A certain amount of selective morality I think is a safe assumption. In the case of Syria, it is my view that the sanctions being imposed are motivated by US myopia to control the world. The Middle East is a critical component in this grand design and oil is the key. Syria has some oil, but its greatest value is its strategic location smack bang in the centre of the largest oil-producing region on the planet. Because it is not amenable to advice from the Americans but even worse, is allied to Russia, this I suggest is the reason why we have America embarking on its usual foreign policy.'

'And that "usual foreign policy" is?' Doug obliged to the obvious cue.

'If the US does not control then chaos should reign,' concluded the professor with obvious satisfaction that she had been able to round off her homily with such an emphatic finale.

Pausing to peer over her spectacles again as appeared to be her idiosyncrasy, the professor cautiously continued. 'Of course there is the additional problem with Pakistan. It is a nuclear power, the only Islamic nation with nuclear capability right now.' Producing a map from her sheaf of papers, she then pointed to Israel. 'Just for a moment let us step beyond Syria and consider its strongest ally in the Middle East, Iran. Imagine for a moment if the Israelis lose the plot entirely and attack Iran with a nuclear device?'

'Pakistan might lend Iran a bomb?' contributed Bryce, which the professor acknowledged with a condescending smile.

'Finally,' she hurried on before any questions could be asked, 'Russia! This country has long enjoyed cordial relations with Syria. This Russian Bear along with the Chinese Dragon took a poke in the eye when their abstentions from vetoing a NATO incursion into Libya resulted in flagrant abuse by France and Britain in particular. You will recall, I am sure, the enforcing of a no-fly zone by Gaddafi forces, and the persistent targeting of Gaddafi ground targets and potential hideouts which could shelter the dictator and his family. Little wonder then that these two military and economic giants delivered a resounding rejection of the American-sponsored UN mandates for foreign intervention in Syria.'

'That's an objective summary?' enquired Bruce as he sought a response from her.

'As objective as I can be,' the professor replied. 'I see no point in pandering to the preferred point of view of either the East or the West, depending on which audience one is speaking with. The only caveat I put on my lectures is that I never say who I think is right or wrong. I present the facts as I understand them and the conclusions which fall from logical analysis.'

'Perhaps we can move onto the legal position Bryce confronts,' suggested Doug as he moved onto what was his third cup of coffee.

The professor shuffled papers and produced a sheet dotted with bullet-pointed paragraphs, to which she referred. 'US sanctions can be applied under its law and they apply to its citizens and corporate bodies. For example, the Syria Accountability Act 2004 prohibits export of goods containing more the ten per cent American components. There is the USA Patriot Act of 2006, which specifically targeted the Commercial Bank of Syria. All transactions with the Commercial Bank were suspended. There also exists a third category – those emanating from Executive Orders from the President. This may specifically deny certain Syrian citizens and entities access to the US financial system. Sanctions under this category are invariably prefixed with accusations that the parties targeted are involved in the proliferation of weapons of mass destruction.' This time the professor raised one eyebrow in a gesture of questioning cynicism. 'But since George Bush and Tony Blair were so comprehensibly exposed as being misinformed at best, or blatant liars at worst, over this vexed issue, allegations of weapons of mass destruction today are dismissed as facile.'

Not getting the specificity of answer he was seeking, Doug pressed a little harder. 'Tell me Sarah,' he said, choosing to use her first name as a subliminal message that he regarded her as an equal and therefore she should not get too domineering. 'Specifically, how do these American laws affect those who are not Americans?'

Professor Middleton adopted her Sarah look, usually reserved for those in class who ventured perilously close to a put-down in front of all present. 'Well actually Doug, they don't apply.'

'There appears to be nothing to stop a country boy from New Zealand selling butter or lamb to Iran or Syria?' It was a question posed with hopefulness.

'Food is often excluded from sanctions,' the professor responded quickly. 'But, to capture the ethos of specificity which you seek, it is correct that as a New Zealander you are not subject to US law when you are not in America. However, America invariably seeks to use its international clout as a trading partner, to convince or intimidate – take your pick – other states to toe the line or follow the example set by its sanctions. Japan's recent cessation of oil imports from Iran is an example of a nation doing what the Americans want.' She took a sip of coffee.

'Bluntly speaking,' she continued, returning to her theme. 'The US Ambassador might well inform the Prime Minister of New Zealand that if this country permitted the export of goods the US had blacklisted, to a country it had blacklisted, the probability is New Zealand would have its access to supply beef to the American hamburger market slashed.'

'And because the quota of beef exported to the US is negotiated at Government level, and not between private companies..,' Doug let his question linger unanswered.

'Precisely, but usually countries historically aligned with the US simply follow its requests. I mentioned the Japan example over Iran as a case in point. Canada is another classic example. They imposed a ban on the export of software for monitoring telephone and internet communications. Canada also froze all assets of Syrian individuals and prohibited economic dealings with individuals and entities associated with the Assad regime. This was over and above their ban on the import of Syrian oil and petroleum products.'

Silent until now, Susan pushed her hand up, like a child in a classroom seeking to catch the attention of the teacher. 'But what about nations friendly to places like Iran and Syria? Surely their friends don't simply do what America wants! I mean, if American law doesn't apply to them, why would they make their laws to stop their own people trading with historically friendly nations?'

With a smile of indulgence, the professor answered her student. 'The best example of that is the Arab Union. The Arab Union; that is all of Syria's Middle East neighbours – countries which have endured a similar level of colonial repression and exploitation during the preceding century – have filed sanctions against Syria. Travel bans against individuals and the assets of Syrian business and political elite in these neighbouring countries, frozen. And most hurtful to Syria, a ban on transactions with not only the Commercial Bank of Syria but the Central Bank of Syria. Even the US has not taken that step yet.'

'What do you mean? Bryce asked. 'Would that be the same as a ban against trading banks in New Zealand, such as the ASB, ANZ, BNZ and Westpac, being the equivalent to Commercial banks in Syria?'

'Yes, replied the professor with some alacrity. 'And also a ban against the Reserve Bank of New Zealand! This was virtually unprecedented in the game of sanctions. Invariably a loophole is left for behind the scenes trading, out-of-sight stuff that goes on at Government level in spite of the rhetoric and public posturing and sabre-rattling about banking bans. In the case of the Arab Union however, they locked out transactions with Syria's equivalent of our Reserve Bank.'

Silence followed, but finally Bryce spoke. 'What if one was to route money as payment for something like cement purchased from Syria via Malta or Turkish Cyprus? Both of these countries, I am informed, operate their own banking services –independent of the European Union, in the case of Malta, and independent of Turkey, in the case of Eastern Cyprus?'

This question took Doug somewhat by surprise. Bryce had obviously been doing his homework.

'I am not aware of the latitude those two states enjoy,' the professor admitted. 'I have read reports floating around the EU and UN which comment on the maverick conduct of these two island states. In the past they have operated as safe havens for Russian, Chinese and other entrepreneurs seeking to stash wealth made in their countries, which they want to remove from their homelands, for whatever reasons. But I don't know what their status is at this moment.'

'I suppose any transaction involving US dollars could be stopped by the Americans, irrespective of which bank the money was channelled through?' Doug said uncertainly.

'Exactly,' the professor said, more conciliatory toward him than she had been moments ago. 'The Americans retain a virtual stranglehold on transfer of money, globally, particularly where transactions are in US currency. At some stage US dollar transactions go through New York. So, if for example you were to purchase something from Syria, when it came to time for you to make payment, the Americans would block any transfer of money from your account in New Zealand to that country.'

Bryce made a show of looking at his watch. 'Thank you Professor. I appreciate very much the time you have given us at such short notice,' he said with aplomb and maturity. 'Your knowledge on the matters we have discussed is impressive and you have been most helpful.'

The professor nodded acceptance. 'You should thank your wife. I simply could not refuse a request from such an outstanding student. Goodness, she might have taken slight and transferred to a history major instead of staying with us in political studies.'

At ten pm Damascus time – eleven in the morning Auckland time – Doug's phone buzzed. Lisa had already taken one call but had instructed Alain to call back on the hour. Snatching at the handpiece, Doug dropped it and lost the connection.

'Bugger!' he said with genuine feeling.

Moments later the phone buzzed again. 'Bryce, is that you?' asked a patently agitated Alain. 'What kept you? Do I stay or do I come home?'

Bryce demurred then said. 'You sound grumpy, a bit like Doug this morning when I called him at three am for the meeting you demanded at that hour.'

'Okay, okay, but let's have it. I need to advise the Russians whether or not I will be at a meeting tomorrow or whether I am on the plane home.'

Bryce took his time answering. He had given a lot of thought to his predicament. From Sarah Middleton to an all-day brainstorming session with Doug, Bryce pretty well figured he had explored all the options, as presented by the Syrians.

'Alain,' he said calmly. 'Tell the Syrians I want exclusivity of phosphate exports to New Zealand and Australia.'

Alain digested the instruction. 'Anything else?'

'Yes, if I am going to put my neck on the block, it must be worth my while. Exclusivity for Australasia is not negotiable,' Bryce decreed.

Alain decided to take the new direction in his stride. 'What if they already have a contract to supply the Australians?

'I have thought about that. That Australian Government is so subservient to America that there is no way any Aussie will be doing business with Syria in this environment. That's got to be grounds for voiding a contract and who is going to stop them trading with a new client if they so decide?'

Bryce continued, with steely determination. 'This crap with Syria is not going to last forever and it is my reading that the American economic dream is now past its apex. They are hanging on to their position as precariously as Assad. They will not be the force they have been these past fifty years. So, I will buy Syrian phosphate, but I want contractual certainty that I have exclusivity for Australasia – into the future. Twenty years. I also want the contract with the Basrik Company and not the Syrian Government.'

'Keep talking,' Alain urged.

'If I have a contract with the Syrian Government and they decide not to honour it, I am knackered. There will be no point in seeking redress. It wouldn't be possible for me to win a court case in Syria against the Government any more than it would be possible for an Aussie to win a case against me in Syria for taking his contract with the Syrian Government. You agree?'

Alain thought for a moment then agreed.

'Conversely, if the Government is rolled, Basrik Enterprises will in all probability still be an operational phosphate mining and export company. Agreed?' the younger man said.

'Yes, you're probably correct,' Alain replied. 'In fact, I'd say it would become very important as an instrument to galvanise commerce.'

Bryce concurred. 'My thoughts exactly. Any new regime coming into power in Syria will likely have a Western penchant. It will want to show its credibility with the West. For Western business the issue is always the sanctity of a contract. So if I have a contract when these events transpire ... do you get my drift, Alain?

Alain answered in the affirmative.

'Look mate,' he said. 'Your logic is fine but there are a couple of missing links here. The first is how we get any product you buy to New Zealand. The second issue is how you make payment from New Zealand to Syria. Now before you tell me which of the options you prefer as offered by the FSB and Mr Yasin, I have to ask if you are quite sure you are prepared for the backlash. I mean, those bloody Yanks are not going to like this and the inevitability of them putting pressure on our own government to block the phosphate being landed, can't be ignored.'

'Thanks for reminding me. I should have explained. I have taken advice from a New Zealand university professor, and Doug and I spent the rest of the day brainstorming. Trust me. I have breathed this issue every second since we spoke this morning,' Bryce advised. 'I have thought about the American reaction but the reality is that unless I can break out from under the heel of the local phosphate so-called mafia here, I will be forced to become no more than what the rest of the smaller companies here have become. I'll forever be a sub-contractor to the big guys, buying phosphate from them to sell to my farmers who will be very disappointed I will no longer be able to produce the eco-friendly fertiliser which is the cornerstone of my business.'

Bryce needed the older man's approval and support. He had come this far on adrenalin and hope, now he needed someone with the sort of experience he lacked to take over and run the programme in the Middle East. 'What do you think, Alain?' he asked, by now his voice tinged with a hint of uncertainty.

Finally Alain responded. 'You have the passion to fight and win, my friend.'

Bryce grinned at Doug and cocked a thumb.

'But you still haven't said which option we take to buy and pay,' Alain solicited.

Speaking from the far side of his office, Doug spoke for the first time. 'Which option do you recommend my friend? Bryce has made the call at this end, but we need your counsel now on which road to travel.'

Alain had expected this question and countered. 'Are you okay if I call the shots over here then, Bryce?

'I am sure you will do your best for us,' Bryce replied. 'We are in this together. We're a team and to that end I insist that both you and Doug take up ten percent of the company each, at no cost to yourselves. I have spoken with our accountant about this and he agrees entirely. Two times ten gives you collectively twenty percent, which means you actually have influence on the board if you act together. It's an important consideration as it means you will not be merely impotent pillion passengers. But let's fine tune that later. Right now, it is over to you to lead the way.'

'Hey, there's no need for that my friend,' Doug admonished. 'You're paying me as a consultant. That the deal and that's fine with me.'

Bryce shook his head in rejection of Doug's declaration. 'No, you and Dad were good mates. He would have approved. Besides, I have some serious battles coming my way so if anything, I'm passing you a hand grenade.'

Alain listened with interest to what was undoubtedly an intriguing new twist to this particular saga.

'Well, if that's what is going to be, I won't be taking a fee for my services,' Doug said with a strong air of finality.

'And you, Alain?' asked Bryce.

'Retirement as a director on the most controversial company in New Zealand? You're passing me a bloody hand grenade, as you say, and it's a live one. But what else does one do with the sixth decade of life looming? I accept in principle. Like Doug I will forgo my fee, but I will need my disbursements paid. This trip is costing a bloody fortune.'

Bryce was emotional. 'Thanks fellas. This involves really big stakes. I am confident of my abilities in economics but it's the politics and reaction from competitors back here which are going to test not only my abilities but my resolve.'

Doug reached across and shook hands with his younger colleague. 'First item on the agenda Mr President,' he said in jest.

Bryce took the cue. 'First item gentlemen, the Famagusta option or the Belize option?'

Alain discarded one option immediately. 'The Famagusta option is already extinguished. Today the Arab Union drew a line in the sand. It was always on the cards. Have you heard about that yet?'

Both men chorused that the professor had alerted them to the probability a few hours earlier.

'It is still possible to fly into Turkish Cyprus and set up a bank account the same day,' Alain proffered. 'This differs from most, if not all of the countries within the EU who demand proof of a period of residency a before they will open an account. It's because Turkish Cyprus is outside the EU, even though it is a virtual province of Turkey. But today the Turks put their foot down. Famagusta will no longer transfer cash to Damascus.'

'Malta apparently is also a free-wheeling port. Many Russians have bank accounts in these island states - somewhere to move their ill-gotten gains to. It's seen as a safe haven which doesn't ask too many questions. But for our purposes, this option is now extinct because Malta has folded to US pressure, just as the Swiss did a few years back.'

Bryce and Doug looked at each other forlornly. 'Cyprus would have been my first option,' called Doug across his office.

'Mine too,' Bryce chimed in. 'I suppose it was too simple. We transfer money to Cyprus which transfers the money to Syria and to hell with the Yanks. But now that won't work.'

'Yep, so that leaves the Belize option,' Alain confirmed from Damascus.

'Shouldn't we really be referring to this option as Russia option?' enquired Bryce.

The delay in Alain's response drew questioning looks from both Bryce and Doug as they waited. Finally Alain replied. 'I think we best leave that detail to Hong Kong. I think the Rooskies were hoping it would be Famagusta too. No involvement by them. But Belize will, I suspect, need to be signed off in the Kremlin.'

Chapter Twelve
Damascus, Syria

Porter Julian liked these people. He had a good relationship with the Education Minister in spite of the most fervent objections of his CIA chief. Although both men were gay, their relationship was professional and cordial. Porter was well aware that homophobes like Dwight believed every gay man wanted to bed every other gay man. This was as illogical as every straight male wanting to bed every female he came upon. What is more, in Porter's case, after a brief period of experimental sex with the denizens of San Francisco's Arabic quarter, he had rejected that consummation of gay behaviour. His existence had become lonely, with no wife as a partner and no gay companion in the sense of an intimate relationship. Instead he opted for a career and put his heart and soul into his job.

Damascus suited Porter. He knew he was doing a good job for his country. He accepted criticism of his own Government, believing it would be churlish not to acknowledge that mistakes had been made and that the position of America on the world stage had suffered hugely because of President George W Bush's ill-considered invasion of Iraq. He also accepted, unequivocally, that the greed, avarice and mismanagement within its own economy as the precursor to the global economic crisis which spread, like leprosy, far and wide in 2008. Porter Julian was intelligent enough and big enough to identify these events as having undermined the country he cherished. He lamented the fact that only the architects of economic mismanagement, such as chief executives and board chairmen, had faced courtroom sequels, but that architects of political mismanagement on a massive scale - George W Bush sprang readily to mind - rode into the sunset, avoiding all culpability.

Looking to the future with hope in his heart, Porter knew he could make a difference to how American behaviour affected the Middle East and how the rest of the world might judge his nation. He believed he had the mandate and the ability to steer a stable course, and to that end, he would lock down Dwight Arnold junior, and the people like him, if it was the last thing he ever did for his country.

Porter pressed the intercom button, advising his secretary, 'Send him in, Sally.'

The side door entrance from the reception desk exploded inward, rocketing into Porter's ambassadorial suite as if it had been propelled by cannon.

Dwight had his beige panama in one hand and a sheaf of paperwork in the other. Striding forth as if it was his own office, he slammed the papers, which Porter saw also contained photographs, loudly onto the mahogany desktop.

'Our Kiwi terrorist left Damascus yesterday morning on Austria Air,' the CIA's head man in Syria exclaimed. 'In Vienna he caught the evening Korean Air flight to Seoul and from there he flew to Hong Kong. He then booked in at the Regal Kowloon and he hasn't moved.'

Leaning back in his chair, Porter let his gaze fall on the documents and pondered. Calculating the time it would take for his CIA chief to accept his lower rank and realise that his entry had been excessive, even for him, Porter paused momentarily. 'I'm not surprised he hasn't moved from his hotel. That's a lot of flying.' He did not offer his CIA man a seat, nor did he indicate by eye movement that an invitation was implied.

Porter leafed through the documents which had been so rudely dumped on his desk. 'I don't see any sign of the five hundred words I asked you to submit with your recommendations on how to deal with this ... New Zealand businessman.'

'He is up to something, sir,' Dwight insisted. Cognisant once again of his superior's status and importance, he had moderated his tone and thrown in a measure of respect.

'I delayed submitting the report until I got a better handle on him. The day after our trip to Homs he was with Wakid Mashreq, the Minister of Mines and the chief executive of Barsik Enterprises for twelve hours! Twelve hours!' he repeated emphatically.

'That adds up to a commercial transaction of phosphate. My people in New Zealand insist he is seeking to buy a substantial volume on an extended contract. There is no question, this man is going to attempt to break our blockade and in the process he will embarrass the American people if nothing else. Well, it will be nothing else 'cause there is no way in Hell he is going to get shipments of phosphate out of here, let alone landed there.'

Porter picked up a pencil, noting for the first time as he twisted it between fingers that the item had been made in Germany. Resisting any temptation to rebuke the CIA chief about his dramatic entry, the Ambassador said, 'Okay, I agree. The signs suggest some negotiations about buying phosphate took place. Where were our friends from the FSB while all this was going down?'

Dwight had forgotten to mention the Russians and obfuscated to disguise his omission. 'Well, of course they were there, sir. Did I not state the obvious?'

'No you did not,' Porter replied. 'It is always a good idea to state the obvious. It reduces the possibility of messages not being properly delivered.'

'The colonel was there in her usual glamorous persona. They also have a new boy on the block. He's quite a big fella and seems to be assigned to Foveaux.'

'Where did he come from?' the Ambassador asked, seeking to surreptitiously probe the efficiency of his CIA contingent in Syria.

'We haven't had this guy on our screens before. We've got no name so we can't back track him. I'll get it though, don't worry about that,' Dwight enthused.

'Any phone calls from his hotel?' the Ambassador enquired. 'What did you pick up there?'

Dwight shook his head. 'We tapped his room while he was at the meeting, but no phone calls in or out. We have a lock on his mobile, but again nothing. Nothing in and nothing out, voice or text. But we can be sure someone is briefing him.'

Porter then turned his attention to the New Zealand businessman, in whom the Americans were most interested. 'Looking at the dossier you have on him, it seems to me he is an old hand at your sort of business. I don't see that he needs advice in that direction,' knowing that if there was one thing that would annoy the CIA chief it would come from being beaten by another professional in his line of work.

'I see he was a captain in Vietnam - promoted in the field at the same time he was recommended for Military Cross.' Porter raised his eyebrows as he powered through the report, verbalising its content. 'The Cross was never awarded - accusations that he shot the wrong people. They stripped him of the recommendation but left him with his promotion. Then repatriated to New Zealand and discharged,' he exclaimed, tossing the reports lightly across the desk. 'This man might better be serving Uncle Sam in your division somewhere out there! Have a seat. We need a plan – in fact we need two plans, one to cover the situation if he goes home from Hong Kong and another if he comes back here.'

Dwight gratefully took a seat. 'I am having him monitored in Hong Kong. I should have a report by six am tomorrow - that will be midday over there. Something should come up by then.'

The diplomat leaned across the table. 'I need a report from you at eight o'clock in the morning for New Zealand. That should set out all that Mr Foveaux has done since he arrived in Syria. The report you receive from Hong Kong can accompany your own and my report to New Zealand, which will then go back to the States. Confine yourself to the facts Mr Arnold. What you put in your report for your own people is not my concern, but the report I attach to my missive should be confined to the facts. I will draw my own conclusions in my communiqué.'

The CIA chief nodded approvingly but was aware of the changed tone and that Ambassador was issuing him an order he should not fail to obey. 'And if he returns?'

Porter didn't respond, knowing he was, at that moment, devoid of a suitable solution. One thing he did know for sure was that he was not going to let Dwight and his henchmen drag Foveaux in for the proverbial chat. Thinking aloud he said, 'If he goes home it doesn't mean he has not already negotiated a deal with these people. So, either way we need surveillance on any attempt to transfer money from New Zealand to Syria. No need to go crazy here. Syria demands US dollars in trades and as you'll be aware, any attempt to send money into this country can be traced. That covers initiatives by Foveaux and his crew to use a Trojan horse. Tracing that horse will ultimately demonstrate its origin in New Zealand if Foveaux sources the money from within his own country. We can pretty much presume he will do so because I doubt he has proxies around the globe who will stand in for him. His people in New Zealand are, after all, a relatively small outfit.'

'We should have a code name for this operation,' Dwight urged the Ambassador. 'Is operation Frog okay with you?'

The Ambassador shrugged indifferently. 'How did you arrive at that name?' he enquired, with distinct indifference.

'Foveaux is French. A Frog is a Frenchman, just as a WOG is an Arab and a WOP is an Italian and a Hun is a German and a Spic is ....'

Porter swiftly raised both palms in mock defeat. 'Okay. Enough. I get it.' The penchant of his CIA chief for pejorative appellations dismayed the diplomat, but he was well beyond having the remotest interest in trying to re-educate the man. Shaking his head, Porter brought the discussion back to their plans.

'So, we have objective reports from you attached to the Hong Kong missive and my covering report going back to New Zealand and then over to the States. Tomorrow morning, nine o'clock Syria time.'

Dwight nodded acceptance and recorded the order.

'We need to place a monitor alert on currency transactions, as discussed. You can do that when you leave my office,' Porter said, consciously pointing his German-made pencil at Dwight. 'We also need a monitor on activity at the phosphate plants.'

'Already in place,' Dwight advised, a little too excitedly, as a schoolboy might announce to his teacher that he had put out the class rubbish without being asked.

'And if Foveaux comes back to Syria?'

'Operation Frog is ready to go. He will be under constant surveillance, physical and electronic,' announced Dwight, once again seeking to demonstrate that he was really on his game.

The Ambassador felt it was perhaps time to offer some encouragement and subtly proffered an olive branch. 'That's great. Thanks. Meanwhile, I will be in contact with my counterpart in New Zealand. We need a handle on where their Government might place its sleeping mat. The New Zealanders have been tepid allies since Iraq. Actually, that was the case further back, since they were shut out of ANZUS, our Australia New Zealand US military alliance, because they adopted anti-nuclear legislation preventing the visit of our battleships unless we confirmed that they were neither nuclear-armed or propelled.'

'Which of course we don't do,' interrupted Dwight indignantly. 'Who the hell do those turnips from down-under think they are?'

Porter avoided verbalising his thoughts. The Kiwis had forced the Americans to their knees. And they had caused the abandonment of a key plank in US foreign policy in the Pacific – ANZUS.

'The latest reports I have on New Zealand is that the present Government has made positive steps to get back into our boat. So I will ask my counterpart to get a handle on exactly what that administration would do if a shipment of phosphate left port Tartus here in Syria with the stated intention of landing it in New Zealand.'

Chapter Thirteen

Hong Kong

Alain had always regarded Hong Kong as the anus of the Empire – the British Empire that was – and nothing had changed since the transfer of sovereignty to the People's Republic of China in 1997.

It was the last outpost of colonial domination, abuse, commercial exploitation, and literally, the rape of its women, by American, French, English, Russian, Dutch, Austria-Hungary, Italian and Japanese colonists who dispensed Christianity while trading in opium and slavery until the final vestiges were erased by triumphant communist forces led by Mao over Chiang Kai-shek in 1947.

Their hotel was packed. An international Rugby Sevens tournament had ensured the mid-range hotels were overflowing, in turn putting pressure on capacity in the better establishments. Alain went straight to bed. Twenty six hours of waiting at airports or in the air had taken its toll on his soul. Egor however had other thoughts in mind, anxious to find a nubile young Asian girl, preferably two, with which to relieve his tensions. But this was not to be. A bland-faced block of a man with short-cropped hair and unmistakable origins in Kazakhstan had met them as they had exited the passport control. Alain was bid adieu in the foyer of the hotel by this block of granite, while Egor was marched unceremoniously back to the limousine which had brought them from the airport. Alain could only speculate at the fate of his travelling companion, but was too tired to devote more than a moment to this sentiment.

Eight o'clock the following morning Alain was woken by a persistent buzz. Eventually he lifted the phone from its cradle. '*Doobrya ootrya* Alain,' the caller proclaimed.

'Good morning,' Alain responded in a state of automatism.

'We have a meeting with our people in sixty minutes. Will you join me for breakfast? Our car will collect us in the lobby in an hour,' Egor advised.

Right on schedule, Alain and Egor climbed into a Russian embassy Mercedes and within forty minutes, they walked into the office of Caruthers and Associates, Hong Kong.

Alain placed Richard Caruthers at sixty five, carrying too much weight for his one hundred and seventy eight centimetres. He was a flashy dresser of Asian sub-continent parentage. He was probably the result of an illegitimate liaison with between a British military attaché and a local woman in crumbling post colonial China.

'Delighted to meet you,' Richard said as he extended his hand to Alain.

'*Rad poznakomeetsya Yegor,*' he said to Egor with impressive fluency in Russian.

'*Gavaretya prooski elee angleeski*?' he said, addressing them both.

'English if you don't mind,' replied Alain. 'I don't wish to miss a detail in this session.'

Richard smiled accommodatingly. 'Worry not. This a proven path trod by many a rich man and woman, good and not so good alike. Ask as many questions as you wish.'

The two men were ushered into what seemed to be a drawing room, an English legacy with opulent furnishings from sixteenth century Europe. Probably pre-Revolution France, mused Alain, and money clearly no object to the host.

Fifty minutes later Alain asked if he could recount what he had been told.

'By all means,' agreed the host. 'I will make notes where it seems you require further edification. Please tell me what you have learned from our session.'

'Firstly,' said Alain, 'the purpose of establishing companies with bank accounts in Belize, the British Virgin Islands and Hong Kong, is to set up a network through which Kiwifert in New Zealand can subvert the American financial transaction blockade on Syria and pay Barsik Enterprises in Syria.'

Richard smiled approvingly.

'Secondly, you will set up a company of which I am sole director in Belize. By your description, Belize is an island state in the former British Honduras which has a population of less than half a million and is a shit-hole infested with snakes, malaria and criminals of the worst description, many of whom are accountants and lawyers. Furthermore, in spite of its British colonial antecedents, it is regarded as more Central American these days and any white man who ventures forth into this pestilent paradise is more likely to die of lead poisoning than snake venom.'

Richard nodded. 'It is my opinion.'

Alain took a deep breath before continuing. 'Thirdly, the place survives as a haven for gun-runners, drug lords, Russian oligarchs and anyone wanting to transfer money beyond the jurisdiction of America, and the key to transferring money internationally and beyond the purview of most authorities is to form a company in this Island of Paradise.'

'Correct,' said Richard in mocking surprise.

'To achieve this objective I pay you the sum of fifteen hundred US dollars.'

Richard smiled ingratiatingly.

'This company I set up in Belize – let us call it Ajax Company – then sets up a company in the British Virgin Islands, or BVI. This cost me another fifteen hundred US dollars. The BVI company, let's call it Exeter Company, then sets up a company here in Hong Kong which we will for the sake of convenience name Achilles Company. This costs another fifteen hundred US dollars.'

Richard raised his hands and clapped ceremoniously. 'Well done. The chronology is correct. Each company will of course have bank accounts in the respective countries. Now please the rationale.'

'For some less-than-precise reason, BVI companies which come to Hong Kong receive preferential treatment from Government authorities, such as the taxation department, securities commission, the police, customs and other like-minded agencies?' said Alain with no attempt to disguise his scepticism. 'And the best you could explain this arrangement seems to be a desire by the Chinese Government not to scare away potential investors who historically have had a penchant for the BVI doorway, and to maintain a robust banking network in Hong Kong but within ultimate control of Beijing.'

'Smoke and mirrors, if you will,' Richard said by way of exculpatory statement. 'When China took over the territory of Hong Kong they were anxious to retain the banking and commercial hub fostered under British rule.'

Alain paused, still calculating the reasonableness of the labyrinth he was now traversing. 'Company tax in China is fifteen per cent and that alone attracts many companies to domicile in Hong Kong. As long as you pay your taxes, the Government pretty much leaves you alone.'

'A very important aspect of the programme,' ventured Richard unctuously. 'To pay your tax,' he added to avoid any confusion.

'To revert a moment, if I may, to the preferential treatment aspect,' insisted the New Zealander. 'The reason for this you are unable to precisely quantify, but you assert that the practice is a convention and therefore has effect of unwritten law.'

Richard nodded approval.

Alain shrugged indifference at this incomprehensible dimension of Chinese banks. 'However,' he continued, 'Hong Kong does co-operate with Western agencies, such as the United States, when it comes to disclosure of who owns the companies which operate out of their territory. This includes BVI companies which publicises the names of shareholders in companies registered there and thus the names of BVI company shareholders who participate in owning Hong Kong companies become public. Belize, on the other hand, does protect the names of company shareholders. That country has a strict policy of non-disclosure, irrespective of who is calling. Before Switzerland lost its nerve and folded to American pressure, that once safe haven provided a similar level of anonymity for its client base.'

Richard once again clapped ostentatiously. 'Yes, but at the moment Belize is one of a dwindling few who have not been intimidated into subservience by the Americans.'

Egor too was keen to erase any question of confusion. In fact it seemed to Alain that the Russian had been particularly vigilant, not only in paying attention to Richard's lecture, but on the journey to the office he had been either highly alert or anxious.

'*Tak*,' said Egor. 'If I wish to hide the identity of the shareholders of a company registered in Hong Kong, I open a company in Belize which protects disclosure in face of all pressure?'

'This is correct,' repeated Richard. 'Protecting company confidentiality is imperative to the future of their economy. As I said, many wealthy people and organisations depend on the integrity of the Belize Government, which in turn depends on the revenue generated from providing this unique service. The island is a very poor state and its people depend on this industry.'

The two visitors to Richard's den seemed to communicate with mental telepathy. Trepidation flowed as a magnetic field. Feeling the need to break the spell, Richard interjected. 'Neither of you however have mentioned the banking disbursement benefits of a Hong Kong company.'

Waving an admonishing finger, Alain denied he had forgotten the most important component of the matrix - how the money from New Zealand reached its destination. Quickly he continued. 'Kiwifert pays Basrik for a shipment of phosphate by transferring funds from New Zealand into the Hong Kong bank account of Achilles which has no connection to Syria.'

'Correct,' Richard repeated, a little cautiously.

'Payment to Achilles in Hong Kong can be on invoice to Kiwifert from Achilles. It is also possible to use this matrix for any phosphates you may acquire from other countries, such as Russia. Once the money is in Hong Kong it can be dispensed to approved persons or by way of cash card issued on the Hong Kong bank.'

'You okay with this Egor?' asked Alain.

Egor nodded but seemed unconvinced. Alain frowned. 'There's something missing here – the documents showing where the shipment of phosphate came from will be required in New Zealand. I agree, there is no legal impediment to Kiwifert at this juncture, but the fact the shipment is from Syria and the invoice is from Achilles are two dots which any half competent

Customs officer is going to join together. Therefore, even the CIA is going to be able to deduce that Achilles is a front for Syrian business.'

Taking a seat on a stool, Richard agreed with this deduction. 'That is not a trade transaction which is prohibited in your country. But the critical element is that the people behind Achilles remain faceless – because of the network back to Belize, and this is important for the Syrian Ministers and military people who want their commission.'

Commission was an interesting way to describe theft, Alain thought, but he did not say this.

'A company like Achilles would be used as the point from which money would be allocated to cash cards. A bank card which has money in savings which can be withdrawn anywhere in the world at any ATM by any person with the PIN number,' said Richard. 'And if that proves too easy for the Americans to intercept, we can transfer money to Ajax in Belize, which in turn can distribute cash to other bank accounts we might set up - for example, in Lichtenstein or Cyprus. Although Cyprus is now denying transfers to Syria, they are not restricting the issuing of cash cards.'

Alain murmured. 'By the time the Yanks caught up with one outlet, another could be in place and so on.'

Smiling again, Richard agreed. 'This is the nature of my business Mr Foveaux. To be one step ahead of the world's self-appointed policeman.'

Rubbing his chin, Alain pondered then said, 'Ultimately it seems to me even the CIA will be able to join the dots which appear on their spy software and lock into any card we issue from any of the banks we set up, won't they?'

Richard agreed in principle. 'Technically that is possible, but once we have these three companies set up, there are a multitude of combinations, including additional bank accounts, which we can put into place. This will provide ample time for disbursement of funds to whomever you chose to disburse to, before the CIA can intervene.'

'The ultimate money launder matrix?' Alain replied derisively. 'So what do you need to set up these companies?'

'Four thousand five hundred US dollars cash and the names of the parties to go on the company register in Belize,' said Richard, a little too smoothly.

'So there is no requirement for me to fly anywhere? It is all done from your office? I give you my full name and an address I presume, but what evidence of identification do you require?'

Richard smiled slyly. 'You come well recommended,' he said, casting a glance at Egor. 'A copy of your passport will do and any address you feel inclined to furnish. No proof of occupancy required.'

Alain paused again, reminding himself that he was not there because he liked the place, but rather because Valentina had recommended this course. It was also as he had discussed with Bryce and Doug and he had their approval. Sure Richard had doubled the price quoted by Valentina but that was still small change in the overall scheme of things. Alain handed his passport to Richard, who proceeded to scan it.

Egor then handed Richard two more passports, one bearing the Russian crest and the other being an EU variety. Alain raised a querying brow.

'I have been instructed to present these two passports to be included as shareholders in Ajax.' Egor spoke softly, swiftly and with downcast eyes.

'This is news to me,' Alain said with concern in his voice. 'When was this decision made? This is not the proposal as outlined by Valentina in Damascus.'

Alain looked at Richard, deducing immediately that he had been aware of this change of plan. But this was not the time to throw his toys from the cot. There had to be a reason for this. The Russians wouldn't pull this stunt without good cause. 'Egor,' he said finally. 'I'm disappointed that you did not discuss this with me earlier. I need to call New Zealand.'

Egor pulled a chair out and sat. 'I apologise. I am told of this only first time yesterday when we arrive in Hong Kong. You go to bed, I go to FSB office. I can explain you why this is.'

Alain pulled out another chair and sat too, reasoning that this could be a long day. 'Please do,' he said, surprised at his own calmness in the face of such chicanery.

In spite of saying he could explain, Egor fumbled his words. Finally finding some composure he spoke. 'Colonel Valentina tell me in Damascus that Kremlin agree to make shipments of phosphate to New Zealand for two reasons. First reason is for pride - to defeat American blockade is big victory for Russia. Kremlin not worry about phosphate for farmers in New Zealand.'

'That seems reasonable,' answered Alain. 'An eminently believable explanation in fact. And?'

Egor hesitated. He was nervous and a slight perspiration appeared on his upper lip. Suddenly and without premeditation, Alain demanded Richard leave the room. Richard evaporated like a mist before a hurricane.

'Okay, it's me,' said Alain. 'Cut the crap. What's going on?'

Once they were on their own Egor began to talk more freely. 'Second reason, Kremlin know Yasin make demand of Syria that his name be shareholder in Ajax company in Belize. Yasin is a powerful broker I think you call it. He make many deals for Iran to sell export goods for cash. Also he arrange sale of Iran and Syria gold for cash to ease the crisis of each country which is caused by sanctions. Yasin is man who knows all Belize people behind the screen. Many Arabs use Yasin to make private money transfers. Colonel Valentina tell me he is crazy man - very dangerous. America has bounty on his head.'

'Behind the scene,' Alain corrected the Russian automatically.

'Thank you. My English is not good on slangs or when am I nervous.'

Alain thought for a while before speaking again. 'So, Yasin wants a cut. You know what a cut is?

'Is slang for share of money?' Egor questioned.

'Very good. But this still doesn't make sense. If Yasin is a hoodlum, why would the Syrians let him in on their deal?'

'How Colonel Valentina tell me, Wakid Mashreq and Minister of Mines are corrupt. They expect a cut,' Egor said, demonstrating his new lexicon. 'Wakid Mashreq and Minister have bank accounts frozen by America. America freeze bank accounts of Syrian apparatchiki.'

Egor turned and asked if Alain knew this word. The response was in the affirmative.

'All Ministers take cut when Syrian enterprise makes sale - oil, cement, phosphate, not matter. Always is big corruption, which is reason for many Syria people to fight Assad on civil war,' Egor professed.

The reasons for rebellion in Syria were varied, but Alain did know that corruption among the elite was a burning issue of contention among many of that country's people.

'Yasin is only man Wakid Mashreq and Minister can use to help them take cut now America shut down their international accounts. Best way now for Wakid Mashreq and Minister to take cut from phosphate is with help of Yasin,' explained the young Russian.

'And steal money,' Alain added definitively. Egor smiled weakly.

'So what we now have is a three way split - Kiwifert; FSB; Syrian elite' said Alain, to state the obvious.

'Colonel Valentina tell me Russia want name on company for control. Russian must know what is happen with Ajax at all times. Not interested in cut. Too small money for Kremlin.'

That's generous of them, thought Alain with some sarcasm. Shrugging dismissively, he said, 'Who are we to reason why, my friend. As long as Kiwifert gets its correct measure of phosphate for the dollars paid, we are not going to worry. The parties who will be short-changed are Basrik Enterprises and the Syrian Government.'

Again the two men locked eyes as Alain considered the latest twist. 'Yasin is involved because he has the Belize and BVI connections and is known to Wakid Mashreq and the Minister as being the professional whom one approaches to do these things under the radar, like you say. Yasin therefore holds the shares in Belize on behalf of Wakid Marsreq and others from the corrupt elite.'

Feeling much relieved at the manner in which Alain appeared to be taking the change of plan since they departed Damascus, Egor said encouragingly, 'Yasin has reputation for deliver the goods. This is also slang?'

'Cliché,' Alain corrected, 'but it's the same as slang.'

'Arab elite must have much care to steal from Government,' Egor proclaimed with certainty. 'Same is in Russia when bureaucrats siphon money from Gazprom and other Russian conglomerates. Must have person who is trustworthy with access to networks. Yasin has this repute. His success as broker depends on his integrity.'

A gentle knocking reminded the two men they were guests. 'Have you gentlemen made your decisions?' Richard asked as he timidly pushed the door ajar.

'Yes we have,' Alain determined. 'Do join us again.'

As Richard prepared more paperwork, Alain asked, 'May I presume that you are an employee of Yasin?' Richard was clearly unprepared for such a question, his flustered body language answering the query without words.

'Dangerous playmates you have,' Alain proclaimed, looking directly at their host. 'If he knew you were doubling up on his charges for setting up this labyrinth, I suspect he would take a dim view of your perfidy. I'll tell you what. I have here two thousand two hundred and fifty US dollars; that is the amount the Russian colonel in Damascus quoted your fee to me. Any problems?' Richard had none.

Alain handed over the cash, in crisp new American greenbacks. 'So when do we set up the bank accounts?' he asked.

Richard smiled unctuously. 'Actually, I took the liberty of getting all the paperwork in place prior to your arrival. The accounts can be opened at the bank across the road.' Separating the slat blinds over the office window, he pointed to the edifice of a well-known international bank. 'We can pop across there now if you wish?'

'Yes we will,' Alain acceded. 'I agree to the multi-shareholding, but I must be one of the co-signatories for all financial transactions, and what is more, I insist that my signature is biometric.' He held up his index finger. 'That means accounts can't be accessed unless I scan in my fingerprint.'

Half an hour later, as they waited on the street for their limousine to appear, Alain observed, 'That was simple enough.'

'Is very good idea you make,' Egor replied, making reference to the insistence of a biometric signature.

'I think that Richard very much likes little boys,' Alain proclaimed from the side of his mouth.

'*Ya Torsha*,' Egor replied. 'I think this too. But I think he is doing all things proper to help Ajax, Exeter and Achilles. Him very afraid of Yasin.'

This was a conclusion Alain had also reached before he had given his final assent to the project. As he was to explain to Bryce and Doug later, as long as Kiwifert got its phosphate, he did not mind who got the money or who Richard preferred in his bed.

As the embassy car pulled into the curb, Egor asked, 'What is Ajax, Exeter and Achilles? These are names from mythology?'

'Maybe,' Alain replied. 'But they are also the names of ships. Achilles was a New Zealand cruiser which together with two British cruisers, the Ajax and the Exeter, forced the German pocket battleship Graf Spee to be scuttled in Montevideo. The German captain was later executed I think. It was one of the first big naval encounters of World War Two and the Germans not only lost their best fighting ship and its crew, but they suffered a mortal blow to their naval supremacy on the high seas at that moment. Some say it was a turning point of the war.'

'Stalin say different,' Egor countered. 'Only reason Germany lose war is because they make attack on Russia. Churchill say this also. Russia entry into the war was turning point. Not Graf Spee and not Pearl Harbour.'

Chapter Fourteen

Damascus, Syria.

The Damascus heat crippled Porter and his people from about two in the afternoon until about nine at night, sometimes later.

'It's impossible to get any meaningful work from these people after noon,' he lamented as he signalled his CIA chief to take a seat. 'What happened in Hong Kong?'

Thrusting forward his jaw in the provocative manner he'd used in high school when lining up against his opposite block on the gridiron pitch, Dwight raised an admonishing index finger and glared spitefully at the Ambassador.

'Foveaux and this new Russian were treated like royalty by the local FSB. Special limo taking them to an office complex which included firms specializing in setting up shelf companies and bank accounts in Hong Kong.'

'Taxation relief,' said Porter.

Sitting upright, Dwight challenged that assumption. 'Maybe but more likely part of a clandestine network in the Caymans or Luxembourg or BVI simply to cover their tracks.'

Porter nodded. 'Probably both,' he conceded.

'Our people out there are working on the fine detail,' continued Dwight. 'It's not an easy place to penetrate commercial intrigue but disclosure of company registrations is mandatory which means we simply trawl and trawl until we come up with the names. The point is, Mr Ambassador,' he hurried on, 'this is evidence Foveaux is putting into place a vehicle to defeat …or should I say try to defeat … our blockade. He is doing this with blatant assistance from the Reds and that means, Mr Ambassador, that we have a duty to stop him.'

Porter let the moment linger. His CIA chief had a point. US legislators had made it abundantly clear that they were reluctant to challenge Executive Orders emanating from the White House, and the President had by his actions demonstrated that he was pretty much running the Middle East by Decree. Recent Executive Decrees were providing a virtual carte blanche for people like Dwight to run amok. If he didn't work with him, Porter realised that he would be left in the dark completely by his local CIA operative; a man he considered to be bordering on unstable.

'Here,' he said tossing a report across the desk to Dwight. 'Read this cable, just in from New Zealand.'

'What's it say?' demanded Dwight as he snatched up the document and furled through the pages. 'Jesus. Those guys down there know how to keep the paper industry in business.'

Porter smiled at the hackneyed joke but regrettably concluded that it was now time to give his hound dog his lead. Therefore it was in the best interests of operational efficiency and information exchange that Porter momentarily buried the hatchet and not in Dwight's thick skull. 'It will take a while for you to plough through in its entirety so I will summarise for you and we can make preliminary plans.'

Great, thought Dwight, believing that he now had his superior well and truly by the balls.

Porter took up the issue. 'The bottom line is that our people don't believe the Government in New Zealand can stop shipments of phosphate from Syria being offloaded there.' He paused to be sure the bottom line had sunk in. 'The present government is more pro-American than the main opposition, which is a collection of our equivalent to Democrats, and a surprisingly large Green block which as we know, are no great fans of America.' That last utterance would grate with the CIA man, thought Porter, secretly satisfied at getting that particular barb in without challenge.

'So, even though we have an incumbent government more disposed toward the US than the rest of their parliament, the advice I receive, and you will find it comprehensively annotated about page fifteen as I recall, is that the Foreign Minister and the Prime Minister will lead a tirade against this fertiliser company for dealing with Syria. But it will not stop that company from importing phosphate from Syria because it cannot.'

It was all was too much for Dwight. 'Bullshit!' he exclaimed loudly enough that the receptionist clearly heard the muffled outburst through what were supposed to be sound-proofed doors. 'They stopped the crews of our ships taking R and R in their ports because they legislated against visits by vessels with nuclear capability, so they can certainly legislate against a shipload of potential explosives from Syria.'

Once again Porter was stunned by the display of arrogance and silently sought divine intervention, or simply the arrival of someone who could provide relief from a man he had long ago decided was a moron.

'I am sure the New Zealand authorities would not need to justify legislating against exports on the basis the material was, or might be, used for weapons of mass destruction,' he explained to his CIA man. 'When you read the report thoroughly you will see that it is the opinion of our people - our experts over there – that their Government will make a noise but it won't legislate specifically against importing phosphate from Syria.' Pausing for effect Porter concluded by adding, 'Phosphate is a critical component for their economy. They use it in agriculture, not to make bombs.'

Porter reached forward and with a back scratcher extended his reach to flip over a couple of pages in the document on Dwight's lap. 'That graph diagrammatically demonstrates the volume of exported agriculture products from New Zealand – including to Iran. The point is, agriculture is big business. As our experts on the ground in New Zealand deduce; it is not politically practical to discriminate against phosphate which is used to grow food – and not to make fucking bombs!'

Porter caught himself. He had raised his voice and it was a very rare occasion for him to swear. To use obscene language was virtually unheard of in his manner of speaking, but his CIA chief's insistence on seeing a terrorist under every woman's skirt frustrated him immensely.

'I'm sorry but it is not politically practical for the government of New Zealand to blacklist phosphate from Syria which is used to grow food, while at the same time the country is selling mutton to the Ayatollah.' In exasperation he emphasised, 'This is advice from our people on the ground in that land, far away our usual network of intelligence gathering! They tell us that it would be unprecedented for a government to legislate in such a manner. It has never been done so before. And according to my counterpart, the Prime Minister and Foreign Minister, while great showmen on camera, are totally devoid of backbone when it comes to making unpopular decisions.'

Porter could see Dwight was livid; near apoplectic.

'Fuck. Fuck. Fuck,' the CIA operative said, but this time he kept the decibel count low. 'We saved those mothers from the Japs in forty two! And this is how they repay us?'

Porter let Dwight get his emotions under control then picked up the thread again. 'With no help likely from our friends in the South Pacific, I therefore, must require you to submit three options on how the CIA might deal with this problem,' Porter decreed. 'I do have genuine concern about the damage this fellow Foveaux could do to the image of our country.'

From the slouched and defeated posture he had slumped to four minutes ago, Dwight was now bolt upright and his mind razor sharp. 'I'll have Operation Orders for three scenarios for Operation Frog, by early tomorrow morning. Sir.'

Alain and Egor were collected at Damascus Airport by the Alpha Force karate instructor who had nearly torn off Egor's arms during his first refresher. During the weeks which followed however, Egor had demonstrated conclusively that he deserved the Chidokan black belt awarded to him in New Zealand. As a result, Sergei and Egor had established a bond. Their abilities in the martial arts were well above those of all other Russians on assignment to Syria. Having a colleague with good self defence capabilities had been welcomed by Sergei for too often he had been assigned to tasks of some danger where the back-up he could call upon when in trouble, was uninspiring. Although he had always been able to fight his way out of a dark alley, he was astute enough to know that this run of luck, in his line of business, could not go on forever.

When Egor passed through the diplomatic channel with Alain close on his heels, Sergei expressed relief that his new friend had returned safely.

'That's an odd thing to say!' suggested Alain to Egor. 'If my Russian is correct, your friend was concerned for our safety?'

Egor nodded but did not reply. He asked Sergei if there were any problems but the response was curt, probably, Alain surmised, because Sergei was reluctant to speak openly in his presence. In broken English Sergei said, 'I take you both on colonel. Is why am I have colonel's machina.'

'Nice car,' said Alain, noting the upgrade in engine size, body weight and internal luxury from the standard Mercedes Kompressor which had been his chariot from the Omayed to the meeting with the Syrians several days earlier. Valentina is doing well for herself, he thought.

With little more to be said among the men as they drove into the city, Alain and Egor were quick to catch some rest. Both were tired. Their flight from Hong Kong back to Damascus had reversed their earlier Vienna-Seoul route but with no stopover.

As shadows cast by the setting sun extended their tentacles across what Alain perceived as a truly beautiful landscape, he noticed a couple of burnt-out vehicles. Curls of smoke lingered over the south east of the city and from time to time he saw placards praising President Assad. There were no active signs of rebellion in the streets but this was Damascus, not Homs or Aleppo where opposition to the regime was centred.

As they passed by Shoukry Al-Qouwatly intersection with Ath Thawra boulevard on which they were travelling, Alain roused sufficiently to catch a glimpse of the massive Four Seasons hotel edifice towering above its environs. At Baghdad Avenue they crossed left over their carriageway then turned right then left then right then left, by which time Alain figured they were close enough to walk to the Russian compound. It would have been quicker than their vehicular progress which was frustrated by the myriad one-way alleys to be negotiated.

Darkness was closing as the driver slowed to a stop behind another of the many delivery vehicles which had often blocked their passage often for up to five interminable minutes. Suddenly, before Alain could comprehend more than the fact that their vehicle had stopped, his head was thrust forward with violent G force as their driver slammed the Mercedes into reverse and accelerated. Within seconds Alain's head jerked up and back, a searing pain burning somewhere near the base of his skull as the Mercedes slammed into a vehicle which had followed them into the alley and blocked any retreat.

The next thing Alain saw was the base of a police-style door rammer aimed directly at his door window. One man had the rammer; another had a sub-machine gun. Both men were younger and dressed similar to the young people whom he had seen in Homs week earlier.

'*Sadeetyes! Sadeetyess*!' yelled Sergei.

Involuntarily Alain ducked as the bash of the rammer against window exploded like a stun grenade. To the other side of the car Alain saw other men, one of whom had a M16A4 standard NATO-issue assault rifle aimed at Sergei. In the fleeting glimpse he had of the man and the weapons, Alain recognised the modified form of the model of weapon he'd purchased for the Omani army during his time as logistics commandant over a decade earlier. For a moment time stood still as he contemplated death delivered by an old friend. He knew well that the weapon in the hands of the man standing on the pedestrian strip would rip holes in one side and out the other of the Mercedes.

'Sit!' repeated Egor in English. 'They cannot get in. This car is bulletproof.'

Suddenly the gunman on Sergei's side of the car opened up. The noise was deafening and instinctively Alain and Egor ducked but quickly lifted their heads when they realised Sergei had not flinched but was studying where he could ram their car past the vehicles to their front.

Alain's head lurched backwards again as the G forces of five litres of Mercedes at full power surged forward, over a curb and through some rubbish cans, smashing beneath it a tree the size of Alain's leg which had barred a clear passage down the footpath. Moments later Omar Ben Al Khattab street signage flashed past Alain's peripheral vision and he knew the Russian Embassy compound was within spitting distance; a destination at which he was most grateful to arrive moments later.

Alain was not introduced to the Russian Ambassador and for that he was also grateful. Watching the Ambassador kick a tyre of the bullet-scarred embassy limo, Alain felt the ferocity of the man's anger permeating the courtyard. Several embassy staff stood around but all some distance from the short, powerfully-built former Red Army general.

When Sergei and Egor were taken off to another part of the compound, Alain suddenly found himself alone on Russian soil – without a visa! His rescue from no man's land appeared from the shadow of the entrance pagoda.

'*Tovarish*. You are well?' she asked, her voice as soft as velvet.

'I am well comrade,' he said smiling at her use of the now obsolete idiom and grateful for her appearance.

'Is well you are in my limousine. CIA make plan kidnap you but not calculate change of taxi.'

For the first time since the incident, Alain realised he had not analysed why the attack had occurred. Rapidly now he processed data input, the events which happened in the alley not thirty minutes ago juxtaposed against events which transpired over the previous ten days.

'You serious?' he asked.

'Attack not by local bandits,' she replied with an open hand gesture of stating the obvious. Alain smiled quickly at her use of the term bandit, an idiom used by Russians use in place of the word criminal. 'Attack on Mercedes is not attack on Russia. Attack for kidnap you, *Tovarich*.'

'Okay,' said Alain reluctantly conceding the possibility she was right. 'I suppose you're right,' he replied. 'But what makes you say the attack is on me?'

'To stop you buy phosphate and embarrass America. Attack to take you from car. Only when people cannot open car much frustration and then shooting. Attack not to kill you or bomb is used. CIA make instructions to bandits - capture you. But they fail and when angry they shoot.'

Alain sat on the steps, savouring the cooling night air. Some element of shock was beginning to manifest; this he knew from experiences in Vietnam many years before. Shootouts always produced delayed reaction in people. Only machines were immune to such weakness. Retracing the event in his mind, he turned to Valentina. 'One of the gunmen was carrying the latest US standard army issue assault rifle. I saw him aim the thing at Sergei and thought at that point, it was all over.'

Valentina nodded and he saw in her at that moment only the colonel. 'I make change limousine for reason. Hong Kong FSB follow CIA who follow you and Egor. This I know. CIA same, always same. Make surveillance for make plan. Valya think CIA make plan on Damascus for you. Ambassador he not agree. He say America not kidnap you. So I make small plan - change car, just in case.'

'I am grateful that you did. Thank you. You very clever FSB colonel.'

Valentina smiled. 'When Valentina soon tell Ambassador of American ammunition on street, Ambassador also think this.'

'This is bloody crazy! Why would the Yanks do that? Christ, I am only a businessman. I am not a bloody terrorist.'

Valentina moved closer beside him. It was an astonishingly beautiful night.

'I tell you in café you are in dangerous place in Syria. I tell you in café you are old man. Not fast reaction like Vietnam. I say America will assassinate you. You make big problem for America; is self respect problem. All peoples in world see small man beat America blockade. Is worse problem than have Iran break blockades. Iran big. You small but big problem. I tell you in café, Russia your only friend.'

Looking at her again he searched for the woman, not the colonel. An overwhelming desire engulfed him. More than anything in the world, at that moment he wanted to embrace her; to hold her; to take her away from the danger; to be with her forever.

Leaning towards her he looked into those eyes of a hungry blue eyed wolf he had once romanced in Croatia.

'*Nyet,*' she said.

He paused, motionless.

'*Nyer troiget.*'

Don't touch. The woman is psychic. She reads me like a book. Can you feel Valya, the strength of emotion surging through me now, at this moment? This is not raw sex. This is desire born of love. I want you Valya. Would you marry me now? But he did not say these things.

'You must not return to Omayed. Is guest room on embassy for you. Ambassador has tell me this. Not cost money. Tomorrow is serious talking. Breakfast at seven thirty am.'

And as always, she was gone.

Midnight! What the hell's gone wrong now? thought Porter as he rolled from his bed to the dresser where the red light on the phone console blinked and buzzed with urgency.

'This is the Ambassador,' he said using the standard response all his staff knew to be the elementary security check preferred by the ambassador. Porter waited for the caller to enter a four digit pin which would stop the red flasher on the console and identify the name of the staff member on the digital display. But the caller entered instead a six digit pin and the light kept flashing. Porter listened to the first two sentences then cut the caller short.

'When and where can we meet?' was all he said.

Fifteen minutes later, dressed in beige slacks and a light pink and grey silk shirt, Porter walked into the grand entrance of the Four Seasons hotel. Silk, as a fabric, Porter found was warm in the evenings but cool in the day temperature which consistently hovered above thirty degrees at this time of year.

The hotel was massive and as grand as any he had ever been in.

'Tammam. What a pleasant surprise to find you here,' he said extending a handshake to the Education Minister who feigned surprise.

'Mr Ambassador!' replied Tammam, loud enough for reception desk employees to hear, before mischievously asking, 'What brings you out at this hour; the pleasures of night life in Damascus?'

Taking the cue, Porter replied, 'Needed a night cap, Minister,' adding in an admonishing tone, 'And as you well know international hotels are the only place I can buy a good Jim Beam.'

With exaggerated display the Minister beckoned a waiter. 'A Jim Beam for my friend the Ambassador if you please and mint tea for me.' Turning to Porter he enquired further in impeccable English but as characteristic of many Syrians, with a slight French accent, 'Ice?' Porter nodded to the waiter and the two men retired to lounge chairs in full view of the lobby. 'We must smile, Porter. This is an agreeable perchance encounter. We have a serious problem my friend.'

Porter followed instructions as best he could but his nervousness affected his ability to maintain the composure of casual gaiety. With growing anxiety he listened as Tammam revealed a horror script no ambassador would ever wish to be woken to.

At one am Dwight read the Ambassador's code on his mobile. 'Morning Ambassador. To what do I owe this...' was all Dwight managed to say before the Ambassador cut him off. 'I can be in your office in thirty minutes, sir,' he replied. Another hiss down the line. 'Fifteen. Okay.'

Dwight sat motionless reflecting on the day's events. From the moment he'd realised the black Mercedes was a different vehicle to the grey Mercedes the Russians had used to ferry Foveaux to and from meetings in the city, he'd had the first twinges of doubt about the plan. Riding shotgun into the city from the airport it had occurred to him several times that he should pull the pin and wait for another chance. But the closer Foveaux stepped inside the Russian tent the more difficult it would be, so he elected to take the chance that the black Mercedes was not heavily armoured. Damn Russians had so many vehicles he had not bothered memorize which were cars and which were tanks in drag. In the end, he had not pulled the plug and the worst scenario imaginable had unfolded before his eyes.

Langley was not a problem. This ambassador was.

Porter was standing in his favourite corner of his office; the corner with the distorted view of the compound and garden. He had changed into a bedroom robe and slippers.

Porter's voice raised with the tempo he delivered his first response to Dwight's initial defence.

'But you, predictably I might add, went to the other end of the spectrum and started a God damned war with the Russians!

Dwight was quickly on his feet. This was not a run of the mill friendly chat with his boss. This was him in the trenches defending his career which was on the line because he had defended his country.

'Option three was and still is a good plan. Foveaux to be taken out by freedom fighters holding as hostage a businessman trying to prop up the Assad dynasty.' Dwight was now yelling at his despised Ambassador. 'If the damn Russians hadn't changed vehicles, the freedom fighters would have Foveaux, now. We would have clean hands. The Reds would be up to the anus in shit. No matter what they said, supporting an Assad sympathiser would now be causing them serious grief, both internationally and here in Syria. The plan would have exposed those assholes for precisely what they are; a totalitarian regime supporting another totalitarian regime.'

Porter rubbed his unshaven chin. The CIA chief had a point. The plan was plausible. Successful abduction of Foveaux would have really upset the Russians, more so than merely having one of their limousines shot up. The plan by the Russians to emasculate the American financial transaction blockade of Syria, would itself have been emasculated. But the plan had not gone according to script.

'Ahh, what the hell!' cursed Dwight. 'Nothing lost. The Reds and these WOGs will shut this down. There is nothing to link us. They can think what they will, nothing changes there. Mutual hatred - things are as they have been. We'll get another shot and next time it will be a shot and not a snatch.'

Porter remained passive, thinking, rubbing his chin from time to time. 'Nothing to link us to the hit?' he said, as much statement as question.

'None of our people. No way the perpetrators will put up their hands and confess. Police won't find them in this jungle. Too many firefights in Homs and Aleppo to worry about a shootout they may not even be called to by locals after all the contestants have gone home. I wouldn't mind wagering the locals would never say a word.'

Porter let his chief have a few moments of respite, then he said, 'Wrong.'

Dwight's jaw dropped.

'I was informed earlier this morning by an impeccable source deep inside the Syrian fortress that the Russians and Syrian authorities have been in closed session over this since it happened. That means they are collaborating.' Porter held up his hand, preventing Dwight from responding. 'Predictable, you might say. However, Syrian Intelligence operatives attended the scene of the shooting where they took possession of NATO ammunition shell cases. This ammunition is inconsistent with the weapons being used by defectors from the military and other freedom fighters who are using Kalashnikovs.'

The message was clear enough even for Dwight. The Syrians and the Russians would sooner or later use that evidence to support a claim that CIA was agitating behind the scene.

At four am - three pm New Zealand time - Porter placed a call to his counterpart, the Ambassador in Wellington.

Like a gnarled parody the bougainvillea twisted around the pagoda over the breakfast porch of the Embassy; petals of crimson beauty disguising protective thorns lurking beneath the foliage. Beauty and the Beast, his mother named this serpent.

Breakfast on one table consisted of various cereals, prunes, dates and apricots in abundance; boiled eggs; gherkin and tomatoes as big as a large peach and so soft the flesh melted in one's mouth. On a second table was bacon, poached egg and some foul smelling fish. Freshly squeezed fruit juices and mint drenched tea complimented coffee one could stand a spoon in.

'Astonishing tomato,' Alain commented to the Ambassador who had invited him to cross the dining room and share his table. 'I vaguely recall tomatoes like that when I was a kid but the product they sell now in the supermarkets in New Zealand has skin so thick you can literally bounce them off the wall.'

'The reason for this Mr Foveaux is because your vegetable growers have been captured by world food production giants who genetically alter the foods we once knew so they ripen in the shop and not on the vine. Another tool of America: commercial warfare,' explained the Ambassador condescendingly. 'Bulgaria is best for producing tomato and fruit which is not poisoned by these artificial hybrids. Like Syrian tomato but better. You have been to Bulgaria?'

Alain shook his head.

'Not recommended by your tour companies,' laughed the Ambassador. 'Nor is Syria but you see the astonishing world heritage on display in this fascinating land. Perhaps if the Western tourist came to enjoy these vistas, their presence would also facilitate a meeting of two cultures.'

'Come to think of it, New Zealand tour companies promote the tried and tested pilgrimage to London, running of the bulls in Spain, dinner in Venice and debauchery at the Munich beer festival. Not much advertising is given to Prague or St Petersburg; Budapest or Belgrade. This is a great pity,' replied Alain.

'May I suggest to you that this syndrome is more a matter of manipulation of tour companies by American interests. It would not do for the peoples of the West to become unafraid of the peoples of the East.' The Ambassador was grinning jovially, but Alain challenged him on this assumption.

'I agree with your concerns about American interference with the food chain but the choice of vacation destination by Kiwis is more a matter of flowing tradition and family roots. The values and customs of Londoners are very similar to those in New Zealand and this is a comfort zone for Kiwis when they travel. But Damascus, Tehran, Istanbul!' said Alain with some uncertainty. 'These are different cultures which many Kiwis prefer to leave to a later trip, which due to the cost and distance often never happens.'

A dismissive shrug suggested to Alain that the Ambassador thought his point had been sustained.

'Tell me Mr Foveaux,' invited the Ambassador as they took seating at a table. 'How do the peoples of your country now view Russia; now that she has shed the yoke of strict Marxist Leninism and has no military forces beyond her own territorial borders? Are we perceived differently to how we were perceived in Brezhnev's day; days when you and I my friend may have been looking at each other with binoculars across a hostile jungle in Vietnam?'

Alain was a little shocked. He hadn't reasoned that the man he now sat with for breakfast and who in a matter of minutes had demonstrated an empathy with human interaction beyond the capacity of many; might thirty odd years ago have had him in a gun sight. The question made Alain think. He did not answer immediately and his host did not press him. Eventually he replied.

'I suspect most New Zealanders still regard Russia as potentially the ultimate foe. Yet as I think about your question and try to formulate a response, the answers I find are embarrassing for their foundation is rooted in ignorance and prejudice.'

A slight inflexion of the head and raised eyebrow conveyed to Alain that the Ambassador was thinking, 'Is this not what I have just been speaking of?'

'You have stated a perception which is not borne out by the facts,' responded the Ambassador. 'Russia did go home after the Berlin Wall collapsed. America did not. It still has military bases in most western European countries. Germans tire of this constant presence. Japan and South Korea have been converted into gum chewing baseball players; this is not their culture. But Poland, Czechoslovakia, Hungary, East German! These countries liberated from Nazi Germany by the Red Army are now free of Russia and so too is Ukraine and the Baltic states. It took time for Russia to go home but the Soviet Arm did go home. But America however has not gone home from the countries it helped liberate in the West.'

Alain had to concede some if not all of the Ambassador's thesis. The description of baseball-playing, gum-chewing South Koreans from whence he had flown only hours before might be anecdotal but it made the point.

'In recent years Russia has intervened,' continued the Ambassador. 'In Georgia and other regions in the Caucasus, but these responses were and are in all logic, motivated to preserve Russia's immediate boundaries. Even Afghanistan, which was a big mistake, is actually on our southern border! Conversely, America has been striding the globe like a colossus, pouring napalm and bombs on Vietnam; cruise missiles on Belgrade and land armies in the Middle East with the inevitable rape, plunder, torture and abuse which accompanies any invading force. Take the case of US marines urinating on the dead bodies of Afghanistan freedom fighters!'

The ambassador paused, searching his memory for facts. 'Ah!' he exclaimed with obvious satisfaction. 'I recall now. Was it not New Zealand SAS soldiers who registered their disapproval in a respected magazine, of Americans torturing the prisoners the New Zealanders captured in Afghanistan and handed over to America for safe keeping!'

Alain did recall the disclosure in mid-2011. The ambassador smiled gently.

'These theatres of unrest can hardly be claimed to be on the immediate boundaries of America and a threat to the security of the Land of the Free. But under the guise of spreading democracy as America would have it and religion as America would prefer was the path to God, America has left a trail of murder and mayhem.'

The Ambassador poured them both a coffee. 'Black?' he asked and Alain nodded.

'A succinct and sobering synopsis Ambassador which subtly demonstrates my contention that New Zealand's perception of Russia is based on ignorance. But to put a fine point on my answer to your original question, I think most New Zealanders would still look upon Russia as the Bad Guys,' concluded Alain.

A pleasant smile caressed the diplomat's face. 'My research, if you will permit a humble former soldier to be so vain, suggests New Zealand, like Australia, has been exposed to mass American indoctrination via films and television. Western movies of the fifties and sixties portrayed a bold and courageous America. American film stars became your household heroes and heroines. Time passed and television replaced most else as your form of entertainment and through the decades, generations of ANZACs as you call yourselves, absorbed American sitcom values to the extent they destroyed the cultures of your young people.'

This was one male who, perhaps by his powerful physique but more likely by his supreme confidence in the strength of his opinions, demonstrated not the slightest complex about his height or his antecedents. To be in his company was refreshing.

'What exacerbated this indoctrination was monopolisation of world news media by America.' The ambassador opened his hands in a gesture of defeat. 'Aljazeera television appeared momentarily as an independent voice and because of the world's thirst for another point of view if not the truth, attracted a massive following not only in the Middle East but internationally. Alas,' the Ambassador paused to sip coffee. 'Alas, America took an interest in a voice they could not shut down.' Again, the open hands gesture of defeat and then he said, 'Money, Mr Foveaux. Every man has a price. Tell me Mr Foveaux. What should we do about your predicament?

The change of subject threw Alain. The humble soldier's rendition in flawless English of history playing tricks on the minds of the unwary, had unsettled him, and his own plight paled to insignificance.

'Aahh! Colonel Goloshapova. Do join us. You are late,' the ambassador said, interrupting Alain as he made to respond to the question. Alain stood as Valentina took her seat. He was unsure whether the Ambassador was displeased with the colonel being twelve minutes late.

'My apologies, Mr Ambassador,' said Valentina as she swiftly poured herself a coffee and commandeered the remaining croissant on the table.

'I think I shall start up a tour company when I am deposed from this post and target New Zealand and Australian tourists. Surely there is more art and culture in St Petersburg than there is in London. Tchaikovsky, Rachmaninoff, Shostakovich, Tolstoy, Puskin, aaaahh! These are masters of their universe, all Russian! Have you ever feasted your eyes upon the boundless architectural genius of Moscow and the Kremlin in particular? And of course, we were the first to put a man into space, Yuri Gagarin, so we do not atrophy in the past.'

'A capital idea,' agreed Valentina but with such emphasis on the word capital Alain did not miss her subliminal reference to the requirement of capital for such bold initiatives.

'There is a problem we now share Mr Foveaux,' commenced the Ambassador, changing subjects yet again but this time in earnest. 'Yesterday an attack was made on a Russian embassy vehicle containing two embassy employees and yourself. I am satisfied the attack was an attempt to take you hostage; the use of a device specifically designed to smash entry into a vehicle aimed at the window of the door where you were sitting, is instructive. I accept the reconstruction of my investigators who have been assisted by Syrian government agents that once the attackers realised they could not break you out of the embassy vehicle, at least one hundred rounds of ammunition were fired from at least three weapons into the car.'

At this point the Ambassador paused. Alain felt disinclined to say anything and Valentina remained stoic.

'The fact none of our staff nor you were injured is a testament to the manufacturers of bulletproof Mercedes,' he said with a smile. 'It is also fortuitous that Colonel Goloshapova had the foresight or intuition, I am not sure which, to assign a heavier duty vehicle to your uplift from the airport on the return of yourself and your fellow countryman, Egor Rostov.' The Ambassador acknowledged Valya with a slight dip of the head.

'My people have informed our Syrian friends that you have returned from Hong Kong where you were on a mission accompanied by a Russian embassy employee, to expedite commercial activity between Syria and New Zealand which will benefit both parties but in particular Syria during these difficult times for the country.'

Once more Alain could not be other than impressed with the succinct and objective description of his recent activity.

The Ambassador continued. 'In the circumstances I am authorised to inform you that the Syrian government at the highest level, which includes Wakid Mashreq and Mining Minister al Shaar with whom you are already familiar and Nabil Rafik who is commander of the Presidential Guard, recognises the close relationship which has evolved between the Russian embassy and yourself. They will co-operate with the Russian embassy to protect you and will provide assistance to ensure shipments of phosphate begin as soon as payment structures are confirmed to the satisfaction of Wakid Mashreq.'

'Mr Foveaux,' said Valentina in Russian and unexpectedly, but which Alain later reconciled as being a stage managed entrance, 'This is an unprecedented level of co-operation between Syria and Russia. We are allies but collaboration in matters as sensitive commercially and politically as is your mission, has not happened during my service in Syria.'

'*Nyer gavarete tak beestra parzhaloosta, po-rooski oochen troodna*,' responded Alain, requesting Valentina slow down her speech because translating her sophisticated Russian was difficult. 'I am embarrassed but I cannot follow some big words,' he said in apology to Valentina and to his host.

'Small matter,' responded Valentina, showing no sign of offence. 'Mr Foveaux,' she continued, this time in her best English. 'First you must accept that in Syria, Russia is your only ally and only Russia can help you commercially. Also you must understand America is angry; already make kidnap attempt. You must have protection.' As an after comment she added, 'Egor he is okay for you?'

Alain made to answer but she held up her hand to silence him. 'You want to telephone partners in New Zealand maybe. Big decision. If you now walk away, is okay. But walk away later, not good.'

Alain felt the full gaze of the Ambassador who made no attempt to modify or dilute the bluntness of the message being delivered by his colonel. The best Alain could respond with was, 'I understand. You need assurance that if Russia commits to help, we will not abort the mission if the going gets tough.'

The impassivity of the Russian faces spoke volumes.

'Helicopter arrive here ten thirty am,' said Valentina, breaking the silence. 'You will go to Homs and visit Barsik phosphate complex. Your friend Bassam he meeting you. Egor also he go to Homs.' Valentina turned to the Ambassador and Alain thought he saw him make a hand movement of caution at which Valentina abruptly stopped speaking.

'I must leave,' said the Ambassador pushing his chair back from the table and stretching to his full height. 'It has been a pleasure meeting you Mr Foveaux. I enjoyed our chat. We may not meet again; in fact I trust we will not for it is inappropriate for me to have, how do you say, "Hands On" with operational matters. Colonel Goloshapova has my full confidence. She is commander of Operation Kiwi. *Da sveedanya,*' he said, shook Alain's hand with a crippling vice-like grip, smiled and retired from the breakfast room.

Sitting beside her, alone, Alain again felt the surging desire to be with her, always. But how silly, his mind protested. Who am I to impose upon this woman of career? At a time like this I need a clear mind. Damn it man. Wake up.

'Love's not Time's fool.' She was looking directly into his eyes and quoting Shakespeare. Alain was speechless. Does she understand the verse? Of course she does; she quoted it for Christ's sake. How did she know what I was thinking? I am that transparent?

'Valya,' he said breathlessly.

'Come,' she said. 'We go armoury. Ambassador he not want listen when we talk of *pooshka.* You need a weapon, just in case.'

Alain was handed ear muffs as he entered the basement shooting range. He could see the facility was only for small arms short range; pistols, sub machine guns, sawn-off shot guns. Egor and Sergei were already at the mound. A short, beefy but attractive young woman handed him a semi-automatic pistol.

'*Takarev ee Makarov,*' she said grinning and pointing to two weapons lying in a tray she said, '*Stari ee Novarya.*'

'*Toot,*' said Alain pointing to what seemed to him to be a newer version which also happened to be the weapon the woman had pointed to saying, Novarya. Valentina took the older version.

Fifteen minutes later Alain had fired forty rounds; five drills of eight rounds. Twenty metres standing; twenty five metres kneeling; thirty metres prone; sprint twenty metres, pause, two second draw and shoot times eight; sprint fifteen metres back, drop to prone, shoot, roll, shoot, roll, times eight. At the completion of the drill, Alain was puffing. I need a swim, he thought. My cardiovascular is suffering without my regular fifteen hundred metres twice a week.

The score board illuminated:

'Blue. Possible 400 Score 300

'Red. Possible 400 Score 386

'Green   Possible 400 Score 300
'Yellow   Possible 400 Score 400
'Were you yellow? Alain asked Egor.
'Not me. I was blue.'
'Did you have a new or an...'

'New,' snapped Egor, unhappy at not bettering Alain's score. 'I am wanting old. Much better. My grandfather tell me. Is very good.

'I think the sprinting and the falling down and the rolling affected my aim more than the age of the pistol,' said Alain. 'By the way, who was yellow?'

Chapter Fifteen

Homs, Syria.

At ten thirty am precisely a Squirrel helicopter dropped into the Embassy compound. Alain had expected a military aircraft and was surprised to see a compact new emerald green Squirrel with the Basrik Enterprise logo making the machine as near to a private corporate as possible at the top end of the business sector. He was also intrigued to see a motif on the door of a kangaroo standing on a banner reading, Waltzing Matilda. He was even more surprised to be welcomed on board by a strong Australian accent.

'Gidday mate. Climb aboard. Watch ya step there cobber,' said the pilot, a man of medium build in his mid-thirties, whom Alain guessed could have Mediterranean antecedents.

'Gidday,' responded Alain.

'Was tempted to throw a sickie today,' said the pilot, unsettling Alain somewhat. A pilot who contemplated sickness to avoid the trip was not a comforting thought. 'Been watching the Maroons thrash the Blues in the State of Origin,' he continued. 'Great game to watch mate. Meninga is on a roll. You a league man or a rugby man? Probably rugby I reckon, bein' a Kiwi.'

Alain settled into the co-pilot seat feeling some relief that the pilot was not contemplating aborting the trip because of a small thing like a raging civil war waiting to greet them at their destination, but rather because a rugby league game had precedence.

Egor and Sergei made up the load.

'These blokes with you; they speak English?' enquired the pilot. 'By the way, name's Artie. Reckon I was named after Artie Beatson. My old dad was a St George man. Could never figure that, us bein' Queenslanders from Beaudesert.'

'Nice to meet you, Artie. One of my escorts speaks English. Yes, I am or was a rugby union man but I prefer to watch the league these days. More naked aggression. A game for real men.' Alain thought he'd add that final touch to humour the driver.

'Flight time two hours to our destination which are mines and a processing plant south east of Homs. We are going in the back way. Don't need to attract attention. Should be all quiet up there. Not like yesterday, mate. We have to drop into Palmyra; you ever been there? Bloody amazing mate. Need to collect a passenger. Old mate of yours. Samer Kaakarli.'

Damn, Alain cursed silently. Valentina had mentioned the name Samer in her briefing at breakfast but the trip to the shooting range had interrupted his thoughts and he'd omitted to seek clarification from her.

Fifteen minutes later Alain's headphones crackled. 'A Melbourne investment group is behind me and this machine, in case you are wondering.'

'Yes, I was wondering,' replied Alain.

'Since Nauru Island ran out of bird shit, getting phosphate has become a bit of a problem for us down under. Your mates in the back there; they have big reserves of the stuff in Siberia or somewhere but getting the stuff to a port for export means dealing with the Russian mafia and that presents problems for long term supply security,' explained the pilot amicably.

'What problems for long term supply?' asked Alain as he had been cogitating whether to explore the Russian option himself.

'I'm just the jockey here mate,' replied Artie self depreciatingly, 'But I hear the odd conversations which go on here in Matilda. Apparently as soon as a supply route is settled and the economics are good to go, these boyos start demanding more cash for the same supply and once that threshold is reached, six months later it starts all over again.'

Artie interrupted his dissertation to point out a settlement below. Half a dozen tents loomed out of the vast blinding desert sands below. Alain wondered how people survived in such harsh landscape.

'Is like Siberia in winter,' Egor's voice crackled through their head sets. 'Only Siberia is not desert sand. Siberia is tundra. All snow.'

I suppose the climatic hardships in Russia are similar to what is down there, thought Alain, his mind lost in a fantasy of intrepid journeys across the landscape below.

'Can't pop down to the local for a few quiet beers down there mate,' said Artie cheerfully. 'Anyway, like I was explaining. It's getting hard to get a good supply of phosphate. Algeria has the stuff but from what I hear on these headphones, the locals over there would cut your balls out for dinner. Morocco has the stuff but they got a civil war too down in the Spanish Sahara or somewhere where they mine the stuff. Egypt is a bloody mess with all their scrapping over who is going to replace Mubarak. Saudi produces poor product and is controlled by some US mafia. So my blokes decided to try here. Product is top grade. The Melbourne crew reckoned Syria was worth a punt. Mind you that was back in 2007 when they first came here.'

The helicopter began to descend and Alain picked up man-made structures looming out of the wilderness. The pilot maintained his discourse. 'It's taken our boys over five years to negotiate with these people. Crippling bloody costs, much of it poured into the pockets of ministers and generals who keep swapping chairs. In the meantime a bloody civil war erupts. I tell you Alain, I'm lucky I'm still being paid. The Melbourne boys are so deep in capital invested here they can't pull out. Real fucking mess mate. But for me I reckon this is still safer than flying tourists into Papua New Guinea. At least these blokes only shoot you when they get you. Those black fellas in Papua eat you.' He chuckled. 'Welcome to Palmyra. A jewel in a desert. Going in now.'

From his view inside the helicopter, Alain was overawed by the spectacle of Palmyra's classic Roman ruins. Dating from around the second century AD, Palmyra once stood as an Ozymandias of the desert; astride a crucial oasis on the Silk Road of trade that ran between the Mediterranean Sea and Persia and then interminably across wilderness and mountains to the land of Chin.

Artie alighted from their flying taxi, ducking his head as he ran to meet a group of men waiting in nearby black Mercedes ML's.

'Is not correct,' said Egor as he leaned forward from his seat in the rear of the helicopter.

'What?' asked Alain. 'What is not correct?'

'Pilot. Is not correct he say Russian mafia control phosphate extraction in Russia. Government make big companies with private sector. Maybe oligarchs but not mafia.'

Alain smiled to himself at the sensitivity of the Russian, a characteristic of most Russians he had discerned. 'I don't think he meant mafia as with guns, Egor. I think he was referring to the corporate control. No different to the dairy product and meat export industry or log export industry in New Zealand. Any attempt by entrepreneurs to break the monopolies these big companies enjoy, is stamped on. Just like Kiwifert, our New Zealand fertiliser company. The reason we are now sitting in the middle of a civil war trying to source phosphate is because some big companies back home behave like a mafia. The pilot is using a euphemism. He doesn't mean mafia like in Al Capone or Sicilian brothel owners.'

Egor was not placated.

One of the men detached from the huddle near the MLs and, limping heavily, followed Artie to the helicopter. As the two men approached the aircraft, momentarily Alain thought he recognised the stranger. No, couldn't be, he reasoned. Seventeen or eighteen years! Couldn't be! But as the stranger climbed aboard and their eyes meet, the recognition in both men was instantaneous.

'Samer!'

'Alain! Is good to see,' said a smiling overweight Samer. 'I am wait for this moment many days. Can it be the same man?'

'What? How is this? Why are you here?' burbled Alain.

'We speak soon. In private.'

Alain's mind was reeling. How did Samer, his contact from Bosnia seventeen years ago, fit into this deal? Yes, Samer was a middle man for weapons transfer. Perhaps he was the middle man for cash transfer? Beating the blockades was his specialty. He also got me from Bosnia to Syria even if I was seasick for ten days.

Homs loomed on the horizon then suddenly they were above a metropolis streaming beneath like a colourful carpet on a dull floor. Black smoke curled into the atmosphere on the northern fringe of the city and was soon lost to sight as the pilot dropped from the sky into a wire fenced compound the size of several football pitches. Heavy earthmoving machinery littered the compound, and had been immobile for some time it seemed to Alain. Near a large ironclad shed, rusting from the sulphur in the phosphate, Artie cut the engines and their chariot lay silent but let in a sound unmistakable to a Vietnam veteran: howitzers. Distant but all the same; howitzers.

As the group climbed out of the helicopter, two black Mercedes MLs drove into view, stopping some distance off before proceeding slowly; their darkened glass windows denying identification of the occupants and portraying a sinister silhouette.

Samer appeared at Alain's side. 'It is good to see you my friend. Is bad we not have time for talking. Take care with these men. Be careful.'

Yasin emerged from one of the MLs accompanied by Basam. Several young men with Kalashnikov armaments fanned out; a precaution, thought Alain, against freedom fighters or terrorists, take your pick.

'Allo Mr Alain, is good to be seeing you again,' responded Bassam, but Yasin remained passive and aloof.

'Ah! It is you Samer! Is surprise. You are represent Australia, is true?' Bassam spoke to Samer in reasonably good English.

Samer nodded without extending a handshake. 'My principals asked me to be here for contract signing and inspection tour. Make sure all is okay. My job.'

A feeling deep in Alain's gut started a constant throb. I don't think these boys are on the same page, he thought. Turning to the helicopter pilot with his back to the others, in a subdued tone he asked, 'What's the story here mate? Who is your boss? Where are these Aussie investors?'

Artie grinned unreassuringly. 'Like I said mate, I am lucky to still be paid. I haven't seen the Melbourne team for some weeks; they went home when the wheels started to fall off Assad's trolley. But they needed someone to keep an eye on things and that turned out to be me. I have transport anywhere in the country or out of the country if it comes to that, at my disposal. Like I said, what I don't hear in Matilda leaves little to the imagination. But Samer here is the numero uno. He is the chief negotiator for the blokes back home watchin' the footie, live.

Alain became aware of Bassam at his elbow. 'Come Mr Foveaux, we show you crushing plant. Also inside is laboratory. People not work today. Is Friday.'

Friday is the Islamic equivalent of Sunday, this Alain knew. But he could also hear the howitzers which he reasoned might also be a reason why the work benches at Basrik phosphate plant were empty.

'Raw phosphate is mined all around this complex,' explained Bassam, casting a gesture of wide embrace as he commenced a tour of the plant without any sign that things might not be normal. 'These machinery is some only. Many more machine at quarry. See over other side of building? That is crusher. All crusher plant and caterpillar machines is from Australia money. Syria government make joint venture. Foreign investor is Australia, must make machine and plant. Syria government make land and mining consents. Together is joint venture.'

Pretty standard, thought Alain as he followed Bassam into the gloom of what transpired to be a massive area under roof, quite misleading from outside appearance. Fifteen minutes later the group assembled in a cafeteria adjacent to the laboratory, staffed by a young man in military fatigues.

'So,' said Alain making his first contribution to the discussion for several minutes. 'This is where we get our phosphate.' It was a statement, not a question.

'Is quiet now but phosphate here is best in world. RPR specifications and sulphur as you demand,' answered Bassam and waved vigorously at the cafeteria assistant.

Alain noticed Samer had not spoken during the tour. Yasin too had remained silent but that was his style as Alain recalled their previous encounter in the Minister's office.

Some liquid, possibly coffee, was produced by the orderly. Egor and Sergei, whom Alain knew were both armed, took a coffee each but stood at opposite ends of the cafeteria. Can't be taken out together, Alain mused absently minded as he took a coffee and drifted to where Samer was sitting, alone. 'You represent Melbourne?' asked Alain pleasantly.

'Yes my friend. But they have problem with own government. Australia is much friend of US. US and EU have sanctions against Syria. Australia government make pressure on Melbourne to stop export phosphate,' explained Samer.

'Yes, but US and EU sanctions do not apply to Australia or New Zealand. Only UN sanctions and as I read the situation, Brazil and India as members of the Security Council, don't support sanctions; they are apprehensive any UN sanctions will be followed by UN remits for NATO to intervene militarily; like Libya. So as long as Russia and China and India and Brazil stand up to the American pressure?' replied Alain shrugging. 'Your Melbourne team should be able to export.'

'Not simple for Melbourne,' replied Samer. 'How you say, de facto pressure applied. Taxation department. Money laundry enquiries, Internal Securities police. This is government level pressure. Private sector level banks make different rules to comply with America. Banks is not like government. Government must make hidden pressure, how you say, latent, but banks not restricted like government. All make big problems for Melbourne.'

It had occurred to Alain that breaking the blockade, even though the Hong Kong matrix would disguise the final destination of money paid by Kiwifert for its Syrian phosphate, was not a simple operation. He needed to speak again with Bryce. Sooner rather than later.

Yasin and Bassam were in deep conversation, perusing documents Yasin had produced. Contracts, thought Alain. Then he remembered Samer's warning. Turning back to his old friend he asked, 'Why you warn me be careful?'

Checking that Bassam and Yasin were out of hearing Samer said, 'Yasin is represent elite peoples in Syria who steal money from government. Always generals and politician steal money but now is big rush steal much money. Maybe end come soon for old elite. Samer think Assad soon fall. Not all way down but fall some and Syria is big chaos. Perhaps three years, perhaps seven years. Yasin is now agent of big thieves. He is dangerous man.'

'And your job, Samer?' asked Alain.

Samer smiled softly. 'My job is protect Australia investment. My job is to get full monies from Kiwifert into Australia bank. Melbourne is good to Samer. Pay good money in good times. Now bad times. Samer make repay. My job is get most money for Melbourne. Yasin he want most money for elite. Hong Kong ...'

Samer stopped speaking as Bassam and Yasin, folding the documents, walked over to Alain and Samer. 'You are okay you see true phosphate plant? Is good phosphate? Can make many shipments,' said Bassam.

I've got to obfuscate here a bit, Alain reasoned. Things are not quite right. Best to query the mining process rather than the money transfer. Don't want to make them nervous out here in no-man's land.

'I was just asking Samer about the capacity of the mine to produce the amount we require. You must excuse me Bassam, but the place looks pretty quiet at the moment. If we start locking in hundreds of thousands of dollars in LC's; sure we can retrieve the money if the product doesn't arrive but we can lose six months; we lose use of our money and we end up with clients back in New Zealand leaving us because we don't have product!'

Masterful! Alain congratulated himself. Would fool me if I didn't know my real concern is now about where the money goes and what is the real game.

Chapter Sixteen

New Zealand.
Minister Foreign Affairs suite. Wellington.

Murray McIntyre had been a Member of Parliament for twenty one years. He had seen out smarter, more energetic and more principled colleagues. He recognised early in his career that the best way to longevity as an MP was to be pleasant to all, never hold an opinion and always lick arse; particularly the arse of the boss.

From his first term Murray set a *modus operandi*, a course of conduct which he was confident would propel him near to the top one day. Like flotsam in a tank of putrid water. Sooner or later it floats to the top. That's what Murray's mother told him once on the farm up north when he was a kid. He'd never forgotten that early lesson in life although he realised some time ago that he had forgotten all he had been taught at school in chemistry.

Murray was well aware that parliament was like a tank of putrid water, and as his first wife reminded him until the day she departed with half his future parliamentary pension earnings, he was rubbish. By extension of elementary logic, Murray calculated he would one day get to the top; if he just floated around long enough.

The pension problem however, was more to do with the first wife discovering the identity of a mistress when he texted in error the wrong message to the wrong woman, and nothing to do with him being flotsam or stupid.

After eighteen years Murray had made it as far up the ladder as he was ever going to climb. Number five in Cabinet and Minister of Foreign Affairs was nothing to be sneezed at, after all. The job had perks! International travel and introductions to rich, famous and infamous was great for the ego. Nor were the duties intellectually challenging. If one looked back over the Foreign Ministers the country had recently produced, two he knew were alcoholics and one had a preference for young boys, and none, in Murray's view, were ever likely to have topped the class. All of which made Murray feel very comfortable as his last term in office drifted quietly to a peaceful conclusion and a listing in the following year's Honours. "Sir Murray" had a nice ring to it.

Television New Zealand ground out another uninspiring rendition of CNN international propaganda and local fodder about how good everyone was feeling about the national rugby team.

Murray was a great believer that the game of rugby was a foundation stone of the nation. The fact most women could name most of the All Blacks seemed proof to Murray that rugby was the cement which bound together the nation of New Zealand. The fact that twenty five percent of Auckland, the largest city by population in the country was now Chinese or Korean or some other Asian offspring, and that probably ninety nine percent of these new immigrants didn't give a fig about rugby, seemed to have evaded the Foreign Minister's usually sharp antennae. In any event the unpleasant adjustments the nation was going to inherit whether they liked it or not, heralded as they were by the changing demographics, wouldn't be his problem. He was to retire in eighteen months.

Moving his corpulent frame from the settee in front of the television to his office desk chair, reluctantly he scanned the list of meetings for the evening session. Christ! He had forgotten. The US Ambassador was due at seven thirty pm.

Wayne knocked and entered. 'Evening Chief,' he said with his usual unctuousness and slipped into the chair reserved for private secretaries. 'The US Ambassador will be here in five minutes. Very tight lipped out the subject matter. You happy for me to sit in and bolt for backup if he drops a curly one?'

'Good idea,' said the Minister, relaxing now his Chief of Staff was available to handle any crisis.

Urbane. That is how the US Ambassador presents, thought Murray, as he struggled to maintain attention. The adrenalin rush precipitated by the shock of realising that he had forgotten the Ambassador was calling had worn off, and the effects of a bottle of Riesling with dinner began to reappear.

Battling the fog, Murray still maintained enough pride to be offended when the American insisted that New Zealand "owed America" (for what he didn't specify) and should therefore put a stop to any maverick businessmen who might dare to break the self imposed American blockade on Syria.

In fact, as he recalled the events of Gaddafi's demise, Murray had held the view that the Libyan President for Life was not much better than Mugabe, another President for Life somewhere else in Africa if his memory served him, which often it did not. As he recalled the way NATO forces had abused a UN mandate to equalise the skies and instead, starting attacking Gaddafi and his mates, in the end he had been in Gaddafi's corner. Not something he would disclose in Cabinet of course, but rooting for the underdog seemed to be a characteristic which pervaded the Kiwi psyche. And now he had an American Ambassador in his office telling him, a senior Minister of the Crown, how to run his own country.

In fact, as Murray took stock of the situation, the American ought to shut the fuck up and get out of his office!

'While the Minister understands the predicament this chap Foveaux might be putting New Zealand in, as regards its relationship with the US,' said Wayne the Chief of Staff for Minister Foreign Affairs, 'the fact is the government does not have the legal prerogative to stop commercial transactions between this country and Syria. US and EU resolutions have no force of law in New Zealand. UN resolutions are a different matter, particularly where New Zealand has voted for a remit which imposes sanctions, but that is not the case here.'

Couldn't have said it better myself, thought the Minister.

'I give you an assurance Don,' said Barry resorting to the lowest trick in a scoundrel's bag by calling the other chap by his first name, 'I will take this matter up in Cabinet, but before that I will also discuss the greater implications,' he said emphasising the last phrase which the Ambassador himself had used, if Murray was not mistaken, as an implied threat that something terrible would befall the nation of great rugby teams. 'I will also discuss the greater implications with the PM at our private breakfast session.'

At eight am the following morning at breakfast with the Prime Minister, when Murray explained the issues raised by the American Ambassador during his visit the previous evening, Murray was very grateful he hadn't told the ambassador to "shut the fuck up" half way through his diatribe.

'I am very pleased you brought this to my attention before Cabinet,' said the Prime Minister. 'Wayne was correct. This is not an easy fix for us as far as our American friends are concerned. I think it best not to put the matter on the Cabinet agenda. There is no guarantee we would have majority support even in our own team. And if Cabinet stick with convention, which is actually the course we would have to adopt even if there was a majority in favour of blocking the arrival of a ship from Syria, once the matter is in Cabinet minutes, it would be even more difficult to implement a pragmatic solution.'

Murray maintained a watchful eye on his bacon and eggs as the Prime Minister tapped the side of his nose with an index finger.

'Meet me at one thirty pm before Question time. I'll bring in Doug and Jim. Let's discuss options to have their departments take an interest in the commercial activities of Kiwifert. No one but no one enjoys the IRD or Securities Commissions sniffing round the back yard.'

'Quite right, Prime Minister. We need to get onto this promptly. The Ambassador said he had been called by their chap in Syria and shortly afterwards Langley called him,' commented Murray, conforming to his MO.

'I am not surprised,' the Prime Minister responded. 'A shipload of phosphate arriving here from Syria while the Americans are trying to garner support in the UN would make them look very silly. It would also undermine all the progress that has gone into restoring relations between us. This simply cannot be allowed to happen.'

'Wheels within wheels, eh Prime Minister?' Murray laughed at his own parody but the Prime Minister was already walking out of the dining room.

Auckland

Bryce entered Doug's office like a tornado, tossed his jacket onto the sofa then started pacing the Persian carpet.

'Your news good news or bad?' he asked Doug.

'Bad.'

'Then you go first. Mine's diabolical.'

The door opened slowly, Lisa's ostrich egg buttocks pushing it open as she backed into the room bringing two coffees. 'Black, one sugar. Twice,' she said, depositing the mugs then retreating.

Doug stirred his coffee. 'I just had a call from someone. Well, you should know so you can judge its reliability. My son. He is office manager for the Hamilton IRD desk. His job is to allocate staff. Human Resources. He's not one of the bastards who trawl through your affairs. Don't mention it for Christ sake. It's his job's worth. Anyway, this morning he received a directive from Wellington to put together a team of, listen for it: ten! Ten fucking IRD snoops. Can you imagine assigning ten investigators?'

'To do what?' asked Bryce curiously.

'Oh. To investigate Kiwifert! Us!'

Visibly shocked, Bryce grabbed the back of a chair. 'You're kidding me!'

Doug shook his head. 'No I am not. Darren said he often gets a memo from Wellington to put together a posse. Hamilton is the largest IRD office in the country. When a major investigation is launched, he supplies the troops. He said this is a full team.'

Bryce thought for a moment. 'How did he know I am the target? Did they mention my name?'

'It's not your name but the company name. The IRD have a name for all these investigations. In this case it's Kiwifert. He thought nothing of it until he remembered that I'd told him a couple of days ago I have taken a parcel of shares in Kiwifert.'

Doug let the news sink in then said, 'This has got to have come from Wellington. It's too much of a coincidence that we are putting together a sanction busting operation which we know will really piss off the Americans and all of a sudden, ten investigators are assigned to a small company that has never had a tax blemish. I assume I am correct on this last point.'

Bryce nodded. 'You are. Never been late with a GST return. Books always made up on time by a reputable accountancy firm. I'd better warn them.'

'Hold on a minute, mate. Don't do that for Christ's sake. If you alert the accountant he will be compromised. Sooner or later the IRD will ask him if he knew what was coming. If he says yes the backtrack will stop with my son and he will be out of a job and blacklisted.'

'Sorry,' apologised Bryce. 'Wasn't thinking.'

'It's okay. Darren said he expects to be asked some questions at some stage, particularly if someone on the investigation team makes a connection between his name and my name on the share registry. But he thought that through before he called me. He says it's easy enough for him to deny knowledge, particularly as the transfer of shares is recent. He'll just say something like, "Dad's a big boy. He doesn't call me on everything he does". Darren will be fine as long as our end does not expose that it has been alerted.'

Sitting now, Bruce asked the older man for advice. 'What should I do now?' He was worried.

'Been thinking about that too before you got here,' said Doug. 'When the investigation unit arrives, be polite and act surprised. Then and only then call the accountant and tell him to co-operate, not that he has a bloody choice. You say there is nothing out of order. Let these people waste their time. At least they are not like the police. They are not going to fabricate a case and they won't suddenly find cannabis in a file cabinet.'

Downing the last of his coffee Doug then postulated. 'This can only have come to pass because the Americans have got to the Prime Minister. Only he could put pressure on the IRD like this. He would have had to pull in the Minister of Inland Revenue and probably that drunk in Foreign Affairs. But it is illegal for a Member of Parliament, and in particular a Minister, to interfere in the operational affairs of a government department. This being the case and it can be the only explanation, the Prime Minister has actually walked onto thin ice.'

Reaching this logical deduction brightened Doug's day. Working his way through the issue carefully and methodically was his forte. Like the tortoise. Slow but sure.

'Actually,' he said with renewed enthusiasm. 'We've got the bastards by the balls. When the shit hits the fan about Kiwifert busting the blockade, your, or should I say our, company, will be in the limelight. It's not a quantum leap for the news media to find out that we have suddenly been hit by the IRD in the most unusual of circumstances.'

Smiling now he said, 'This tsunami could surge back and drown the lot of them! What's your news?

It took a few minutes for Bryce to make the transition from hunted to hunter. 'Whew. I hope you're right on that, Doug. You sure your reasoning is sound, no offence but?'

'If there is one thing I have learned during my years as a political lobbyist, it is how the system down there works and about the rules of engagement,' he replied. 'Trust me. Our Prime Minister just bent over once too often when Uncle Sam walked in his door. This is another Dot Com fiasco'

Hunching his shoulders Bryce sat on the sofa arm, cogitated then said, 'Alain called.'

Doug waited for the younger man to continue. 'Things got a bit messy over there,' he said, 'But I'll start at the beginning,' and proceeded to relate Alain's account setting up the companies in Hong Kong.

'Interesting,' said Doug when Bryce had finished his sermon. 'We had a rough idea of what was going down in Hong Kong. Seems a little cumbersome but I guess if it was too simple too many would be into it. Good to hear though that we have the network in place.'

Bryce then told Doug what happened when Alain returned to Damascus, starting with the shooting and culminating with the amicable chat with the Russian Ambassador.

'Makes the pending attack on us by the IRD pale in significance,' responded Doug who found the account of the shooting an incredibly exciting deviation from the humdrum of daily life.

Bryce then went on to apprise Doug of the Melbourne syndicate involvement which drew a more sober response.

'Warning signs here my friend, said Doug. 'If those bloody Aussies can't match the pace over there, I reckon that is a definite warning sign that our extraction operation, which is minor in comparison to a full blown operation, is not going to be a cake walk.'

A grimace preceded Bryce's next revelation. 'How perceptive you are,' he said with irony. 'Seems the fellow we are actually now doing business with is a bloke by the name of Yasin.'

'Shouldn't that make it easier; streamline the process? As long as Kiwifert gets its true measure of phosphate; money for value, do we really need to be involved in how they share the loot?' said Doug.

'With a big sigh Bryce recounted what Alain had tried to explain on the phone.

'It seems for most if not all products exported from Syria where the State has some ownership, be it oil, cement, or as in our case, phosphate, senior ministers with responsibility for the sector concerned and selected senior military and secret intelligence agency bosses, all take a percentage.'

'That seems to be par for the course in many countries,' said Doug. 'Of course the majority of New Zealanders think this sort of thing doesn't happen in New Zealand but in one way or another, it does. Allocation of local government construction contracts is a good place to start if you're interested. So, nothing scary yet from this Yasin chap.'

Bryce stood and started to pace the carpet again.

'This is different to some outfit getting a garbage contract for a backhander. Alain tells me, as an example, that when we deliver let's say one million dollars to the account of Achilles...'

'Who?' interrupted Doug. 'Oh, yes, the company; our company in Hong Kong.'

'Aha,' continued Bryce. 'The Kiwifert Letter of Credit with the German bank releases the million bucks when the phosphate enters New Zealand territorial water. Oh! I forgot to mention. That was a compromise by Alain to get the US two hundred dollars per ton CIF agreement. Payment when ship enters our waters in case there is a union strike or commercial sabotage and unloading is delayed. So, when the million bucks are transferred to Achilles, at that point Yasin takes control.'

Doug nodded. 'Also, we only release the money when we have an invoice from Achilles, correct?' queried Doug.

'Correct. And we sure as hell are going to need that invoice with IRD now climbing all over us,' said Bryce.

Doug shrugged. 'Continue please.'

'In a helicopter Alain met up with some bloke he had known in Bosnia years ago. This old mate is apparently employed as a minder for an Aussie group in Melbourne who have put a shitload of money into Basrik. You following me?'

'I'm following you.'

'Well, this friend of Alain's, Samer is his name; he reckons Assad or what's left of his enforcement team, is either too weak to stop this Corrupt Elite from rifling the till at this time, or he is turning a blind eye as part of an understanding he has with this Corrupt Elite, that they support him quid pro quo.'

'And?' prompted Doug.

'Well, whereas Assad may be turning a blind eye, these Melbourne blokes aren't and their emissary, or maybe he is a mercenary if Alain's description is anything to go by, is insisting that the Kiwifert money for phosphate goes to Melbourne. But Yasin is saying the first cut should go to his mentors, the Corrupt Elite.'

Doug grinned. 'This really is a viper's nest. Bloody interesting I have to say but we are close enough to those bloody vipers to get bitten. We need to be very careful.'

Bryce's frown wiped the grin from Doug's face. 'So Yasin starts his allocation. Some cash is allocated to the Syrian phosphate company, Basrik and then the rest goes to the Corrupt Elite.'

'As I already said, how Yasin allocates the money among the Corrupt Elite and then Basrik and the Melbourne syndicate if they are different or the same - this is not our problem, is it?'

A quick upward flicker of eyebrows by Bryce signalled there actually were some problems.

'Alain says the Corrupt Elite are decidedly nervous. They don't have the confidence they once had that Assad is going to ride this one out and are concerned about their future ability to clip the ticket and transfer other ill-gotten gains. There is a sense of urgency and Yasin signalled to Alain that he would be using Achilles to launder millions of dollars from other sources on behalf of the Syria Corrupt Elite.'

This time Doug demurred before responding. 'You mean Yasin wants to use our network to launder other money, money that has nothing to do with phosphate?'

'Seems that's the plan. Alain said Yasin was not forthcoming about detail when pressed and in fact got quite unpleasant when Alain pressed the point.'

'I can imagine,' said Doug. 'As a senior shareholder in Ajax, the name of our Belize company if I recall, and the ultimate authority in all this, my concern is that if we let Yasin have his way, Ajax will come under a different level of pressure. Being home base for a company ignoring American sanctions which don't apply to New Zealand is quite a different thing to laundering money from some heavy dude out of Iran!'

A mobile phone buzzed.

'That you or me?' asked Doug.

Bryce pulled his mobile out of his jacket pocket. 'Hello, Bryce speaking,' he answered. 'Are you sure? When? Did they say why? Have we done something wrong? Unbelievable! What should I do? Yes. Yes. Co-operate all the way. I agree. Let me know if they want to speak with me. Let me know if it gets worse. Thanks Stu.'

'That was your accountant, no doubt?' said Doug when Bruce terminated the call. 'Those buggers don't waste any time. Are they there already?'

'No, Stewart just received a call from the IRD advising him they were sending in a team to conduct a spot audit. Routine, they said.'

'Routine my arse. You did well there my friend. Just play the game.'

Bryce was pacing again, faster and with more energy. After a few moments he said, 'That really makes me angry. I could tell by Stewart's voice he was petrified. Stu is nice guy. Honest. Wouldn't cook the books if I paid him triple rates. These people have terrified him and they haven't even arrived yet.'

Moving across the office Doug placed a restraining hand on Bryce's arm. 'Take it easy. This isn't a personal thing. We're just small pawns in a big boy's game.'

Bryce stopped pacing but turned to Doug with fury in his face. 'Wrong! This is personal. Fuck them! Who do these bastards think they are? Half way around the world they paralyse the planet with their bully boy bullshit about who has the biggest bombs, and when they might drop one on some poor bastard who doesn't want to embrace America's Happy Clapper version of Christianity or who doesn't want an American military base in their backyard.'

Bryce was getting into full swing. Doug let him go. It was important for him let out the frustrations and anger.

'Until that call from Stu, I was thinking that we should pull the plug. Taking the Iraq option seems such a sensible thing to do; so easy! But at the end of the day, do we trust the Yanks?'

Doug hesitated. He'd discerned already that Alain had gone totally feral on America and now Bryce was demonstrating all the signs of taking the same path. 'I've been thinking about this and nothing else for some days now,' he conceded.

'Well?' asked Bryce.

Doug grinned warily. 'Having given the situation due consideration and putting myself in your shoes, I am bound to say Bryce that I think Alain's recommendation to take the Syrian deal is the best way forward. At least we will get a decent load of phosphate and in six months' time it will be an entirely new game.

Bryce smiled. 'Recommendation my arse!' he retorted. 'He has bloody well committed us to virtual open war with the Americans and our own government.'

'He has committed Kiwifert to receiving at least six months' supply of phosphate at a bloody good rate and our company has not broken any laws which apply to our country,' replied Doug nonchalantly.

Bryce stopped his pacing. 'If I don't get a new line of phosphate, Kiwifert is fucked. Truth be known, that's what "the system" wants. The majors will be involved in this too. Bet your boots. They would have been pulling someone's chain trying to get us knocked out of Syria for their own commercial gain. Who else to enlist to help but the Yanks who have their precious reputation as international policeman to protect?'

'Bryce!' said Doug definitively. 'Your original decision was courageous. Remember: The Gods like bravery and defiance. The Gods loath uncertainty and cowardice.'

Chapter Seventeen
Damascus, Syria.

Originally inhabited as early as 8,000 BC, this astonishing metropolitan labyrinth of winding paths and alleys, where walls collide above to block out sun and starlight, conceals treasures of architecture, gold, and humanity. Unpleasant odours are disguised by the potency of spice and herb aromas wafting on gentle air streams. Along the ancient network of internal pathways, veiled women chat noisily, confident in their security but competing for space with donkeys carrying goods as has been happening from time immemorial.

After spending the entire morning lost within the walls of the Old City, Alain was in need of refreshment. Tapping Alain's arm, Egor beckoned that he should follow and soon both were admitted to an oasis within this man-made desert. Egor identified the café entrance by chance, noticing two women suddenly vanish. Unobtrusively the women had slipped through a bland door behind which Egor caught the briefest glimpse of palms and daylight.

Once through the door the two men were enchanted by the decor; French colonial Alain estimated, decorating the two level quadrant courtyard. The transition from the metre-wide ancient footway where mules fought against man for walking space as they carried their loads deep into the bowels of one of the oldest cities in the Middle East, to a modern open sky café, was breathtaking.

What appeared to have been the home of a Sultan, or a very wealthy denizen of Old Damascus, had been converted into some thirty metres square and two levels. Palm trees filtered the blue sky directly above and a water fountain played softly.

The two female shapes which had lured them to this hidden garden, now chatted with animation in this sanctuary; the preserve of girls uninhibited. Their hijab headwear draped over a spare chair, both ravenously embraced a water bowl hookah pipe, paying scant attention to the many young well dressed and handsome Arab men who made up the majority of the clientele.

The atmosphere inside the quadrant was intoxicating. Alain savoured every moment of the unique experience. It was as if he was in a paradise, momentarily transported back in time. But his odyssey was disrupted when he became aware that one of the young women they had followed was now looking intently at them. Her unafraid stare was in stark contrast to the servility of most indigenous women when in the presence of European men.

'Mint tea I think, and I'll try a kebab,' said Alain, a little flustered by the girl. 'Do what the Romans do when in Rome.'

But Egor's constantly alert bodyguard's focus was not on the food. 'Man behind my right shoulder; thin man, look like Italian but Arabic. I see him when we walked by Saladin statue near mosque. This is not accident he is here. Best look in mirror other side of room. He cannot see you look at him.'

'Great,' replied Alain after watching their shadow for several minutes. The face was unfamiliar but the person Egor described was definitely though surreptitiously observing them. 'Man finds the most astonishing watering trough and is driven out by the local thug before repast.'

But Egor demonstrated no interest to leave as he became aware of the intermittent stare he was now receiving from the young Arab woman. 'Maybe that goon is her chaperon?' suggested Alain as his eye contact flicked from the fellow behind Egor to the girl who sat opposite.

Securing no response, Alain sought to reconnect to Egor by turning the conversation to his predicament beyond the walls of the café. 'Egor, I am concerned that the Ambassador will tire of my lodging at the embassy. I should move back to the Omayed.'

'*Nyet*,' said Egor, turning his attention back to Alain and responding in Russian as was the arrangement between the two men; an initiative to compel Alain to improve his Russian. 'The Ambassador instructs the colonel that you are very important person. For Russia it is important that you succeed in your mission.'

'With at least one shipment? Is that not what I overheard him tell Valentina the other day?'

Egor's reluctance to respond confirmed for Alain that his Russian was improving and that his hearing was fine. Alain was also rapidly coming to the conclusion that their entry into the café where he now sat, was not by a chance following of a couple of shrouded female shapes. His minder's attention was clearly no longer on the discussion Alain was trying to generate.

'Mind telling me what the fuck is going down here?' Alain asked finally, his irritation manifest.

'Woman at table. She make arrange to meet me today. She is daughter of wealthy businessman.'

Alain was stunned. 'How the fuck did you met her? When? Where?'

Egor shook his head. 'Is Embassy work. Colonel Goloshapova she make instruction for me to meet this girl who has message for colonel.'

'Are you telling me you were intending to come into this café all along?'

Egor shook his head. 'I am told to look for two women who would be watching for us when we passed by Saladin statue. I am told watch for two women when enter café. Is why I am constantly pulling you on street; this way, that way. In café, girl is to pass message, but man following girl is problem.'

'Thanks very bloody much mate,' said Alain with rancour. 'Look, don't get me wrong. I don't care what you bloody Russians are up to, but I would prefer to be told in advance if I have a part to play in some clandestine affair. That chap watching us has a distinctly unpleasant odour about him and I don't want to be caught in another shootout.'

'I make apology but I am Russian officer and must obey my orders. Russia help you with phosphate and is only fair you help Russia with small problem.'

The way that girl is looking at you, thought Egor, she has more on her mind than passing state secrets.

In fact the more Alain was able to absorb of her without too much of a display, the more she appeared to be almost a replica of the stunningly attractive woman he had encountered on his first visit to the Minister's office some days previously. Many

American women, it seemed to Alain, fitted into the blonde hair, blue eyes, wide mouth, Barbie Doll stereotype. But in Damascus, Angelina Jolie look-alikes seemed to emerge as a characteristic among women sufficiently liberated from religious taboo by social status, who dared to frequent coffee bazaars unaccompanied.

Alain shook his head disconsolately. 'Come. Let's eat then get back to the embassy before that spy over there shoots us both. I have new instructions from New Zealand. I need you to listen to my call to Yasin.'

Reluctantly Egor nodded his approval. The girl was not going to be able to make contact with him with her tail sitting across the café. Something had not gone to plan but Egor was not in a position to know what or how to remedy whatever was the problem.

'You want Russia to listen to your conversation with this Yasin?' asked Valentina cautiously.

Alain smiled at the colonel. I'm sure you listen to all my calls to New Zealand. But better I use the secure line of Russia than use the insecure line of Syria and have the CIA listen.'

Valentina also smiled. 'Okay. Why is you want tell Yasin, Kiwifert will make deal.'

Alain looked at the woman he loved in earnest. 'Valentina. The reason I embrace Russia in this, shall I say game, is because Russia has helped Kiwifert secure phosphate supply which is critical to its economic survival. Without a new supply Kiwifert has no future. Many twists and turns happen. The kidnap attempt here in Damascus was one extreme. In New Zealand the young owner of Kiwifert is now being hounded. Persecuted! The Prime Minister of the country has been seduced by America and puts their agenda ahead of the survival of Kiwifert. This is understandable, but America must learn that a young man in New Zealand, which is not bound by American or EU law and sanctions, puts his company first. You understand?'

She nodded.

'It is also obvious to Kiwifert that its competitors have played a part in our problems,' he continued. 'For these reasons, the young owner has decided to fight. And both I and another minor shareholder in Kiwifert support him in his courageous stand.'

'Alain, how can two containers, fifty tons of phosphate, save Kiwifert? Soon war is here and no phosphate will flow. This big trouble for small gain, no?' she said.

Alain let a little time elapse then he said, 'What does Russia think? What do you think?'

Leaning back now Valentina paused then said, 'I am colonel FSB. I wait for shipment to New Zealand. This is good for Russia and Syria. America domination damaged. This very good.'

'And what does Valentina the woman think?'

'I think boy in New Zealand is brave but stupid. Long life to come.'

Egor interrupted the moment when he brought a phone to their table. 'Is call from Yasin.'

Alain wasted no time.

'Yasin. Alain speaking. New Zealand tells me to increase the first shipment from twenty five tons to twenty eight thousand tons. This is urgent. This is one full shipload not two containers as we first ordered. This must be the deal. New price US one hundred and eight dollars CIF New Zealand territorial waters when LC payment of US five million on German bank will be released. Not negotiable. Confirm within thirty minutes or it is *Do sveedarnya.*'

Alain terminated the call.

Valentina put her hand on his thigh. Embarrassed by this show of personal intimacy, Egor dropped his eye contact, collected the phone and left the room.

'Very clever boy is in New Zealand,' said Valentina. 'One shipload is good now supply for six months? Time for make new supply other country. Ambassador already suggest me tell you come Russia for good supply. Russian government make sure no mafia problem. I go now.'

'Ah!' Alan raised his hand. 'I have a question for you Valya. Today I found my sightseeing excursion in the Old City interrupted. Initially I thought amidst a young lovers quarrel but as events unfolded and Egor was left with no choice but to make some explanation to me, it seems I was caught in the middle of some espionage exchange!'

The pause then her sagging shoulders was sufficient body language for Alain to feel he had the advantage, so he pressed her. 'I appreciate the help you people are providing, Valya, but I don't like being used as some stooge for a clandestine rendezvous by Russian spies. It is dangerous enough in this city without that sort of carry on. I would like to be told when I am piggy in the middle.'

'Girl from wealthy family. Girl loyal to President Assad. She has information about her father's friend who make plan for transfer money out from Syria. Girl pass small note to Russian professor in university but difficult for information transfers. Girl cannot come to Russia Embassy so we find a way to get close to girl. Egor meet girl in university cafe one time but dangerous for her. Girl also cannot be alone, her status too much big so I send Egor to meet her on university cafe. Many times try make meeting. Today one more time fail. Sorry.'

The fact the girl wanted to pass information did not seem to Alain to be unusual but the complexity of such a simple task, when explained by Valentina, made him despondent. A beautiful young woman risking her life to expose people close to the President who might not be loyal. All the makings of a Shakespearean tragedy, he thought.

'Well, you might also have a budding romance on your hands,' he said. 'That girl had lust in her eyes, if I am any judge.'

Valentina shrugged dismissively. 'Young people is always take risks for love,' she said. 'Remember?'

A flicker of eyebrow was his only acknowledgment. Returning to the substantial he said, 'This sort of money transfer happens not only where pariah countries are involved but in the west. Businessmen constantly seek to launder money to avoid taxation.'

Valya nodded. 'I know this. Also happens in Russia after Perestroika. But girl in café her father is close by Wakid Mashreq. From these people there is much power and girl in big danger to pass information.'

Alain sighed, a little despondent. 'Well,' he said resignedly. 'I guess I am fortunate it doesn't involve me.'

A look of something between despair and contempt registered on Valentina's face. 'You are getting old my friend,' she said. 'I suspect reason the girl risks her life is because her father's companions are planning to use the company structure you set up in Hong Kong, to launder money out of Syria. The girl sees these people as traitors. How you say, having each way a wager?'

The new day dawned suddenly but Alain had been awake for some time; the call of first prayer by the nearby Imam ringing across the stillness of a still slumbering city had become his daily alarm to daybreak.

This day he was to meet Samer again. A relief from the boredom of compound living. A week had passed since Yasin confirmed a full shipment of phosphate would make up the first transaction. Yasin had procured a ship from Russia and Alain sensed Valentina's hand in this. A Letter of Credit had been lodged with a major German bank whose integrity, where honouring the fine print of an LC was critical, was to the satisfaction of all parties. Arrangements had been made for Samer to pick him up, literally, in the helicopter to fly east and view a border post between Syria and Iraq as a respite from the boredom. Artie was to descend into the compound in his chariot at eight thirty am.

Two hours at least before pick up, Alain swung his legs to the floor then staggered to the toilet for an early morning pee. A quick shave and toiletries followed before he returned to his bed to commence a daily routine. One hundred sit ups, using the soft bed as support for the base of his spine. How many years had it taken him to figure out that damage to the base of his spine caused by sit ups on the hard surface of a rugby ground could be ameliorated by doing the same exercise on a bed? Then dropping to the floor, ten sets of twenty press-ups was the plan but usually five sets were enough. Slipping across the courtyard, Alain was pleased to find the pool unoccupied. Forty laps would follow, before the rush. By mid-afternoon the pool would be like Bondi Beach.

At seven thirty am Alain left the compound to take a stroll around nearby streets as shop keepers unfurled their wares in preparation for another day of uncertain selling. It was a regular beat to tread, most mornings passing the spot where the gunmen hired by the CIA had made an attempt to capture him. Bizarre, thought Alain. Absolutely bizarre. Often he wondered what the Americans might have in store for him next and he remembered the tail which had followed him and Egor inside the Old City.

'Mr Foveaux, a moment of your time, if you please.' The interruption to his thoughts momentarily startled him. The accent was unmistakably American. The apparition tending a stall of wood carved artefacts seemed anything but. 'I have a request,' continued the pleasantly mannered smiling male of Syrian appearance. 'The Ambassador would like to meet with you. Perhaps you will telephone the US Embassy? When the prompter asks, please enter the pin code of your birthday. This will connect you to the Ambassador. It is a pleasant morning in this beautiful city.'

Alain had not moved. Adrenalin pulsed through his body, as instinctively his mind calibrated another kidnap attempt. Though a surprise, the encounter was over before Alain could formulate a response as the man had slipped between two street stalls and disappeared.

With consummate skill Artie dropped the Squirrel behind desert dunes near Al Waleed. Alain, Egor, Sammer and Artie climbed out of the helicopter then scrambled to the top for a view some five kilometres to the East where lay the border with Iraq and a military check point. 'Is best we not stand up. Keep below the horizon. Use binocular. Is good view,' said Samer.

Egor and Alain devoured the sight before them. A border cross point. Long queues on either side, like serpents resting in the sun. At regular intervals, slashing forward like the tongue of a snake constantly scenting the air, another vehicle would speed away from the checkpoint. 'Fuel tanker,' commented Egor as he focused the binoculars.

'Many fuel tankers,' corrected Alain. 'And many four wheel drive jeeps and small trucks. A hundred vehicles in the queue on this side alone.' Both men watched in astonishment as vehicle after vehicle pulled out from the check point after cursory inspection. 'Too many vehicles each day for big search,' commented Samer.

Fifteen minutes later Alain said, 'This is fascinating Samer. These vehicles; these are small traders in furniture and household goods?'

'Many things,' said Samer. A black market is the life blood for both countries.'

'And the oil tankers?' Samer coughed a cynical grunt. 'This is, as you see, oil. Stolen from the pipelines in Iraq. Transported through this border post for sale in Syria but now is bad time and it's transported to Aqaba as alternative.'

No response was invited. Shortly Samer continued. 'America condemn Syria for allowing smuggler to cross the border. Look either side of this border post. Miles of desert. Syria has not the troops for surveillance. America she has the drones and many surveillance aircraft but you not see America patrol the border from Iraq side! Why is just Syria guilty for this thing?'

'What interests me, said Alain, 'are these tankers. Vehicles stop on the Iraq side. I suspect the guards are Iraqi and American. Then the vehicle is sent forward to the Syria side. A short stop and off it moves, another tanker into Syria.'

'I have been through that border post, Alain,' said Samer. ' Is true what you see. Iraqi and America soldier. No officer on checkpoint. Only soldier is in sun. Sun is hot. Officer is seat in that dark grey bunker. Is cool inside. See Sky TV dish. Luxury for officers. Captain. Sometimes only lieutenant. But always is officer American.'

'Let me guess,' said Alain as he pushed himself up from the desert rock and handed his binoculars to Samer. 'American officer keeps record of oil tankers and later payment is made to the colonel or the general of the border control battalion.'

Samer smiled. 'America is corruption and is everywhere is America.'

Twenty minutes later Artie dropped out of the clear blue sky and landed beside a café at the junction of highways separating Palmyra and Damascus. 'Café Baghdad?' said Alain enthusiastically. 'Ironical perhaps?'

'Pardon?' asked Samer.

'The name of the café. First stop after the border with Iraq and smugglers can relax in Baghdad?'

'Is popular name I think,' said Samer as he led the way into a private rear room. The dome-shaped building afforded an unexpected coolness. Mint tea was served.

Presently Samer said, 'I like to show you reality of American occupation in our lands. This why we fly to border post. Also Alain, I ask you today for serious talking. We have problem.'

Sipping the piping hot, sweet but refreshing tea, Alain invited his old friend to be candid.

'Yasin tell Kiwifert make changes to phosphate shipment. Why you not tell Samer?'

Alain paused his sipping. 'I did not disguise it from you Samer! I was told maybe six days ago by New Zealand. I didn't realise I needed to tell you. In fact, it never occurred to me. I supposed the Minister would tell you as the Melbourne joint venture partner agent.'

'Why you make change to shipment of twenty seven thousand tons and not two container load?' Samer enquired after a few moments.

'As we are old friends and as I trust you I will be candid,' responded Alain. 'Kiwifert has many problems in New Zealand. Americans put pressure on New Zealand government. The government cannot stop Kiwifert importing Syria phosphate. New Zealand is not bound by US and EU laws. Only UN sanctions apply to New Zealand, but Russian and China and India and Brazil say no in United nations.' Alain paused. 'Do you understand what I say?'

Samer nodded.

Alain continued. 'New Zealand government has no power to stop phosphate imports so they sent the taxation department to Kiwifert to cause troubles. The owner of Kiwifert is a young man. He is angry at the government. Also Kiwifert learned that commercial competitors in New Zealand made contact with America to try and stop Kiwifert buying Syria phosphate. Young man got more angry. If he cannot buy phosphate he will lose the business his father built for him. So he made the decision to bring a big load of phosphate. One shipment is all he can afford but one shipment will make many months of fertilizer for Kiwifert. Maybe the situation will be better in six months?'

Alain's answer seemed to appease Samer. 'Yasin is big man. Many friend. Very powerful. Very dangerous.'

Alain remained quiet, sipping at his tea.

Presently Samer spoke again. 'Yasin not to pay money from New Zealand to Melbourne partner. Yasin say Syria generals want move money fast out from Syria. Yasin say Melbourne must wait for payment for phosphate.'

Alain stopped sipping his tea. 'Bastard,' he said quietly.

'You're right there mate,' chipped in Artie. 'Melbourne boys have been pouring money in here for five years as I know. They want a dividend.'

'Has Yasin explained how he is going to,' Alain paused, searching for an appropriate word, 'misappropriate our payment for the phosphate?'

'Your bloody Hong Kong bank mate,' said Artie with scorn.

'Yasin is shareholder for Syria in Hong Kong bank you make. His people in Hong Kong also make company for you. He has much control,' explained Samer.

'Yes, Richard in Hong Kong put the papers together but I went to the bank with him and in the presence of two bankers with good English, made certain that nothing moves from Achilles unless it has my signature. Richard is the signatory on behalf of the Syrian consortium which I suppose includes the Melbourne syndicate. I am a joint signatory for Achilles financial transactions,' explained Alain.

Then he added, 'I can prevent Yasin stealing our money. I made the condition that transfers only happen if my signature is biometric. They must have my fingerprint scanned through a special pad. Patent rights by the way for this technology is owned by a New Zealand company.'

Artie emitted a shout of delight. Samer gently nodded approval.

'Yasin also use Achilles for launder other monies. Big monies. Many millions,' continued Samer. 'Yasin is big business for many Syria military and politics. Iran also. He make transfer of components for armaments. Very important man. Very dangerous man. He will kill you if you try stop him.'

Well, I guess I am on a learning curve here, thought Alain. 'Five million is hardly worth killing me but I suppose if the quantum of cash being laundered is many millions from transactions unrelated to phosphate purchase, he might. And Yasin will be in breach of international anti-money-laundering laws and Achilles will also be in deep shit!'

Samer shook his head. 'Wrong my friend. In this region people kill for five dollars not five million.' Later he said. 'AML laws don't have any weight with the oldest trading nations in the world, my friend. All Middle East, most of the Asian subcontinent, South American states, Russia, China. These countries see anti-money-laundering laws as an attempt by America to control the world commerce.' Samer smiled for the first time that day.

'Already Arab world is how you say, squeezed between rocks,' continued Samer. 'Oil price is in US dollar but many Arab states want freedom to trade in Euro currency. America not like. My peoples think America make deal with Standard & Poors to downgrade France credit rating as way to undermine value of euro currency. This help make US dollar important for oil trading. America say no this not true but I not believe America. Very sensitive problem and very big problem.'

Samer smiling reminded Alain of a day many years previous when they'd sat together near the Stari Most or Old Bridge over the Neretva River in Herzegovina. Like the bridge and himself, Samer was now an old warrior.

'We must help each other, as we did in the past,' Alain pledged as they strolled back to the helicopter and he placed his hand on Samer's shoulder. 'We must make a plan my friend.'

Dusk was nigh as Artie put the chopper down in the Russian embassy compound. Egor caught Alain and held him steady as his left knee gave out when he stepped from the chariot. A cruciate knee ligament injury from a fall when jumping his favourite hunting steed, with the passage of years and without proper initial corrective surgery, now pained Alain after cramped sitting for some time.

'Thank you,' he muttered rubbing his knee furiously to boost the blood circulation. A shower, some traditional meat and vegetable dish at a local café just outside the embassy gates and solitude beckoned, but as he walked through the pagoda he sensed her presence.

'Valya!' he whispered. 'I can't see you in the shadows but you are there,' he said reproachfully.

'Breakfast at eight am please. You must attend.' Her tone was formal and he was disappointed. 'I was hoping you might join me for dinner; the restaurant across the gardens?' Valentina touched his arm in the darkness. He felt her gaze upon him but he could not see her. Then she was gone.

At nine thirty pm Alain placed a call to the American Embassy then keyed in his date of birth. Several moments later a younger man's voice sounded. 'This is the Ambassador.'

Suppose it's my turn now, thought Alain as he looked at his mobile, half-expecting something else to happen or be said.

'Alain Foveaux. I was told to call this number.'

Another slight delay. 'I would like to meet with you Mr Foveaux. For a late night snifter. Is it possible for you to attend the Four Seasons hotel tonight?'

Midway through a meal and I receive an invitation from the Ambassador of the country which not a week ago shot up the car I was passenger in! Alain's fork hovered above the over-cooked piece of mutton. He prodded the food perfunctorily. What the hell, he thought. But I will take a precaution.

'Okay. See you there in thirty minutes.'

Alain made another call then finished his dinner.

Valentina and Egor were waiting outside the café. Alain recognised the original car he had been collected in at the airport when he arrived in Damascus over two weeks ago. 'No need for another bulletproof transport?' he asked as he ducked into the car.

'We have confirmed the number you called. It was the American Ambassador. Is unlikely he lure you to assassination. Ambassador not CIA,' she said. Alain was not so sure the Russian Ambassador was not FSB though.

At the Four Seasons, Alain once again was in some awe at the size of the edifice, rising as a giant among dwarves; the opulent exception amidst scruffy neighbours.

Egor entered the hotel first. Alain followed some minutes later following a series of clicks softly emitted from a device Valentina had secreted on her person.

Alain saw the Ambassador sitting in one of the lobby chairs. He stood as Alain approached and extended a handshake. Alain reciprocated. He spotted Egor, appearing to be engaged in conversation on his phone across the lobby. Dwight was nowhere in sight nor did there appear to be a clone of the CIA man. But, Alain registered subconsciously, what the hell is a CIA person supposed to look like?

'Thank you for joining me,' said the Ambassador. Smiling graciously he continued, 'I am here alone. No CIA, but I see you have brought your Russian minders.'

With a taut smile he replied. 'I have learned at my expense, the streets of Damascus can be dangerous.'

'Please call me Porter. May I call you Alain?'

'By all means. Do we sit here or is there some private room?'

'I have taken the liberty of arranging coffee in one of the cubicles across the lobby. These are in full view but do afford some level of privacy.'

Taking a seat, Alain sat leaned forward. 'Let's get to the point of this meeting Ambassador. Sorry, Porter.'

Porter took in his adversary. He looked sixty but reasonably fit. It's not possible to calibrate the intelligence of an adversary by physical appearance, except in the most extreme cases, but it is possible to get an inkling of attitude; hesitancy, resolve. Alain's posture signalled to Porter; determination.

Porter hadn't decided whether he should refer to the attack on the New Zealander but he expected the matter to be raised. It was the New Zealander who spoke next, pre-empting any response by Porter to the initial question. Agitation, concluded Porter. This man is determined but he is also angry.

'I met your local heavy, Dwight, and his side kick. Agriculture they told me. A not entirely agreeable visit to Homs, as I am sure you have been briefed.'

Porter smiled politely. Keep this civilized, he told himself.

'Alain, I have been briefed on everything you have done since you arrived.'

'Including the botched attempt to hijack me?'

Cautiously Porter responded. 'I was briefed about an assault on a Russian embassy vehicle in which you were a passenger. There are many reasons why this attack was made, not the least being anti-Assad people displeased with the support the Russians afford the incumbent regime.'

The two men met with a level gaze. Now they had spoken, Porter was able to move beyond assessment of an adversary on the basis of physical appearance alone. This man was also cautious, he concluded, which accounted for his bodyguard in the hotel.

'It interested us that neither the Russian nor the Syrian authorities released details of the incident to any media.' The Ambassador let the issue drop. 'What was your impression of the border crossing beyond Palmyra?' continued Porter smoothly when no response was forthcoming to his previous question.

'Interesting,' replied Alain cocking his head with a slight shrug. A genuine response, concluded Porter who had made body language one of his pet hobbies.

'One thing about this region. Corruption is rampant it seems. Those oil tankers!' Alain shook his head in a gesture of incredulity.

'And America fits into this well, you might conclude?' replied Porter making his first concessionary initiative. The man is not a fool and I would be a fool if I expected him to decide after watching that border post that Americans are not involved in the black market of stolen oil.

A merest head nod gave comfort to Porter that he had won some respect from the New Zealander. Some moments passed then Alain spoke again.

'What is it you want, Mr Ambassador?'

Alain's reversion to the formal title was not lost on Porter. It was time to make his play.

'Alain. We know you are in Syria to buy phosphate. This strategy contravenes US and EU law.'

'But it has no effect on our company which is registered in New Zealand. That country is not subject to the rule of law as America decrees,' responded Alain.

Careful, Porter cautioned himself. This man is angry. These people do not like being bullied. 'There are also AML laws, internationally embraced,' he continued cautiously.

'Paying for phosphate is not laundering money.' This time Alain's hostility was tangible.

It is time to unburden, concluded Porter. It is time to use my diplomatic skills.

'Alain,' he said. 'I understand the economic imperative driving your company. No please. Let me finish. I suspect your commercial competitors have had a hand in your trials. Your objective is further complicated by a civil war in the country where you seek to buy phosphate. And on top of that you find yourself in the middle of a Super Power game of "one-upmanship"; getting points on the board at the expense of the other. In truth, neither of these Super Powers gives a damn about Kiwifert.' Now I have his attention Porter admitted to himself with some satisfaction. 'To make matters even more complex, you now find you are in a business arrangement with Yasin; a man on who's head the US government has placed a bounty of ten million dollars dead or alive. Viktor Bout, the Russian arms dealer and Yasin are in the same category. This, for the United States, elevates the ball game to premier league.'

Alain had not spoken for several minutes. This Yank knew his stuff, he concluded. The man had some finesse; not like that CIA clown, Dwight. Maybe with more diplomats like this fellow the world would be a safer place.

'And?' said Alain finally.

'And, how would Kiwifert respond to an offer from the Iraqi government to buy phosphate from mines in that country?'

Alain took a sip of his cold coffee.

Egor parked the car and bid them good night. Valentina sat, waiting. Finally she said, 'You will tell me what is happen? What is America say you?'

Turning to face her, he said, 'Valya. During this adventure, if I might call it such, my attitude toward America has hardened from ambivalence to contempt. Toward Russia it has changed from fear of the unknown to no fear from knowledge.'

Valentina permitted another of her wispy smiles to ripple. 'However,' he continued, 'that does not mean I am totally infatuated with Russia even if I am totally infatuated with a Russian woman.'

An expression of confusion creased her brow. 'What means infatuated?'

'In relation to Russia, it means I am not blindly loyal to the Motherland. In relation to you it means I am blindly in love.'

Tenderness crept upon her. Her posture softened and once again he saw that somnolent gaze; like a leopard watching from the bush. Alain leaned across the divide and kissed her softly. She closed her eyes and pressed her lips upon him. The moment for Alain was ecstasy but it was only for a moment.

'Valya also is infatuated with you. But I am first colonel FSB. What say America Ambassador?'

Alain slumped against the door pillar. 'The Yanks offer Kiwifert a free hand into Iraq phosphate. The Yanks claim the war; their war; in Iraq is over. They want to see commerce flourish so they can get out from the mess they created and leave them free to fight the war in Afghanistan.'

Valentina sat bolt upright. 'Ambassador. He say this things?'

'Not in so many words. In fact, the spin is mine.'

'Spin?' she demanded.

'Interpretation. But the offer for Kiwifert was made. The Yanks want to save face. This Ambassador is trying to use diplomacy rather than rendition and water boarding.'

'And what says you will do?'

'With the frequency and size of bombs being exploded in Iraq, I think to say the war is over is to draw a long bow.' Alain stretched a leg as best he could in the confines of a Mercedes Kompressor.

'What I should do Valentina, is call Bryce in New Zealand and recommend he take the Iraq offer. Getting phosphate out of Syria will not be simple nor will it be safe. And with respect, getting phosphate out of Russia has its problems. But...' and he paused.

'But what is?'

'But one thing; as I recall the Americans promised to buy the bulk of Australian sugar cane, if the Aussies went into Iraq. The Aussies kept their end of the bargain. The Yanks didn't. So I wonder if Kiwifert could suffer a similar fate.'

'This America promise Poland and Czech and Ukraine and other former Soviet States; America put weapons on your lands for fight terrorism, but true reason is fight Russia. For this permissions promise America make big trades. But not big trades happen. America not tell truth.'

'Regrettably, that seems to be the way they conduct business,' lamented Alain.

'How you know America Ambassador tell truths? Can he make this deals?' she asked.

'I doubt his solution, eminently practical as it is and an astute diplomatic compromise, has been signed off in Washington and Baghdad. This is a jungle Valya. Sadly, to trust is foolish,' he said forlornly. 'Kiwifert must look after itself and to do this I have decided to look after the friends of Kiwifert. Kiwifert will go with the Russians in the Syrian connection.

Again she smiled that transient ripple, like wind on water.

'*Ya lublew tebya,*'he said softly.

She paused, alighted from the car and replied. 'I love you too, Alain Foveaux.'

And she was gone.

Chapter Eighteen

**Tartus Port,
Syria.**

When Captain Valera Laskin took the print-out from his communications officer he reflected with some mirth as he unfolded the document. For how many centuries had the officer in command of a Russian vessel received orders in written form? Pre-Marconi and radio, orders had been delivered by letter on a silver platter prior to sailing. Post-Marconi, encoded orders had been transmitted by Morse code for transcription and handing to the captain once at sea. In this age of instantaneous computerised transfer of data, the Navy still required the communications officer to transcribe inward orders and present the same to the captain on a plate.

That was forty eight hours ago. By Addis lamp flickering across the ocean, Captain Laskin had confirmed his departure from the Fleet; he would not be returning to the comforts of his wife and family at the Russian naval enclave of Sevastopol. Instead he was to proceed with utmost haste to station off Somalia where his mission would be to protect Russian vessels from piracy. En route he was to escort a merchant ship carrying phosphate out of the Syrian port of Tartus through the Suez Canal, into the Red Sea and out to the Indian Ocean.

As the Kasin class destroyer passed through the Dardanelles on its way from the Black Sea into the Sea of Marmara then the Mediterranean Sea, Captain Laskin had informed the crew that they would not be home for another three months.

Two days later, when the ultra-modern Russian destroyer hove to off the port of Tartus where several smaller Russian frigates now also languished, Captain Laskin received a second order on the same plate proffered by the same communications officer.

Captain Laskin read the order then looked into the eyes of the lieutenant who had conveyed the signal. Without breaking eye contact with the lieutenant or turning to look at First Officer Petrenko who was waiting at hand, he ordered: 'At eighteen hundred hours we go to battle ready, level red.'

The helicopter hovered to starboard of the former grain carrier nestled alongside the two hundred and seventy metre-long phosphate terminal at Port Tartus. Harbour tugs were securing their hawsers in preparation to pull the ship's nose toward the open sea. 'She's seen better days,' Artie said of the old style maritime freighter.

Deftly, as Artie manoeuvred his aircraft, Samer took photographs of the ship in the fading light. Jerking his thumb over his shoulder as he completed his photography, he gestured that they should retire. He had seen what he'd come to see. The first shipment of phosphate for export for many months.

Beneath them the once bustling Mediterranean port seemed strangely quiet. Founded in the second century BC the port later served as military headquarters to the Knights Templar from 1152 until Saladin recaptured the city in 1291. In 1516 the Ottoman Turks arrived, beginning a period of long economic decline until after World War One when the French took control of Syria. As Syria gained independence in 1945 life was again breathed into the port providing a lifeline to the dreams of an emerging nation. Now those dreams lay in embers.

Artie cast a nervous glance at his companion. The Melbourne syndicate put a lot of faith in Samer. This Artie knew. But two of the Melbourne team were expats or Syrians who had migrated to Australia a decade earlier. The other partner was a lawyer from Australian bush town of Bendigo, whom Artie regarded as next to useless. Artie's father had embraced the Syrians as his conduit to investment in Syria. He wished his father was still alive. He needed the old man's intuition born of years of business experience. The next twenty four hours were going to take him into uncharted waters.

Artie was a pilot. He'd never expected to have to take over his dad's role in the company but he had seen the necessity. Artie didn't trust the Melbourne syndicate and as his family had fifty per cent of the company, it was a no-brainer for Artie to domicile himself in Syria and keep an eye on things. Concerned he was alone in a wilderness with foreigners with whom he never bonded like his dad had, Artie had turned to the only people he figured would be able to help him.

Initially the people at the Australian Embassy were helpful but Artie soon realised that bureaucrats made poor business decisions. Giving advice where they had no personal financial involvement seemed to colour it with fanciful solutions from which they were quick to distance themselves when things went wrong. Artie got on far better with the bloke doing the military intelligence beat and it was through him that he met Dwight from the US embassy.

The problem now for Artie was, whereas Dwight had been a great confidant over the last few months, in the past couple of weeks when the prospect of the Melbourne syndicate picking up some revenue at long last seemed within reach, Dwight's attitude had changed. Each time Dwight called him, Artie began to realise that the questions being asked, if answered truthfully, could compromise the shipment. Artie found himself between a rock and a hard place. He needed someone to turn to for advice on the politics of the country, and simply another Caucasian to have a beer with. But that same saviour had been insistent to the point of outright hostility that no sale could be made to these Kiwis. It became impossible to reason with the CIA man who isolated Artie more and more with his arrogance. Artie even stopped discussing the plans for the company with his sister back in Australia when he called her twice a week because he suspected Dwight would plug into his phone calls.

The more immediate problem Artie had now the shipment was on the water was how to get his hands on the payment coming from the Kiwis for the load. He knew this problem vexed Samer too. The middle man, Yasin, was proving to be quite a problem for Samer. Artie didn't think Samer was afraid of Yasin but he was certainly nervous about him.

'Well, that's the easy bit. Now to get our hands on our money. How do we deal with Yasin?'

'I meet him tomorrow afternoon in Palmyra. He comes across the border from Iraq,' Samer replied thoughtfully.

Somewhat mollified by this answer Artie changed the topic momentarily. 'Back to Homs?' he queried. 'We should make it before dark.'

'Palmyra,' crackled Samer's voice.

The plan change startled Artie.

'We can't make Palmyra before dark. Air traffic control won't authorise me to night fly and I sure as hell ain't risking being shot down for flying unauthorised.'

'Then take me to Damascus. Russian embassy.'

Artie changed course and called in for clearance from air traffic control. I don't like the way Samer leaves me out of the fine tuning, he brooded. I should be more involved in his plans. The boys back in Melbourne might be happy to let this guy do everything but my family has the biggest stake in this.

Alain meet the helicopter in the Russian compound. Artie waited while Alain secured permission to secure the aircraft overnight and made provision for fuel. After confirming with Artie to meet at the helicopter the following morning, Samer left him to find his own lodging at one of the nearby three star hotels. Resentment burned deep as Artie watched Samer and the New Zealander in deep conversation he should have been part of.

Acting on gut instinct out of frustration, Artie dragged his phone out of his kitbag and placed a call.

Chapter Nineteen

Damascus, Syria

Porter checked his secure phone, again. No sign of a call from Foveaux. Porter was disappointed. It had been a long shot; inspirational and compulsive. Serious initiatives were now coming out of the Secretary State's office, promoting commerce as the key to a stabilizing Iraq now the military had pulled out. He was sure he could pull together access for the New Zealander. But it seemed his best intentions on this issue would never be put to the test. Conversely, the consequences of a phosphate transaction on his patch, Syria, did not appeal.

Porter placed Shostakovich in the CD compartment and settled back with a Hennessey cognac.

'How did these people manage to produce such masters of music?' His lament was lost in the strength of the music by the Russian composer, which drowned his burden.

'Dad would never have been proud of me Mum. You see, unlike you, he knew I was a homosexual. And that is something he could never accept no matter how high in the tree of respect I climbed. I tried Ma, I really tried. But you and dad gave me these chromosomes. Don't you understand? I had no choice.'

Later he also said aloud. 'Yes Ma. I will do my best for my country.' But he was talking to his cognac.

Dwight was anything but happy. Langley had made it very clear; Foveaux was not to succeed. Porter Julian had been an obstacle but whatever his "diplomatic solution" had been, it had failed. Foveaux was now taking a shipload and not just a couple of containers.

Dwight's phone blinked.

'Hello,' he said then listened. 'Palmyra? That's somewhere in the desert for God's sake!' He listened. 'I guarantee you will get your five million.'

'Listen pal. You're talking to the top CIA man in the region. If I tell you your five million is in the bag, then it's in the fucking bag. So what's going down cobber?' Dwight listened with growing agitation.

Later Dwight depressed the terminate call button then pressed the most used key on the pad.

Wilbur placed his Le Carre novel with care in the chair beside his bed. Midnight. No problems. Weekend tomorrow. Sleep in day.

But then his mobile chirped and cautiously he put the device to his ear.

'We got shit going down. Get over here pronto,' rasped the unpleasant and unwelcome tones of his immediate boss. No need to be the resident linguistics expert to decipher that, he said to himself.

Breakfast was served early for the guests of the Russian Ambassador. Alain had some fruit and a coffee. Samer had coffee only. Egor had his usual large serving of bacon and eggs. Valentina had a glass of fruit juice and the Ambassador abstained. Midway through the repast Artie was admitted and like Egor, demolished a healthy serving of bacon and eggs.

'I am able to confirm your shipment has made good progress toward the Suez.' The Ambassador also confirmed that no hostile warship of any nationality or description had been sighted by either of the ships.

'We are most obliged to the Russian government,' said Alain. 'It is beyond my level of competence to pass judgment on whether the Americans would seriously have seized our ship on the high seas. My advice is that this would have been an act of piracy. But,' Alain shrugged, 'America makes its own rules. I can only say again, thank you.'

'Both ships are Russian. It would be an act of war, not piracy.' The Ambassador clasped his hands. 'I think your problems are less maters of State but matters of commerce. And in these matters Russia cannot assist.'

Alain cleared his throat to get their attention. 'Colonel Goloshapova has made it clear to us that Russian embassy staff cannot be involved in Palmyra. I am compromised however, sir. Egor has been my translator during all my negotiations. He is known to people involved in our transactions. He is seen as a translator. It is too late for me to find another translator and this is sensitive stuff as you know. I ask for an exception that he may attend only as translator.'

It was obvious the Ambassador had not anticipated the request. He looked to Valentina for a solution but she steadfastly gazed directly in front of her. Egor had stopped chewing, mid-mouthful.

'I suppose you require him as a driver too?' he asked. Then without waiting for Alain to answer said to Egor. 'Confine yourself to translation of commercial matters only.'

'Thank you Ambassador,' said Alain with genuine appreciation. 'Samer is flying ahead in the helicopter. He has business with Yasin on behalf of the Melbourne partners in Basrik Mines. Egor and I will drive and should arrive after all negotiations are concluded. My presence should only be required to sign, scan and transmit bank documentation pertaining to payment transfer from Kiwifert to the agreed destination.'

He chose not to refer to the question of Yasin's intention to smuggle additional funding from sources yet unknown, at the same time.

The Ambassador nodded and looked at his watch. 'It is a four hour drive to Palmyra. You should leave soon.' He then shook hands with Alain and retired.

Samer, now deep in thought, bowed his head. 'Artie and I must also move. We need to sweep the venue before Yasin arrives. He has his own security but he demands assurance that we have swept for explosives and electronic devices.'

Alain pushed back from the breakfast table. 'So the programme is; you go on ahead and meet Yasin in the Zenobia Cham Palace hotel where you sort out distribution of Kiwifert payment for the shipment. That is a matter between the Melbourne Syndicate and Basrik.' Alain waited for confirmation. Samer nodded assent and stood from the table too.

'When that is sorted you will call me, and Egor and I will rock up. That should be sometime after three pm, correct?'

'Yes. If we cannot agree after two hours, then I cannot account for what might happen,' said Samer.

'All this should have been sorted long ago.' Artie's comment was belligerent in tone and Alain raised a questioning eyebrow toward him.

'I'm not just the bloody pilot here mate,' said Artie. 'My family is the largest investor in the Melbourne Syndicate as you conveniently describe us. This place might not be as dangerous as Papua New Guinea but it surely is not my choice of picnic paradise.'

Turning to Samer, Alain now directed a questioning glance at his old friend. 'You never mentioned Artie was an investor.'

Samer shrugged. 'An oversight of no importance my friend. Artie tell you he is only pilot. I not ask why. Not problem for me.'

I suppose it makes no difference, concluded Alain, but it does explain Artie's testiness.

'Assuming you get your division of profits issue resolved,' continued Alain, addressing his comments to Artie now, 'the next issue is going to be a little more complicated. How we deal with Yasin's intentions to launder other sources of illegitimate cash, piggy back on our legitimate phosphate payment. You were not privy to the lengthy discussions Samer and I had last night but all I can say in summary is, this is very messy and frankly, I haven't a bloody clue how to deal with this man, particularly as he has such powerful backers and according to Samer, is mad.'

'We should go,' called Egor from the passage-way.

Alain followed him with Artie and Samer in tow but turned to Artie as they walked. 'If you had been a little more transparent earlier there is no reason why you couldn't have been involved last night.'

Artie's body language exuded contrition. 'Sorry. I wasn't sure how you fitted into all this when we first met.'

'Okay,' Alain reassured him, 'but I hope you don't have any other surprises for us.'

Fifteen minutes later as Artie lifted the Squirrel into a clear blue sky, Valentina touched both Egor and Alain on the arm and beckoned them to follow her. In her office she shut the door and indicated they both sit. From a drawer she took two Russian pistols; a Makarov and its older version, a Tokarev.

'This for you', she said to Egor as she handed him one of the guns. 'Old model you like.' Valentina then unwrapped the other pistol from what seemed to be brand new packing. 'For you, new model,' she said, handing the gun to Alain.

Instantly the mood in the office was electric. Both men had heard the Ambassador issue clear instructions about the involvement of Russia and Egor in the negotiations to come. Those instructions did not include firearms. Valentina rested her buttocks on the desk and faced the two men. 'Ambassador has diplomat job. I am FSB colonel and have different job. I must deal with Yasin.'

It then became more a matter of what Valentina did not say than what she did say. 'Yasin very dangerous man. He has body guards. Automatic weapons.'

Alain gave a slightly dismissive shrug. 'There is no point for Yasin to kill us. Or to kill Samer for that matter. Yasin needs our signatures and biometric validation to transfer money from the Hong Kong company.'

Valentina glared at Alain as if he was a small child not understanding the dangers of crossing the road. 'I not know what Yasin plan is. I know Yasin kill many people in past. I know Yasin perhaps torture your friend Samer for you compel your consent? Yasin also can also kill you after you consent. I say you many times, Yasin is dangerous man. Unstable.'

The rebuke reminded Alain once again; he was getting old. Addressing Egor, Valentina said, 'If all goes wrong you escape in Roman ruins. Hide and wait for Sergei come with Alpha save you. Makarov for your self defence.'

Alain returned to his room, collected clothing suitable for the cold desert dawn and was about to join Egor in an old blue-grey Opel, when Valentina barred his way.

'I am changed my mind,' she said. 'You not come to Rostov na Dona.'

Her statement stunned him. Bewildered he asked, 'Why? What has changed?'

She stepped forward and kissed him passionately.

'Be very careful, my lover,' she said in earnest. 'I am want on New Zealand. Maybe you make me wife? I can go on Auckland? I am soon finish FSB. Too old. Like you.'

Grabbing her in an embrace Alain squeezed her strongly until she wheezed for him to release her.

'As soon as this is over I will start immigration proceedings. *Da sveedarnya* my love.' And he was gone.

Chapter Twenty

Palmyra, Syria.

Yasin pushed the whore from his bed. Two women a night was the minimum he insisted his hosts provide. He preferred the Latins from South America; he liked their skin colour which was similar to his own but also they were invariably lascivious and compliant. Russian whores by contrast, who were many in Syria, were demanding, petulant and often forced him to beat them which was unnecessary. They were after all, whores who should not need to be cajoled.

Stumbling to the dresser he rubbed a hand over his recently shaven head. The pressure was constant. Altering his appearance from one month to the next. Always moving. But with ten million US dollars on his head Yasin knew his greatest threat was not so much from chance discovery of his whereabouts by random or cross-border check but from perfidy by those closest to him. The meeting therefore with Samer; a respected denizen of the clandestine labyrinth in which they both moved, reeked of danger. For this reason his advance security team had been at the Zenobia Cham Palace oasis retreat thirty six hours before he arrived, twenty four hours ahead of his scheduled meeting later this day.

It came therefore as no surprise but with a tinge of disappointment when his security head, Omar, knocked softly on his balcony window to alert him to CIA people suddenly appearing and seeping through the hotel like waters of a poisonous spring.

'Special One,' intoned Omar with the level of respect and reverence reserved only for his daily prayers to Allah, 'This is a hastily prepared mission unless the Americans have become even more clumsy than usual. At four thirty am we saw a mini bus stop outside the township on the road from Damascus. By six thirty am there were armed men in strategic positions in the grounds of this hotel. They search no rooms. No other buildings have been approached.'

'They have been informed that I am to meet Samer later this day,' responded Yasin. 'Come inside. Sit,' he ordered. Barely had Omar sat when his master gave orders. This was like the Special One, thought Omar. Always he is quick to plan.

'Call in the mobile patrol. They must be seen at hotel reception to demand the helipad be reserved for a special quest at ten am. The men must then demand breakfast and then remain in the foyer in full view. They should be cheerful and carefree.'

'It will be done, Special One,' replied Omar.

'The Americans will be told of this; they will have informers within the hotel and will move their people to secure the heliport. Perhaps they will deploy all of their people to this location if they believe it is I who will be landing.'

Omar grinned his appreciation of his master's strategy.

'When you see the Americans move into position our mobile patrol team must remain in the lobby as a decoy to lull the Infidels into thinking we are not alert. At nine thirty am all Americans will be in position but not in a state of immediate preparedness. Some will be urinating in the bushes; others will be checking their weapons. That is the time you must bring our hotel team from their lair and must strike. How many Americans are here?'

'Five in the hotel grounds Special One. CIA from Damascus.'

An Imam call pierced the early morning. Yasin invited Omar to pray with him before this mission.

Dwight and his team had departed the US Embassy compound at twelve thirty am. Wilbur was his number two who would maintain the mobile HQ and communications link among him and his team. The four men with him were his men, trained and indoctrinated with CIA ethos the way it was and in Dwight's view, the way it should always be.

About ten kilometres from their destination Dwight had called a halt; roused the men from a slumber and put them through fifteen minutes of callisthenics. Coffee and sandwiches from thermos and pre-pack was followed by a briefing Dwight had conceived en route. He put aside the vexed issue of not briefing the Ambassador. This was sensitive ground. On the one hand the Ambassador was head of the mission in Syria with power to veto or approve any CIA initiative which was not a covert Langley operation. On the other hand, the CIA was an independent Government agency. Turf wars among FBI, CIA, the State Department and other government agencies were legendary. But now he was too far to turn back and Dwight had twinges of doubt about being the main character in the next chapter of the book on turf wars.

'God damn it!' he exclaimed on more than one occasion during the journey, each time waking his men from the oblivion they sought in less than comfortable sleeping quarters. 'This is my moment. This is Yasin. Wanted for fundraising for al-Qaeda, transferring terrorists across the Middle East to strike at our boys; laundering money, running heroin from Afghanistan to Turkey. It is my duty to take out this motherfucker.' Then quietly he would concede that it could also be his duty to at least brief the Ambassador rather than leave instructions that the Ambassador should call him the moment he rose for the day. As for Langley, a cryptic SMEAC met his obligations given this was a moving and hot pursuit operation.

Briefing his team in the middle of a desert on the road from Damascus surely amounted to hot pursuit and besides, the mission had a certain panache about it which would make a great bedtime story for his grandkids. One day. But today it was: Situation, Mission, Execution, Administration, Command, in real time. Dwight ran through his Orders Group. He prided himself on having cultivated Artie who had eventually come up with a scoop. But the fine detail was still missing. A few loose ends, he conceded. Until he learned the strength and whereabouts of Yasin and his thugs, inevitably a certain amount had to be left to chance.

By five am Dwight had his team assembled near their vehicle HQ. Fifty minutes and five kilometres later Dwight and his team filtered into the grounds of Zenobia Cham Palace. With no sightings of security people lurking in the grounds or environs, Dwight concluded that Artie's information on Yasin's estimated time of arrival post mid-day was good. The team would have time to reconnoitre, rest and refresh, then stake out.

At seven am Dwight walked into the hotel reception and demanded to see the head of hotel security and shift manager. Thirty minutes later he felt much relieved. There was nothing to suggest a forward security team of any VIP had been despatched to the hotel nor was there any registration in the name of Yasin or any of the aliases Dwight provided to the receptionist. Dwight was astute enough to realise it would be unlikely that Yasin would use his own name or a known alias, but the fact these names were not in the register was comforting.

Dwight was busy briefing the manager when a receptionist poked her head into the office interrupting him but advising that the three men who had earlier been in the breakfast bar, now demanded that the heliport be reserved for a VIP at 10am. Dwight knew at that moment that God was on his side. After all, he was a Christian.

At nine am Artie guided his chariot onto the heliport at Zenobia Cham Palace hotel. Barely had Samer alighted from the aircraft than he was confronted by a hotel manager frantically waving his arms. Samer did not need to be told that he and Artie had intruded onto space reserved for a VIP or who that VIP might be. Leaning back into the helicopter, Samer instructed Artie to park their means of transport on the nearby golf course then return to meet him in the lobby.

Inside the hotel Samer waited for Artie to arrive. At the breakfast bar three men were behaving as if they owned the hotel and he placed them as Yasin's people.

Fifteen minutes later he and Artie obtained the keys to the suite previously reserved as the venue for their one pm meeting with Yasin. Artie carried a small suitcase which was checked by hotel security. 'Explosive and electronic detection equipment,' explained Samer. 'No disrespect to your hotel security but we must double check.'

Inside the executive suite Samer relaxed. 'Lock the door,' he instructed Artie, then froze when he felt the muzzle of a gun against the base of his skull.

Dwight listened in horror at the approaching whump whump of helicopter rotors. At nine am his team were barely in position. 'Damn that Australian,' he cursed softly as he realised he would have to take pre-emptive action the moment the chopper disgorged its lethal cargo. Dwight had made it very clear in his Orders Group that this was a dead, and not an alive mission. But when he realised the chopper was the Basrik Mines aircraft, one sort of panic morphed into another as he anxiously hoped his crew, in their fluster to get into position, would also recognise that Yasin was not on board this helicopter.

Dwight had Artie in the sights of his Heckler & Koch MP5/10 sub-machine gun and could have shot the man with impunity such was the intensity of his anger. But relief flooded his senses when he realised their quarry had not arrived prematurely. He assumed the man Artie had referred to as "the negotiator" on behalf of the Melbourne syndicate, was the overweight passenger who ran ducking under the rotor blades for safety.

Wilbur had made comms with all field operatives before the first helicopter dropped into the Zenobia Cham Palace. Like Dwight, Wilbur was seriously relieved when the first arrival at nine am proved not to be Yasin. By nine fifteen am all operatives were settling into their positions. Standard procedure now required each man to check in every five minutes. By nine twenty six am Wilbur had logged five agents having reported in three times each. At nine twenty seven am Wilbur unscrewed the coffee thermos and took a well-earned break. But when nine thirty five am passed without any check-in from the field team, Wilbur experienced the first twinges of anxiety. Quickly he ran checks and double checks on his equipment. Nine forty five came and went, Wilbur still buried among cables and antennae. By nine fifty am Wilbur conceded there was a problem but not with his HQ.

'What the hell is going on there? Come on guys,' he yelled and bashed his open palm on the table, upsetting the thermos. By ten zero five am with no helicopter arriving, Wilbur was in a state of trepidation and fear. At ten fifteen am he called Damascus. Code Red.

When Yasin entered the suite Samer had pre-booked for their meeting at one pm later in the day, he did so with knowledge that soon five American CIA agents would lie dead, dragged to the refuse zone of the hotel where the bodies would be dumped in garbage collection bins.

Malevolently Yasin glowered at Samer. 'This is not what I expected from you, my friend,' he said.

Samer sat motionless, untied but nevertheless impotent facing an impassive young man with fire in his eyes and a cocked Kalashnikov in his hands. In the corner of the suite Artie quivered like a small child terrified by a large dog. Saliva and mucus dribbled from his lips and nose. A large red welt had closed his left eye but he too was unbound.

Bowing obsequiously, the leader of the patrol team explained that the pilot had tried to force his way out of the suite. Yasin nodded his approval. His men knew he brooked no error on their part; to have allowed the Australian to escape would have brought instant death to the culprit or culprits; however many and however close to the Special One.

'Why did you do this?' asked Yasin, angered that such a long-term associate would stoop to bringing in the Americans. 'Was ten million dollars too much to resist?'

Perplexed, Samer put the same question to his tormenter. 'I might ask you the same thing.'

The two men stared at each other, neither quite comprehending the situation.

Eventually Yasin said, 'The Americans. They are all dead. They cannot help you. Why?'

Samer remained impassive. What was this man talking about? Unable to follow all the Arabic conversation, Artie did understand the words "American" and "death" and these words catapulted him into an abyss of fear. He sobbed uncontrollably.

Samer and Yasin turned to him; Samer in confusion and Yasin with disgust.

Suddenly Artie blurted out, pleading to Samer. 'Samer, it was me. You must explain. All I wanted was to be paid for the phosphate. This is our money. I didn't know how to get the money. The CIA promised we would be paid. Tell him, please. All I wanted was what is my family's.'

In disbelief, Samer tilted his head as if he was hard of hearing. 'What is you say? You do what?'

Watching the saga unfold, Yasin discerned genuine reaction by Samer. 'You inform to CIA? You bring these men to Palmyra? Are you crazy?' spluttered Samer, anger mounting within him.

Distraught beyond consolation, Artie's head sank to his chest as he cried like a child.

Yasin took a .38 Smith & Wesson revolver from his jacket. Plunging a silencer over the short barrel, he fired two shots into the Australian's chest.

'On your feet,' Yasin ordered Samer. 'Follow Omar. If you try to run I will kill you.'

Alain and Egor were still an hour from Palmyra when Alain's phone sounded. Outside their vehicle the desert air was forcing the temperature gauge on an unrelenting upward spiral.

'Maybe problem?' asked Egor, detecting by Alain's silence during the call that something was amiss.

'I think so,' responded Alain. 'That was Samer. There has been a change in plan. We are not meeting at the Zenobia Cham Palace any more. We should meet at the café with the Purple Camel sign. It is in the main street. We must be there at two pm.' Pausing he looked at his wrist watch. 'How far are we from Palmyra now?'

'It's noon. We will be in Palmyra at one pm,' replied Egor.

Alain rubbed his chin. 'Something is not right. Something in Samer's voice.'

'Perhaps I call Colonel Goloshapova,' suggested Egor, producing his phone from its belt pouch.

Alain shook his head. 'I am not certain something is wrong and besides, this is an off limits meeting as far as the Russians are concerned.'

Shrugging Egor fiddled to return his phone to the pouch when suddenly it flashed and buzzed. 'Huh? What is? Colonel she is call!' he said and slipped open the receiver. Suddenly Egor swerved to the road side harshly applying the brakes and sliding to a stop in a cloud of beige dust.

'Is true. Cannot be? Yes Colonel. Please wait.'

The astonished look on Egor's face sent the first tremors of alarm through Alain. Taking the phone from his driver he spoke. 'Yes Valya. What is it?'

Alain listened for some five minutes without comment. Finally he said, 'I thought there was a problem when Samer called me just before your call. He said the meeting place has been changed to the Purple Camel café in...'

She interrupted him. 'You know where it is. Okay. So we are to meet at one pm which is an hour earlier.'

Egor pushed Alain's arm with his palm then held up two fingers when Alain looked at him.

'Sorry. Egor says we must be there at two pm.'

Again she interrupted.

'Yes, now one pm. I am sure.'

Again Alain listened then he repeated her instructions back to her. 'You want Egor and me to wait four hundred metres north of the café near the bicycle shop. Be in position at one pm. Got that. We wait there for you and Alpha to arrive. Sorry, can't hear...'

Static caused loss of clarity momentarily. Alain held the phone upward and soon she was clear again. 'You are already flying?' Alain was surprised. 'When do you arrive?' he asked. 'And what is the plan then?' but the call went dead.

The men sat in silence for several minutes; Egor allowing his partner to formulate his thoughts. 'Well,' said Alain eventually. 'What a fucking day this has turned out to be, mate.'

Still Egor waited patiently for explanation.

'At the hotel where Samer was to meet Yasin, they found five dead Americans. All kitted up; an assault team. Shot in the head. All of them. Close range. One of the dead is that fellow Dwight.' Alain shook his head in disbelief. 'Didn't like him but I wouldn't wish that on him. Poor bastard. Hotel janitor found one body in a garbage can. Then they found the rest.'

'What were the Americans doing there?' asked Egor then answering his own question said, 'Probably went there to get Yasin. But how did they know he would be there?'

'Artie told them. He called the Yanks in last night. Remember, he wasn't with us. The hotel manager found him shot twice in the chest in the suite Samer booked for the meeting with Yasin. Not dead but not healthy, says Valya, and he was able to give an account of what went down at the hotel.'

Egor was by this time visibly shocked. 'Five dead Americans! That is like car bomb.'

'But not as indiscriminate. So,' continued Alain. 'Samer has obviously been taken to this Purple Camel by Yasin. He must have a full team there. Five Americans! Incredible.'

'*Da*,' replied Egor, almost trance-like.

'That's why Samer sounded strange I guess,' speculated Alain.

'Colonel is come with Alpha force,' said Egor, ignoring Alain's comment. 'Sergei! Is good team,' he said, his focus now shifted to what would happen next.

'I dare say the Americans were a good team too, Egor,' replied Alain cautiously. 'This Yasin lives up to his reputation. We must be very careful. Like Valya warned me.'

'What is plan for Palmyra now?' asked Egor, some enthusiasm beginning to stir in the young man.

'Actually old chap,' replied Alain, adopting a haughty English accent, 'I wouldn't have the foggiest.'

Samer followed Omar out of the hotel and into a vehicle. He was then taken, closely guarded, to a time-worn mud brick single room dwelling in the poorer section of town. Narrow access alleys to the meeting place barely permitted passage of the three Toyota Hilux utes in their convoy. This was not a section of Palmyra into which authorities would venture unless in force and Samer knew well, in these troubled times, no local militia commander would initiate a raid for whatever reason unless it was first cleared through Damascus. In the present climate in Syria, law and order was maintained by communities within communities. Apprehension of criminal elements by State authorities could easily be misunderstood by a nervous populace as politically motivated. Police were unlikely to come looking for him in this sector today.

Hustled inside the low ceilinged abode where little light penetrated, Samer was directed to sit on a stool already placed in the centre of the room. Yasin's men stood respectfully near the entrance with one man blocking the rear exit. Soon Yasin appeared, pulled a chair to the room centre and placed it opposite Samer. Now face to face, Yasin leaned over the back of his chair and stared into the face the Melbourne negotiator.

'We must put behind us the treachery of the infidel,' said Yasin.

Samer nodded. 'He was foolish.'

'You did well to place the phosphate on the ship at Tartus. Wakid Mashreq informs me the Russians procured the ship and also have a destroyer to guard the vessel through the Suez.' Pausing, Yasin leaned back on his chair. 'The navy is to protect the Russian crew from the pirates of Somalia.' Producing a sardonic smile he continued. 'This is how allies should treat each other. Like China with Iran. China does not bow to Obama bullying them to stop buying crude oil from my country.'

Samer nodded.

'The only loose end my friend is now the payment for the phosphate. Also Wakid Mashreq informs me the Letter of Credit for payment has been approved by his people and is lodged with the German bank. Payment will be released to this Achilles company in Hong Kong when the shipment of phosphate enters New Zealand waters. This is true?'

Samer nodded again, his mind racing ahead trying to predict what would be the finale at the hands of his very ruthless adversary.

'The New Zealand company must have an invoice from this Achilles for phosphate. This is critical for the taxation reconciliations is it not?' continued Yasin.

'The invoice is essential and conditions on the LC also specify that payment will not be released until the appropriate invoices are received in New Zealand,' said Samer now contributing to the chronology.

Yasin pursed his lips and stared at the floor, thinking through the steps to be taken. Eventually he said, 'This is sound commercial practice. Later when the Americans intimidate the New Zealand government to investigate this shipment, as they tried to intimidate the Chinese not to buy oil from my country, the Hong Kong authorities will disclose the bills of lading originate in Syria and that Achilles is owned by our company in British Virgin Islands.'

'Yes, Exeter,' said Samer, naming the company and stalling for time.

'The BVI jurisdiction will refer the inquisitors to Belize where the owner of Exeter is the company Ajax.' Smiling now, Yasin recited the chronology like a child pleased with himself. 'But Belize they will not disclose that we are the owners of Ajax company and therefore the owners of Achilles! It is a good plan.'

Shifting from one buttock to the other Samer decided his best option was to continue to negotiate as he had intended before Artie was shot; as if nothing had happened. 'My enquiries suggest that we will need to make arrangements beyond Belize,' he said blandly.

Yasin's posture changed immediately. 'Why is this?'

It was Samer's turn to smile sardonically. 'There are already signs America is putting pressure on Belize. Recently the independent economic state of Andorra between Spain and France; it has succumbed. This is what happened already to the integrity of the Swiss banking system which the Swiss value so much. Or perhaps I should say, valued, for they have succumbed to American bullying and now the confidentiality of Switzerland is a leaking sieve.'

Opening his hands in a gesture prompting disclosure by Samer, Yasin solicited a solution.

'Burundi is where we must now move I think,' suggested Samer. 'This is an island on the fringe of the Asian Tigers. As such it is the hub for massive financial transfers from Pakistan and India to China and Indonesia. This is a powerful economic block which a frail American economy cannot defeat.'

Yasin was about to answer when Samer spoke over him, his confidence returning. 'What is most fortuitous about Burundi, is they deal in euro currency and that the country is Islamic.'

Yasin nodded in agreement, his eyes glowing with zeal. 'The country is Islamic. It is the will of Allah, such thing. Like it is the will of God that our Muslim brothers in Pakistan have the bomb and I pray to Allah that he will show the way for a military coup to topple the politicians in that country who are pawns to America.'

Like a cobra coiled to strike, Yasin clenched his fists and hunched his shoulders as he glared about the room, forcing each of his men to drop their gaze in a sign of servile fearfulness. 'This is a good thing what happened in America; this Freddie Mac and Fannie Mae; Enron the gas giant; Lehman, the Jew Brothers! This is good for the world because it destroys the commercial power of America. It is also good for it tells the world corruption is not just the curse of the Arab. Madoff, he is a Jew! He is a thief.'

'On this point we are very much in agreement Yasin,' said Samer feeling a little more at ease now.

Yasin rubbed his bald head. 'Then we must work together to use these three companies or war ships to help the enemies of America as best we can.'

The irony of this was not lost on either man.

'What do you have in mind?' asked Samer, feeling now that they were finally getting to the point of this meeting in Palmyra.

Yasin stood up and stepped back. Appraising Samer he said, 'It is understandable that the Australians want to get their hands on the New Zealand payment, particularly now that the amount is five million US dollars and not five hundred thousand.'

'The Australians have been good partners for Syria. They have poured millions of dollars into equipment and plant. It is only right that they receive a dividend now the mines are selling again,' reasoned Samer.

'Ha! But here is the point my friend. Wakid Mashreq and the Minister; Al Raik and other senior people in the Syrian government have made this investment opportunity possible for the Australians. It is therefore right, as you say, for these Syrians to share in the pot, is it not?

Samer had foreseen this ploy several days ago when Yasin started his manoeuvring and he was prepared to compromise. Now Artie was no longer a dog yapping in his ear, this compromise would be easier for him to concede. Besides, in the present circumstances Samer realised he was not in a strong position to bargain. The bigger question now was whether Alain Foveaux would be brought to this place and how he would respond to pressure to sign disbursement authorities for the money soon to be in Hong Kong.

'This is not a large amount of money Yasin,' suggested Samer. 'Yes, it is larger than the originally intended sale of two containers of phosphate but I'm perplexed that your people are prepared to undermine confidence in the integrity of Syrian commerce, for a mere five million US dollars?'

Yasin made a dismissive gesture. 'Perhaps my friend, but these are troubled times.' Leaning forward he spoke quietly to Samer so others present could not hear. 'There is growing concern among Assad's supporters that he cannot emerge from this all powerful. This will mean a changing of the guard, so to speak. There is now some panic amongst the loyalists and we saw what happened to Mubarak when his supporters changed allegiance. The men I represent today are not fools. They now take every opportunity to transfer their wealth from Syria, and the Achilles presents a golden opportunity to accumulate hard currency outside of Syria.'

Yasin maintained his body position close to Samer. 'These people will reimburse Basrik with the equivalent of five million US but in Syria lira. This is money which has no worth beyond these borders. But it is real money inside Syria which the Australians may retain to remit abroad at a more propitious time. These are my instructions for compromise. At some later time the Australians can recover their investment.'

Twisting his palms together, Samer played for more time while he considered the offer. Finally he said, 'You will need the man Foveaux to agree and sign. Perhaps he will. His interest is to get the phosphate to New Zealand. It is my job to protect the Melbourne syndicate investment.'

Yasin stood up and nodded. 'And you do best to protect the investment of your people in Melbourne if you accept my solution.' In his present predicament, and having watched Artie shot in cold blood, Samer conceded. There would be another day for him to help the Australians recover. This was not a time or a cause to die for.

'So! You agree,' said Yasin sensing the other man's capitulation. 'Soon we will move to a café where is good telecommunications systems maintained by the brothers. I will bring Foveaux to this location and you will tell him what is best.

Chapter Twenty-one

US Compound.
Damascus, Syria.

Hot pursuit? More like blatant mutiny in Porter's estimation, having read and re-read the missive left for him by his renegade CIA chief. At ten fifteen am when the red phone flashed and buzzed on his desk, he was still debating what to do next. It was with foreboding that he studied the phone for several seconds before lifting the hand piece.

'This is the Ambassador.'

As he listened to Wilbur make his report, Porter pressed the audio button, replaced the hand piece, rested his elbows on his desk, and slowly massaged his sinuses.

Five kilometres from the Zenobia Cham Palace in Palmyra, on the side of the road leading to Damascus, sitting in the HQ vehicle of Operation Frog, Wilbur trembled as he waited for the Ambassador to speak.

Unexpectedly, the anxiety Porter had experienced during the two hours or so since he'd woken to the news that he had been outflanked by his CIA liaison, abated. A calmness came over him as he depressed the recording device to capture the precise instructions he was about to give Wilbur. 'And you have heard no shot; no gunfire?'

'Correct, Sir,' replied Wilbur.

'Then you are to now, immediately, drive into the hotel complex, locate the manager and tell him why you are at his desk; explain to him that a US tactical team exercising on the golf course transmitted a communication to say they had come upon unidentified persons whom they suspect as terrorists and have entered the hotel grounds. On that pretext you are to demand the manager makes available to you hotel personnel to search the compound. I will join you imminently. Report back to me on my secure line every fifteen minutes. Move.'

With those instructions issued, Porter buzzed the front desk and ordered his helicopter to be ready in fifteen minutes. The next call he made was to his friend the Minister of Education. Finally he placed a call to Washington.

Chapter Twenty-two

Purple Camel Café
Palmyra, Syria.

'That was foolish, Mr Alain', said the gunman in a quiet but menacing tone. 'Your friend Egor, his weapon has shot dead my associate. This not good for Russo-Syrian relations. You are now in much worse predicament. Please to place your weapon on car roof.'

Alain remembered where he had heard that voice and recognised the man with Arab features. It's Yasin, he thought. No question. Last time I saw him he had hair and was clean shaven. He has shaved his head now and has the stubble.

Alain placed his Makarov on the car roof.

Two men emerged from the shadows of a building and taking the dead Arab between them, tossed his body into the rear of the Russian embassy car. The same men then went to the other side of the car, picked Egor's body from the roadway and tumbled it across the front seats of the Opel.

Alain tried to get a proper look at Egor. There was no question that the Arab who had been shot while holding Alain was dead, but Alain didn't want to believe that Yasin could kill a man of Egor's muscle tone with one blow. He reached in the open door to seek a pulse on Egor's motionless form. He found none.

'Move,' warned Yasin, aiming his .38 between Alain's eyes. 'Walk now, to the café you have been watching.'

A few minutes later Alain was ushered past several men occupying the café; their mere presence a deterrent to all not to enter. A strong hand pushed him forward when he hesitated and he followed directions to pass through the kitchen into an office. The door giving access to an outside alley was barred by an armed man dressed in similar robes to the man Yasin had shot in the street.

Samer greeted Alain with a perfunctory hand wave. No words were spoken.

Yasin appeared in the room and pointed to a chair. As Alain was about to sit he noticed a bedraggled young woman, strapped into a chair. Large red welts were visible on her tear stained face, and her terrified eyes forlornly pleaded in lieu of words she could not utter for the tape across her mouth.

That is the young girl who sat opposite Egor and me in the Old City café some days ago, Alain realised. But he said nothing, partly from shock at seeing the girl and also sensing that Yasin was watching him for any sign of previous connection with her. Instinct told him that recognising the girl would endanger her life even more.

Soon Yasin spoke but his manner was furtive and mendacious.

'Your friend Samer has told that you would come to Purple Camel café at two o'clock but it is only at one pm! You are spying on us?' Before Alain could respond Yasin continued. 'When I come on you from behind I see your driver is Russian from our first meeting. But Russians not say they send FSB for meeting. Why is plan changed?'

Thinking quickly, he concluded that the Russian Ambassador had already informed the Syrian Minister that there would be no further involvement by Russia after the shipment left Tartus. If this information had been passed to Yasin via the Corrupt Elite, he would be confused by the appearance of Egor. But before Alain could formulate an answer, Yasin continued.

'Why you attack my man who is captured by you like a fool with a gun to his head? I have no choice,' hissed Yasin with visible anger. 'I make punish for failure,' he continued rapidly, apparently seeking to justify his harsh response of shooting his own man.

'I am more concerned about my driver,' said Alain cautiously. 'He was loaned to me at my request for translation. He is not FSB. He was sent from New Zealand to help me as a New Zealand company representative,' he continued, regaining some confidence. With it his anger grew. Anger with himself for getting Egor involved and anger that Egor had been attacked without warning.

Yasin displayed no sign that he of accepted the veracity Alain's account of what had transpired. Ignoring Alain's question, he said, 'Samer has agreed New Zealand payment for phosphate is for Syrian Minister and others.' Yasin turned to Samer for endorsement of these claims and to his surprise Alain saw Samer nod.

'I have agreed to the money transfer documents,' said Samer. See them here,' he said pointing to documentation on a table. 'Transfer of payment for phosphate from New Zealand must go first to the Ministers who are involved.'

Alain looked to Samer for sign he had been beaten but there was none. However it was clear his spirit was broken. Perhaps he had capitulated to protect the girl from more brutal treatment. Alain recalled Valentina's warnings.

Glancing around the room Alain computed that there was no way out of the room without a lot of violence and luck, and the young girl was another consideration. So he played for time. He knew Sergei and the Russian Alpha team would by now be somewhere inside the perimeters of Palmyra on foot, making their way to their rendezvous point where an Arab lay dead in the embassy car with an unconscious or dead Egor. Perhaps Egor was awake by now. Or perhaps he had succumbed. The blow he had taken under the chin was a known instantaneous knock-out punch with a high probability of inflicting a fatal neck break.

'What the hell,' said Alain with apparent nonchalance. 'The phosphate is on the high seas and cannot be stopped reaching its destination short of war with Russia. Kiwifert has delivered a blow for freedom of international commercial activity. This is a good thing. No, Yasin?'

'Yasin smiled. 'Is good thing Mr Foveaux.'

'So the issue now is, who gets the money Kiwifert has paid to Basrik Mines via our company in Hong Kong? Samer, you have agreed the disbursement should be to whom?'

Samer smiled his gentle smile of resignation. 'The Minister of Mines, Wakid Mashreq and perhaps other senior people have more pressing reason for payment from this consignment.'

'Then I agree,' said Alain as cheerfully as he could muster under the circumstances. 'Where do I sign? We also must have biometric data transfer of my fingerprint. You have the technology in this café?' he asked turning to Yasin, hoping this technical impediment would frustrate any transaction this day.

Yasin grunted an affirmative reply. Papers were produced by a young man with spectacles and a black and white chequered keffiyeh.

Alain signed and then glanced about looking for a scanning device. He found it. A biometric scanning apparatus lay waiting patiently on a table in the far recess of the room. 'So let me get this straight,' said Alain, a little dismayed as the Arab technician started connecting cables to the fingerprint scanner. 'The payment Kiwifert has made for the present shipment will be distributed to the Corrupt Elite.' He deliberately chose the adjectival phrase for impact.

Yasin turned on him with a half-sneer, but said nothing.

'And what about Artie's team in Melbourne?' enquired Alain, directing the question to Samer.

Samer dropped his eye contact, despair showing in his face. Alain realised he could ameliorate the man's grief by informing him that Artie was still alive as at midday, but he did not want to signal any hint to Yasin that he was cognisant of the events which had transpired at Zenobia Cham Palace that morning.

'There will be time in the future for the Australians to recover the investment,' said Samer cautiously.

'That leaves one unanswered issue,' pressed Alain. 'The concern my partners in New Zealand have about the abuse of our commercial set up in Belize, BVI and Hong Kong.'

Yasin stopped mid step as he returned from the data transmission apparatus. 'What means you this?' he asked with a hint of menace as his glare transferred to the young woman strapped to the chair.

Trying to ignore the malice, tangible as it was, Alain decided to confront this man. 'Somewhere along this journey my New Zealand partners were led to believe that you were going to transfer wealth held by a preferred Syrian cartel. Piggyback on the Kiwifert transfer of funds! Maybe we got the message mixed but I think not.'

Samer translated in Arabic to make certain the message was not mixed again.

'As I assess the situation,' continued Alain with as much arrogance as he could muster, 'It is a simple matter for the Syrian elite to pay the Syrian government in local currency the equivalent to the US dollars Kiwifert transmits to Basrik.'

Again Samer translated.

'To put it in simple terms,' continued Alain finally, 'The people you represent want money they already have in Syria, transferred out of Syria. These hitherto loyal supporters of President Assad, like rats on a sinking ship, then leave him and take their gains made within Syria when they were part of Assad's machine, to another frontier.'

Yasin by this time was leaning against the far wall observing Alain like a serpent watching prey it had followed into a blind alley.

'From the point of view of the New Zealand partners to Ajax, Exeter and Achilles, which provide the vehicles for financial transactions to purchase phosphate, we don't really care up to this point whom you dispense our payments too, for no anti-money-laundering laws, which only apply to specified Western nations, have been breached by any of our companies.'

Alain paused as Samer again translated.

'Where we take a dim view is, when you start to use our matrix of companies to transfer around the globe, money which has been accumulated through heroin sales out of Afghanistan, weapons sales to Iran or whatever.'

Samer did not need to translate this last salvo. Yasin had anticipated it. Pushing himself from the wall with a thrust of his shoulder and signalling his nearest warriors to be alert, Yasin confronted Alain in an aggressive posture.

'Infidel,' he snarled. 'You think perhaps your people have rights over all things which happen in Islam. Sunni or Shiite, to me is the same. There is one God and this God is Allah.'

Without warning and as rapid as a cobra strike, Yasin smashed a backhanded blow across Alain's face with a leather quirt Alain had not noticed he possessed. In the same movement Yasin aimed Egor's Tokarev between Alain's eyes.

Alain quickly realised he had pushed Yasin too far. This was civil war torn Syria, not safe secure little old New Zealand where the violence was largely confined to the Queensbury code of rugby with a referee handy to intervene if matters started getting out of hand.

Menacingly Yasin drifted across the room to stand beside the girl bound to the chair. 'Perhaps you divined these allegations you hurl at me or perhaps you were warned by this divine creature,' he said as he gently stroked the girl's thighs with his quirt. Fear flooded the face of the young woman as a lecherous smirk appeared on the face of her tormentor.

At that moment from the corner of his eye Alain caught sight of movement in the café proper. Yasin saw this recognition in Alain's eyes and turned toward the café as a chair crashed against the floor in the restaurant section.

The next moment Alain was thrown against the wall of the office they occupied. Stunned, he lay motionless, deafened and disorientated by the effects of a stun grenade detonated in the other room. Looking across the floor he located Samer, bleeding from the mouth and nose but alive. The Arab girl had been hurled against a pillar and was motionless, still tied to the chair, with blood streaming from the corner of her mouth.

Reaching forward he grasped Samer's wrist and began crawling backward toward some light he hoped was the doorway to the back alley he spied when he first arrived.

Gunfire erupted as Alain began to squirm his way into the sunlight but a hand dragged on his ankle.

'The girl,' spluttered Samer. 'We must save the girl.'

Cursing in shame for scarpering without taking the girl, Alain crawled across to where she lay, unconscious. Locking his legs around her torso while lying on his back, he began the slow process of pulling her to the door using his elbows as fulcrums, but again he was humbled when Samer, crouching, took one of the girl's arms and gestured for Alain to do the same.

Once in the alley Alain forced himself to his feet. He heard Russian voices; Sergei and Alpha! The firestorm reminded him of an event many years ago in Vietnam where he had led his platoon onto a series of huts known to be used by Vietcong guerrillas. On that occasion villagers were caught in the middle. Now he, Samer and the girl were caught in the middle between Yasin's assassins and the avenging angels.

Black section saw Alain and Samer crawl from the café dragging the girl between them; stagger to their feet, look back, hesitate then stumble onwards toward the ruins.

"Hide in the Roman ruins." Those were the last instructions Alain recalled Valentina giving Egor before they left the Russian Embassy not half a day earlier. Alain had reconnoitred Palmyra's layout as he and Egor drove searching for the Purple Camel. He had his bearings now and stumbled off south west, dragging the girl with Samer's help.

A moment later an Arab emerged, sub machine gun in hand, eyes wide, looking for the girl. A Black section member shot the man at close range, then jerked backwards as he himself was hit in the chest with a .45 colt fired by Yasin who had used his man as a shield. Finding his way momentarily clear, Yasin ran.

When Sergei came upon the embassy car his team approached cautiously from the rear. The discovery of a dead Arab male was sobering. Even for hardened Alpha men the off side of a head from bullet entry never made an appetising sight. But when they found the body across the front seats was Egor, the spirits of the team crashed. Never is it easy to find one of their own.

Colonel Goloshapova roughly pushed Sergei aside, virtually leaping onto the huddled body of the young Russian. Quickly she ran her hands over the body but slowed. Her initial inspection confirmed Egor was alive. 'Medical,' she hissed at Sergei urgently.

'Where are you hit Egor?' she demanded.

Slowly Egor retracted his arm from between his chest and the car seat. 'Here,' he said touching his chin before flopping onto the seats again.

'Let's go,' she commanded, leaving Egor to the medic and lead the Alpha team toward the Purple Camel.

Leading White section, Sergei's team of four, two on either side of the street, ran hunched over toward the Purple Camel. White section, armed with Saiga 12 gauge semi-auto nine shot sawn-off shotguns, would be first to deploy inside the café but poised near the entrance waiting for Black section to get into position.

Black section following were armed with Kalashnikov PPK12 sub machine guns. Their immediate task was to protect White section; to scan the roof tops for snipers. Their ultimate objective was to get behind the target and control any rear exit.

Red section was to take the right of the target building and Green section the left. Both were armed with PPK12 sub machine guns.

Valentina commanded the Alpha group Blue section which brought up the rear. Her section carried a Kalashnikov AK12 2010 version, a Kalashnikov SVS12 silenced laser night-sighted sniper rifle, and base communications. The medical officer was still attending Egor.

Each man in the group had stun grenades, hand grenades and Makarov pistols as secondary weapons.

Valentina and Sergei had anguished over their ability to have only one assault group in Palmyra. Yasin was a powerful adversary; a war lord with extensive resources. But diplomatic protocols determined that while Russia could defend V.I.P.s it should not become involved in military conflicts. Calling in other Alpha groups from the Russian naval compound in Tartus would not likely qualify as a V.I.P. diplomatic protection detail. Besides, the Ambassador insisted the recovery mission was not to become a full scale battle. In the circumstances, if Yasin's men put up serious opposition, she was not confident of pulling her team out in victory intact. After what happened at the Zenobia Charm however, she had no choice but to go in hard. Recovery of Alain, Samer and the Minister's daughter was the mission objective.

The Minister's daughter's capture exacerbated the problem. The girl's constant supply of information from inside the tent of those close to Assad was invaluable. The fact the cartel within the Assad camp intended to use the network set up by Alain to ultimately launder other monies was not unexpected, but she now regretted not having fully briefed the New Zealander for the potential the girl had to be kidnapped. As always where spying is involved, and this girl was a spy, exposure inevitably resulted in someone being killed.

Fifty metres from the Purple Café the White section of Alpha team stopped. Sergei sought Valentina's attention and pointed to his eyes and the roof then held one finger raised before closing his fist. Valentina brought her sniper weapon to shoulder, entwined her left wrist in the carry strap, crouched, frog walked forward two hobbles at a time until she had the guard on the roof in her cross hairs and red dot. Within a second of sighting her target she squeezed the trigger, dropping the rifle to maintain forward motion without having checked that her target had died instantly with a 7.62mm projectile between the eyes.

At the entrance to the café two elderly men sat at a table contemplating a chess board. When the first of the men noticed Sergei, he was looking down the barrel of a 12 gauge. Cautiously the man tapped his companion on the forearm then both men stood and silently evaporated like mist beneath morning sun on the Volga.

As White section moved further into the café a guard slouched in semi slumber at the entrance lifted his head, blinking either in disbelief or terror of the consequences for his lack of vigilance, then slumped back in death. The hilt of Egor's knife protruded from his throat; the end result of an accurate throw from Egor who had backed-up of his own volition. The dying man's foot shot out and an adjacent chair clattered.

Instantly White section threw several stun grenades beyond the corpse on the chair then pressed against the wall. Egor too pressed his body against a pillar and hands over his ears, closing his eyes tight.

Egor identified six targets as he entered the dust and smoke filled room. He knew no shots would come into the room from either Black, Green or Red sections waiting outside for any of Yasin's group seeking to escape. Only White section would kill within the café. Egor was now an unauthorised part of White section but he would face that consequence later. His intrusion into the killing zone was personal; partly because Yasin had humiliated him but mostly because he wanted to find his girl.

But Egor was powerless to stop the fusillade which erupted. 'Wait,' he tried to cry out, but the words either didn't arrive or the cacophony of gunfire drowned out any sound he may have emitted. A torrent of lead sprayed the interior.

Without mercy the Russian Alpha team blasted the dead, the dying, and anything that moved.

Dust and cordite stung his eyes compromising his vision. A fearful tightening in his chest restricted his ability to breath. Panic and terror denied him reason to think. Staggering amidst the overturned chairs, tables and the twisted bodies, Egor searched. Single shots from Makarov hand guns signalled that White section was conducting a routine safety clearance. Frantically Egor redoubled his efforts.

Valentina entered the room. Quickly she took in the situation then turned to Egor, her eyes ablaze with fury. In that moment of diverted vigilance, from near her feet the dying gesture of a mortally wounded man erupted in a single shot.

Alain and Samer lay hunched against some of the impressive Roman columns of the ancient city of Palymra. The girl was semi-conscious but blood trickled from her eyes and ears.

The gunfire subsided.

A silence descended, like the silence Alain had experienced in Vietnam. A silence many in a fire fight experienced when the guns fell quiet and the bodies lay like twisted parodies.

The men decided to make a return to the Purple Camel café but no sooner had they roused to survey the terrain ahead, they saw a figure, hunched over and running directly toward their hideaway.

Friend or foe? thought Alain. Best not shoot. As the figure lurched toward them, Alain readied himself then sprang forward from his hiding place behind a rock column, with a swinging arm rugby league tackle to make Artie Beatson proud. His right arm swing with the full force of his ninety five kilo body weight, propelled with adrenalin fuelled high velocity, connected with the running figure across the throat. Yasin's feet kept running until he was horizontal to the ground but already unconscious.

'Yasin,' gasped Samer in astonishment.

'Two guesses who won the rumble back there,' said Alain to Samer who was now at his side.

Alain and Samer cautiously returned to the café; Samer supporting the girl as she stumbled along and Alain with Yasin's comatose body across his shoulders in a fireman's lift. A silence hung over the Purple Camel like an ominous cloud.

Near the entrance they saw two bodies; both Arab gunmen. Dead. An encouraging sign but neither spoke. At the door Alain shouted in Russian.

'*Tovarish*, it is Foveaux and Samer.'

Suddenly Egor appeared but his face was dark like the silence.

'Alain. Quick. Be quick. Is here. Come,' he said with plaintive urgency. Then he gasped as he recognised the girl was safe. He hesitated for a moment, his face alive with glee but quickly the joy was gone. 'Hurry,' he called and signalled for Alain to make haste.

Instinctively Alain knew the worst. In a daze he released his captive to Egor who with a grip of steel and a glare of utter ruthlessness grasped Yasin by the throat and began to extinguish life.

'Valya,' cried Alain as he stumbled through the doorway, falling to his knees at the table where lay the body of his love. Dark blood seeped from the corner of her mouth. Her eyes flickered when she saw him and for a brief moment a transient smile, like wind on water; a sudden perturbation caressed her lips, followed by stillness.

And she was gone.

Chapter Twenty-three

US Embassy.
Damascus, Syria.

Porter watched from his window as the man who had become the nemesis of not only him but of the America presence in Syria and possibly the Middle East, passed through the Embassy gates check point. Minutes later the same man, whom he noticed walked with a slight limp, was shown into his suite by a marine in resplendent attire.

'We meet again Mr Foveaux,' welcomed the ambassador as he extended a hand shake.

'I extend my sincerest condolences to you, the Embassy, the families of the fallen and to the United States,' replied Alain with genuine sympathy.

Porter indicated a seat and both men sat facing each other across his highly polished mahogany desk.

'Dwight and his team died fighting terrorists in the quest to bring democracy to this troubled land,' replied Porter, reverting to the script promulgated by the Secretary of State when news of the massacre at Zenobia Charm had to be released to the international community. 'The Minister's daughter. How is her progress?'

Alain smiled. 'She was flown to Moscow for plastic surgery to facial injuries. I think also to hide the fact from medical people in Syria that she had been raped by Yasin's men. I am told she will remain in Moscow where to have been raped is not the crime it is considered to be in these troubled lands. She is to attend university.'

Porter nodded a satisfied nod. 'And your minder from New Zealand? He is returning to Auckland?'

A gesture of uncertainty; shrug and open hands accompanied Alain's next statement. 'I am reliably informed that Egor will also return to Moscow. He tells me he has been accepted into a commissioned officer's management course of some twelve months at what I presume is the FSB academy. It is his intention to marry the Syrian girl and remain in Russia with her.'

After a time Porter said, 'You received your shipment of phosphate okay so I read. Your running the blockades seems to have captured the imagination of the multitudes. Your gamble, for I suspect it was a gamble, that your country's parliament would not introduce specific legislation to ban the shipment has paid off.'

A dismissive shrug was the best Alain could produce.

'You intending to make any more blockade runs, may I ask?' said Porter.

'Not on my watch,' replied Alain. 'The government is considering introducing its own sanctions laws. I guess at the moment the US has a compliant government in office in New Zealand.'

A smile of relief drifted across the Ambassador's pleasant face.

'I'd like to thank your people for taking care of the Aussie chap, Artie,' said Alain changing the subject. 'He was very lucky so I'm told.'

'I hear he is coming back to Syria when he has the strength,' replied the Ambassador. 'He wants to maintain some control over the investment they made. They were very pleased to get payment from your company.'

And lucky, thought Alain but he did not say this.

'He wants to be here when whoever wins this civil war, starts picking up the pieces. Remarkable fortitude. When I saw him off home after they released him from the hospital he told me he had learned a lot. Seems he and the local fellow, Samer, a friend of yours, have reached some agreement on how best to proceed.'

Alain smiled a polite smile consistent with the polite conversation.

Soon he said, 'Artie learned something! That's great. I hope we all learned something.'

Porter caste a querying glance at his erstwhile adversary. 'Like what, may I enquire?'

'Well,' said Alain shifting in his chair, 'We learned there are hidden dangers for country boys from New Zealand when they start mixing it with the professionals, like Yasin.'

Porter leaned on his elbows. 'I think we learned some lessons there too Mr Foveaux. Which brings me to a point. Pity you were not able to take him alive or perhaps I should say, keep him alive.'

Alain dropped his gaze to the floor. 'Yes. I too am sorry. I would like you to have had him as at least something to take back. I am sorry I did not trust your offer on Iraq.'

Alain's candour did surprise the Ambassador. 'To use a Clint Eastwood throw away, "Make my day!" The offer is still on the table.'

Alain chose a sceptical look and the Ambassador rose to the bait. 'Trust me. This time I do have the channels open. If you are interested we can start the ball rolling today.'

Alain waited for a sufficient passage of time so as not to appear too eager.

'Done,' he said, holding his clenched fist above the table as either a gavel or the sword of Damocles. 'I will work with your people for Kiwifert to pull phosphate out of Iraq. On one condition!'

'And what might that condition be? asked Porter.

'There is the matter of the reward for Yasin. Ten million US dollars, dead or alive,' said Alain.

'I was wondering when you would raise that matter,' responded Porter.

'I have here the address of a children's orphanage. It is in Rostov on Don, Russia. Kiwifert will buy phosphate from Iraq via the good endeavours of Ambassador Porter Julian, which I hope does enhance your career. But only when the ten million US dollar reward for Yasin, "dead or alive", has been transferred to the orphanage chosen by Colonel Valentina Goloshapova.'

THE END

Postscript

On 25 March 2012 Murray McCully; New Zealand Foreign Affairs Minister, former school friend and parliamentary colleague of the author, announced proposals to introduce legislation which would enable the New Zealand parliament to impose autonomous sanctions.

*****

Please consider posting a review on Smashwords, Amazon.com or social media of your choice.